PRAISE F

RON FAUST

"Faust's prose is as smooth and bright as a sunlit mirror."
—*Publishers Weekly*

"Faust's style is laconic, his story engrossing, his extraordinarily wide variety of characters richly realized."
—Gregory McDonald, award-winning author of *Fletch*

"The kind of stunning writer you want to keep recommending after you discover him."
—David Morrell, author of *Covenant of the Flame*

"Faust is a Homeric storyteller with an eye for the odd character and a fine gift for Spartan dialogue."
—*Library Journal*

"Voluble villains, wise friends and fickle ones . . . Faust writes well . . . charming and violent."
—*Los Angeles Times*

ALSO BY RON FAUST

THE
BLOOD
RED SEA

RON FAUST

TURNER

Turner Publishing Company
424 Church Street • Suite 2240 • Nashville, Tennessee 37219
445 Park Avenue • 9th Floor • New York, New York 10022
www.turnerpublishing.com

THE BLOOD RED SEA

This is a work of fiction. All the characters and events portrayed in
this book are either products of the author's imagination or are used
fictitiously.

Cover design: Glen Edelstein
Book design: Glen Edelstein

Library of Congress Cataloging-in-Publication Data

Faust, Ron.
 The blood red sea / Ron Faust.
   pages cm
 ISBN 978-1-62045-450-3 (pbk.)
 1. Sailing--Fiction. 2. Dominican Republic--Fiction. I. Title.
 PS3556.A98B56 2014
 813'.54--dc23
                                    2013025216

Printed in the United States of America
14 15 16 17 18 19 0 9 8 7 6 5 4 3 2 1

To Gayle

THE BLOOD RED SEA

PART I
Voyage Out

ONE

Draw a circle ten inches in diameter. The scale is seventeen nautical miles per inch. Pencil an X at the center; that's the little sloop *Roamer,* and her position is 19.5 degrees, twenty-nine minutes north; 66 degrees, twelve minutes east. Your diagram represents a great round patch of ocean one hundred and seventy miles in diameter. Pencil in waves if you like, and tiny arrows that show the angle of the southeast trade wind, and insert a dot close to *Roamer's* starboard beam—that's her: Kate.

Now if you are mathematically inclined, calculate the approximate total area enclosed. Convert those inches, at scale, to surface acres or hectares or square miles or square kilometers, any useful system of measurement. So, taking the sloop's central position, and extending a line around the perimeter, you will find that the nearest land, the north coast of Puerto Rico, is exactly five inches—eighty-five nautical miles—distant. And note that the boat is located over the Puerto Rican Trench, not far, in fact, from the deepest point in the Atlantic Ocean, at 28,321 feet. That's almost as deep as Mount Everest is tall. A lot of water, then, beneath the keel, a lot of water all around, and the bright powdery band of the Milky Way above. Surely there are other boats within our circle, but they are below the horizon, invisible to us.

You can imagine how vast this circular patch of sea is, how barren, how deep, what an awful midnight desolation . . .

Now tell me: what are the odds of your finding a lone swimmer there, a woman, in the middle of the night?

TWO

It was an ordinary Monday morning: the incomparable Candace, behind her cluttered desk, held the muzzle of a chrome-plated pistol near her right temple. It emitted the sort of humming that, in sci-fi dramas, signifies the operation of a lethal death-ray device. Candace squinted her eyes shut and then opened them wide in greeting, and shifted the death-ray gun's muzzle to her damp blond bangs.

Three more sad losers were sitting in the straight-backed wooden chairs that lined a wall of the outer office: two men and a woman, all trying to look innocent and hopeful in their misery. Candace complained about the difficulty of doing her work while being persecuted by the stares of waiting felons, but there had been little work to perform until such clients began appearing. And she still had time for her obsessive grooming.

"Good morning, Candace," I said.

She switched off the hair dryer. *"Buenos días, mi caro Señor Pendejo."*

Candace was dating a Cuban who had slyly told her that the word *pendejo*, like *caballero*, could be defined as

"noble gentleman." And so lately she had been address-
ing men as Mr. Pubic Hair, or in the secondary meaning,
Mr. Fool. She called seventy-nine-year-old Judge Levi
Samuelson "Señor Pendejo Viejo"—Mr. Old Pubic Hair.
We did not correct her; we left that to someone who
might be less restrained in his retaliation.

I glanced at the fifty-gallon aquarium that sat atop a
shelf of law books; two more of the bright tropical fish
had died over the weekend, and now, colors dimmed
and tails curled in rigor mortis, they floated above the
miniature sunken galleon and tendrils of weed.

There were two narrow offices at the rear of the
large outer office. Mine was on the left. The room always smelled of dust and mildew after being closed for
a couple of days. I switched on the air-conditioning
and sprayed the room with a chemical deodorant
named Sea Breeze.

I sat at my desk and shuffled through the morning mail, trash-canning all brown envelopes, envelopes
that heralded the chance of a lifetime, and envelopes
with a cellophane window on the face. I opened those
that might conceivably contain a check. None did,
but I found an invitation to a wedding that had taken
place Saturday.

Candace soon came in, leaned back against the
door, and said, "A serial shoplifter, a car thief, and a
crazy woman who thinks the government is tampering
with her womb."

"What are they doing to it?"

"Her womb?"

"Yes."

"They put a microchip in there."

"Why?"

"I don't know. But she wants to sue."

Candace wore a knit dress that was modest in every respect except for the body inserted within.

"Which do you want to see first?" she asked.

"Tell those people I'm booked full, Candace. Send the two men back to whoever referred them to me. Send the woman to a gynecologist. I'm not accepting any more of these wretched cases."

"Thank God," she said, and she returned to the outer office.

I leaned back in my chair and proceeded to deconstruct Candace. First, I mentally eliminated the artificial coloring from her hair. The natural color was a light brown tending toward dusty blond, but her hairdresser bleached it to a canary yellow with platinum streaks. And it seemed full of compressed air. I let the air out, and chipped away at the hair-spray glaze. Excellent. Next I removed her lavender contact lenses, removed the mink eyelashes from her lids, restored all the plucked eyebrow hairs, and wiped away the mascara and eye shadow. Yes. Now the phosphorescent orange lipstick had to go, and the matching orange talons—long, curved false fingernails. I mentally wet a handkerchief and wiped away the various skin enhancers and foundation formulas and liquid blushes that I presumed had names like NaturGlow and PassionFlush. I finished my work and saw that it was good. Candace was now a healthy, pretty young woman with lively brown eyes and an attractive mouth ready to smile. She was not the girl next door, but maybe the sexy girl who lived next door to the wholesome girl next door.

I preferred the natural, unaffected Candace, though I figured that most men would consider my deconstruction a desecration.

The door opened and the predeconstructed Candace reappeared. "There's another one out there," she said. "He says the police framed him on a charge of manufacturing methamphetamines."

"How did they frame him?"

"They planted a meth lab in his garage."

"Send him away, Candace."

I had been a criminal defense attorney, licensed in the State of Florida, for only four months, and yet I had more work than I needed or wanted. Veteran lawyers in the Dunwoody Building tossed me cases as you might toss a chunk of gristly meat to the mutt under the table. Naturally none of the cases was interesting or remunerative. No society murderers, rich drug lords, corporate bandits, celebrity felons, or corrupt politicians. The lawyers cleared files by sending me their mopes: shoplifters, petty thieves, check kiters, scofflaws, repeat DUIs, abused wives and cuckolded husbands, women with microchips implanted in their wombs. A surprising number of my clients managed to have themselves photographed by security cameras while engaged in various crimes and misdemeanors.

There was not much I could do for them. I pled out nearly all of the cases with the prosecutors. A few clients, contrary to my advice, demanded jury trials, got them, and got stiffer sentences than they would have received from plea bargains. I was astonished by the cavalier processes of the criminal justice system: a man might get a six-month suspended sentence by plea-bargaining; the same man, a year behind bars after a thirty-minute bench trial; and three years if he had the gall to inconvenience everyone by demanding his constitutional right to a jury trial. They were vindictive, those judges, those juries—twelve stone-faced, stone-hearted citizens good and true.

Tom Petrie laughed at my outrage. "Innocent," he called me. "Jackanapes." Tom had a rich vocabulary of invective; "jackanapes" was a new insult. "I told you to check voter registrations. You insist on empaneling Republicans."

"I want thoughtful, responsible, solid jurors," I said.

"Republicans, Baptist elders, retired civil servants with pinched mouths, menopausal divorcees, widows of slain law officers. Didn't they teach you anything at those night-school law classes?"

"They taught me that the jury system is the glory of Anglo-American jurisprudence."

He laughed.

"Maybe I wasn't meant to be a lawyer, Tom."

"That's another thing they forgot to tell you at law school."

*   *   *

A young woman was sitting on one of the client chairs as I passed through the outer office. We exchanged appraising glances. Candace, I assumed, was in our medieval lavatory. I hesitated for an instant, staring at the woman, and then went through the door and down the hall. While waiting for an elevator I was embarrassed to realize that I was silently reciting lines from a Marlowe poem: "Who ever loved, that loved not at first sight?" Jackanapes.

The elevator stalled between the second and third floors. The old building had electrical problems. "Where both deliberate, the love is slight." I'd looked up *jackanapes*: it was in part defined as "a cheeky fellow; bounder; coxcomb." (Coxcomb: a conceited dandy.) It could also mean a monkey or ape. A jolly word, jackanapes, but none of the definitions applied to me.

I created a mental image of the visitor. She was an attractive woman of about thirty. Nothing rare in that: there are flocks of attractive native and migrating women around and about Florida. She was a brunette, and that was somewhat distinctive in these days when so many women were bleaching their hair blond and blonder, or dyeing it improbable shades of red.

The elevator lurched, descended a couple of feet, and again halted. A voice echoed down the shaft, but I could not make out any words. The blower had shut off and it was getting stuffy in the old box. A glass-enclosed instruction card advised me to press the red button. I pressed it without hope.

Thick black hair, uncompromisingly black, glossy with silvery highlights. Black eyebrows, gracefully arched, long black lashes, good cheekbones and a firm jawline, intriguingly curved lips, blue eyes—but you could not tell about eye color in these days of contact lenses. Complexion: creamy, maybe, beneath a bronzy suntan.

"Hey!" the man high above shouted. "Hey, Pablo, for Christ's sake, pull the breaker switch!"

The woman appeared alert, sexy, with a level challenging gaze and a piquant half smile. Was I reading too much into this brief encounter? "It lies not in our power to love or hate; for will in us is overruled by fate."

Pablo, for Christ's sake, at last pulled the breaker switch, and the elevator descended the last few yards to the ground floor.

*   *   *

I was half an hour late for lunch and was surprised to see that Petrie was still in the restaurant. Generally, you waited for Tom; Tom did not wait for you.

"Did the loan company repossess your Timex?" he asked as I sat at the table.

Thomas Petrie, Esquire, was a first-rate criminal defense lawyer, one of the best in the state, one of the best in the country according to him. He liked to say that he had been born poor, but born too with teeth bared and claws unsheathed. "I came out of the swamp thirsty for blood." If you imagine lawfulness as a plateau and crime as a precipice, then you'd say that Tom walked very close to the edge, walked on air at times. Together we had been involved in enterprises that, viewed from even the most lenient perspective, qualified us for serious prison time.

"The elevator got stuck again," I said.

"Take the stairs."

Tom's suite of offices occupied half of the Dunwoody Building's top floor; he usually jogged up and down the flights of stairs to stay fit. He was an athlete who looked slow and bookish.

The restaurant was spread through four rooms, yuppied up in a pseudo–Art Deco style and mostly patronized by a generation that believed martinis were blended drinks, sweetened and brightly colored by fruits or fruity liquors. A waitress drifted over, and both Petrie and I ordered mugs of beer and Italian beef sandwiches.

"I just fell in love," I said.

"Tell me about it."

I told him about my brief encounter with the brunette in the outer office.

"Look," he said, "I hate, I really hate to sound like a psychologist—I have my pride. But your adolescent epiphany isn't surprising considering that your former fiancée got married Saturday. You probably fell in love at the precise instant, forty-eight hours later, that Martina said 'I do.'"

"You see a mystical significance in that?"

"I see a drowning man grasping at straws—a brunette straw."

"Were you at the wedding?"

"Yes."

"Speak."

"It was . . . regal. It was like the uniting of two great dynasties. They should have held the wedding at Westminster Cathedral. White doves were released when the golden couple exited the church."

"No."

"A dozen white doves."

"And Martina?"

"Beautiful. Glowing."

"She rarely glowed for me," I said. "Just flickered a little now and then."

"Static electricity, maybe."

Four fresh-faced twenty-somethings sat at a nearby table, and commenced speaking in the new American female dialect, a slurred baby-talk quacking that had originated in California and would only be stopped by the Atlantic Ocean. "Snot what I wanned," one of the girls said. "Swat he wanned."

"Go on, Tom," I said.

"Martina wore a tiara, and a wedding gown that must have cost ten grand. Gossamer, she was enveloped by mist and gossamer and fairy dust. The groom and his courtiers wore morning clothes."

"Mourning, at a wedding?"

"M-o-r-n-i-n-g."

"What are morning clothes?"

"Formal wear for daylight hours. Tails, top hats, all of that, except the color is gray."

"What else?"

"Flowers, elfin flower girls, pretty bridesmaids, unctuous ushers, an Episcopal priest in gold vestment, candles, solemn vows, rice, doves, delirium."

"Jesus. That isn't Martina. She despised ritual. She wasn't churchy, not the radiant bride in white. Not the standard issue. Doves? It's crazy."

"Wake up. People play more than one role in a lifetime. For you, Marty was austere, independent, self-reliant, a tomboy grown into a pretty woman. But for the groom she is the loving bride, the attentive wife, the angelic mother-to-be."

"Christ. That's dishonest."

"She's gone. Give her up."

"Half a year ago she was mine."

"Martina could forgive you killing one man, but the second? That was de trop. Two is one too many. As Voltaire said alter leaving a Paris homosexual whorehouse: 'Once is an adventure; twice is a vice.'"

Our waitress arrived with the beer and sandwiches. Petrie was a food sniffer; he removed the top slice of bread and sniffed the spicy beef, sniffed the cole slaw and french fries, and then began eating with genteel savagery.

I said, "Did you send me the woman with the microchip in her womb?"

He swallowed, drank some beer. "Nah. I keep the microchippies."

The girls at the next table were simultaneously engaged in four separate conversations; listening to them was like rapidly dialing among four radio stations.

"I sent you the car thief," Petrie said.

After lunch we walked down to the bay front for a smoke. Tom fired up one of his fifty-dollar bootleg Havanas; I got out a two-dollar cigarillo. We sat on a sun-heated slab of rock a few feet from where wavelets fizzed up on the sand. It was a blue day, blue sky and deeper blue sea, with puffball clouds reflected on the water and a warm breeze rustling through the royal palms that lined the esplanade.

"What do you see when you look at the lighthouse?" he asked.

"A lighthouse."

He quietly puffed his cigar and then, with fake sincerity, said, "You don't see a phallus? A peppermint-striped phallus? Ellis Slocombe's phallus?"

"I do now, damn you."

Martina Karras had bought the old lighthouse at a government auction some years before. It lay half a mile offshore on a bare rock-slab reef. She lived in the blockhouse and had a studio at the base of the forty-foot tower. It had been my home too, in a way.

"Think they'll honeymoon out there?" Petrie asked.

"I heard they're going to Paris."

"Paris in June. My. Think they'll live out there when they return?"

"No. They'll buy a big house on a canal, join the homeowner's association, join the country club, entertain their peers, produce a couple of brats, grow old gracefully."

"You sound bitter."

"I am bitter. I'm going to go away. I'm clearing my files. I'm thinking about quitting the law."

"After four months? Good. I'll see that the local bar association, in gratitude, throws you a retirement party."

"It's a dreary, humiliating profession."

"It's unfair that you couldn't start at the top, Shaw. So where are you going?"

"I thought I'd cruise the Caribbean in my boat."

"Listen, I need a full-time investigator for my office. You are just a sixteen as a lawyer; at best you can maybe get up to a twenty-four. But you're already a thirty-six as an investigator. I'll give you an office, an assistant, a good budget, more money than you'll ever earn making a mockery of the law."

Petrie was referring to his Laws of Incompetence. The LOI were a flexible work in progress; Tom made them up as he went along, and did not hesitate to contradict an earlier stated law to suit present purposes. His scale ran from two to sixty. The lowest number was assigned to an individual who never got anything right until he died, and then, by thoroughly dying, was awarded two points. A sixty—the theoretical maximum, never achieved—indicated that one was competent sixty percent of the time. Rocket scientists, the standard of intelligence for the banal, according to Petrie, rated an average of forty-one. ("A Mars probe misses Mars by sixty thousand miles. Why? Because half of the team was working in feet and inches; the other half used the metric system.") Petrie ranked himself as a very high fifty-four.

"We have only survived as a species," he would say, "because so far we haven't been competent enough to kill every human on the planet. But where competence has failed, incompetence may succeed."

As we walked back to the Dunwoody Building, I said, "Tom, are you ever intimidated by women?"

"Nah. I had four sisters, two older and two younger. And each of them had girlfriends. My childhood and early youth were oppressed by teenage females. Now, when I meet an intelligent, sophisticated, beautiful woman, I think of how she was at fifteen—sloppy, sullen, scheming, giggly, shrieking, pretentious—and I am at ease. I have been inoculated."

"Lucky you."

"Are you really going cruising on that little sailboat of yours?"

"I think so. Yes."

"Right. Well, I haven't written a will in fifteen years, but for you . . ."

THREE

The state attorney's offices were on the fifth floor of a building across the street from the courthouse. Nestor Naranjo usually kept his door open, though that didn't mean that you were welcome to enter. I stood in the doorframe until he crooked his finger, straightened the finger, and pointed to an uncomfortable armless wooden chair that was eight inches lower than Nestor's leather swivel chair. It had been arranged that way so that supplicants like me had to assume a subordinate position.

"Shaw," he said, removing his wire-framed reading glasses. "Think of the devil."

"You've been thinking about me?"

"Feverishly."

Nestor ran the prosecutor's office while his boss, SA Craig Christensen, continuously ran for political office.

"What have you got?" he asked.

I removed four file folders from my attaché case. "I want to plead out these cases."

"Why come to me? Why don't you deal with the prosecutors I assigned to those cases?"

"Your young prosecutors are merciless, Nestor. It's a

good thing Florida doesn't yet impose the death penalty for shoplifting or stealing fifteen dollars from a parking meter. Anyway, you have to approve the plea deals. I'm just cutting out the middle fascist."

"You sound like Petrie." He accepted the files from me and dropped them on his desk. "I didn't see you at the wedding."

"I wasn't there, but I heard it was something grand."

"An extravaganza of ostentation. There was even a launching of white doves."

"I heard."

"They were kept in wooden crates on the church steps, and when the bride and groom emerged—voilà! an explosion of doves."

"I forgot to ask Petrie. Who gave the bride away?"

"Her uncle."

"Phil? Phil was let out of jail for the wedding?"

"For two hours. The sheriff sent along a couple deputies."

Martina's uncle, Phil Karras, the man who had raised her, was awaiting trial on a charge of Murder One for killing his wife. Tom Petrie, his lawyer, naturally claimed that his client hadn't committed the crime; or, if he had, he was insane; or, if he wasn't insane, the killing was really a generous act of mercy. Alice had been suffering from Alzheimer's, the disease that Phil had terminated with a blast from a double-barreled shotgun.

I said, "I heard Phil's mind has deteriorated badly since he was locked up."

"You heard right."

"What do the psychologists say?"

"The state's shaman says Karras is presently not fit to stand trial. Petrie's tame mercenary shaman says the same thing, of course."

"Have you made a deal with Tom? Maybe a few years in a mental institution for Phil?"

"We haven't ironed out the details."

"You're being uncharacteristically candid today, Nestor."

"I am, aren't I?" He folded his hands behind his neck and leaned back in the swivel chair.

"I can't imagine Craig going along with a deal."

"Craig is testing the political waters. He's found that Phil has some influential friends."

"Do you mind if I smoke?"

"Yes."

"How did Phil behave at the wedding?"

"Eccentrically, let us say. Like he'd wandered into a church when he actually intended to visit his country club. He performed his ceremonial duties well enough, but didn't seem fully aware of what was happening. He laughed at inappropriate moments, pinched a bridesmaid's bottom. Yesterday was one of his bad days."

"This is strange talk from a prosecutor," I said. "Prosecutors always claim that the defendant is faking insanity."

"Phil does a lot of talking down at the jail. He says that you killed a man in Italy last summer. Says he saw you do it. Says, sometimes, that you killed his wife, Alice, too."

"Well, there you are. The man is sick."

"Karras tells a very detailed, credible story about Italy."

"Non compos mentis for sure, poor guy."

"You were in Italy last summer, weren't you, Dan? And Phil was in Italy for a few days after he jumped bail here, wasn't he? At about the same time the man vanished. Coincidentally, that was the same man who had conned many of the rich folks down at Paradise Key out of millions. Trebuchet, he was called here, Arbaleste over in Italy. A woman vanished at the same time—you remember Samantha Ridley, don't you? An old girlfriend of yours, as I recall."

"You're listening to a guy who you just said was mentally unfit to stand trial."

"I've had a couple of phone chats with an Italian federal cop. Nice guy."

"Nestor, I don't think your jurisdiction extends across the Atlantic Ocean."

"The con man who vanished in Italy just happened to live in a Castelnuovo villa next to the villa you leased. Mr. Trebuchet-Arbaleste. Another coincidence, I suppose. Still, you know, people are curious. The Italians are curious. Craig is curious. I'm curious. Just what were you and Tom Petrie and old Judge Samuelson doing over in Italy last summer?"

"Are you going to read me my Miranda rights?"

He grinned. "Maybe someday you'll tell me all about it."

"We were vacationing on the beautiful Amalfi coast."

"Rumor has it that Chester Dalhart and other Paradise Key investors recovered a large part of their money. Maybe our Mr. Arbaleste was coerced into returning the money, and then caused to vanish, along with a reporter—Samantha—who was on the story."

"That's pretty melodramatic, Nestor. Lurid."

"Did you come into a considerable sum of money last summer? You bought a new sailboat, didn't you?"

"Have you been peeking into my bank account?"

"Certainly not." He quickly crossed his heart with an ink-stained forefinger. "That would be illegal without a court order, and we don't have probable cause to get one. And listen, didn't Leroy Karpe buy a very expensive twin-engine aircraft? And old Judge Samuelson—I heard he made a very generous contribution to his college. Why are you smiling?"

"I'm trying to imagine Phil Karras on the stand, testifying to this fantasy. On one of his bad days."

"Phil says it was cold-blooded murder of this Arbaleste."

"Phil is one to talk about murder."

"What have you got here?" he asked abruptly, and he began shuffling through the manila files. Nestor knew everything that went on in the SA's office and nearly as much about the doings—legal, illegal, and quasi-legal—in the county. He had only to glance at the files.

"Petty people, petty crimes. Dopes. Restitution and a year probation for the bad-check chick, Mary Lou; restitution and a year each—sentences suspended and eighteen months probation—for the other two; but this guy in jail, Tiki Sancino, has to do real time."

"How much?"

"This is his third assault in a year. Look at this: simple assault, assault and battery, aggravated assault. He's going to kill someone. Plus this other stuff on his sheet. Five years minimum."

"Confidentially, Nestor, I'd be glad to have the thug

off the street for five years, but he won't buy it. He'll go to trial."

"I'm easy today. How about two years in the pen, two years probation."

"Less time served here in the county jail?"

"What's that?—three months. All right."

"That might do it. I'll try to persuade him to take the deal."

"He's a moron if he doesn't take it."

"He *is* a moron, Nestor."

Nestor returned the files to me. "The community theater is casting for their new play, *Death by Degrees.* A murder mystery. Are you going to try out?" Nestor did all of his acting in the courtroom and at the poker table, but his bossy wife was active in the local theater group and other affairs that might be deemed cultural.

I said, "I might try out if there's a part for me."

"There is. I told you it's a murder mystery."

　　　　*　　　*　　　*

Three of the four clients I had discussed with Nestor were out on bail; I could phone them at their homes to get approval of the plea agreements; but Tiki Sancino was awaiting disposition of his case at the county jail. The visiting room was boxy, painted in the institutional gray of battleships and death chambers, and the metal tables and chairs—potentially deadly weapons—were bolted to the floor. Lightbulbs were enclosed in tough wire mesh. A guard watched us through the thick impact-resistant window on the metal-sheathed door.

Another guard escorted Sancino inside, removed

the handcuffs, and returned to the hall outside. Tiki sat down, accepted the cigarette I gave him, and exhaled smoke through his nostrils. He was twenty-three, not tall, maybe five-six, but big-boned and thickly built, mostly torso and head with short arms and legs. A small teardrop had been tattooed near the corner of his left eye. It was an advertisement, a boast that he had killed a man. But I believed the tattoo was a lie that would eventually prove a prophecy.

"I talked to the Deputy SA," I said.

He watched me.

"I got you an okay deal."

He watched.

You had to choose your words carefully with Tiki Sancino; he was very stupid, maybe brain-damaged. There are gentle stupid men and there are men like Tiki. What he failed to understand made him suspicious and hostile, and he was not able to understand much. He lacked judgment in even the simplest of matters. The man was incapable of reading people—their gestures, demeanor, and intent—and language only increased his confusion. It could be, I thought, that some of his violent episodes had resulted from a simple failure to comprehend. You reached for your wallet; he believed you were going for a knife. You laughed at the TV; he thought you were laughing at him.

I said, "Tiki, the prosecutor will accept a plea." I wondered if he clearly understood what a prosecutor was, other than a snotty enemy in a three-piece suit.

He watched me. The teardrop tattoo, surely self-inflicted, puckered the skin around the corner of his left eye.

"You'll have to do two years."

He understood two years behind bars.

"Deduct time served—you'll be out in twenty-one months."

"Here?"

"No, probably Raiford. Two years of probation after."

I looked into his vacant amber eyes. I could not read him any more than he could read me. He was from another planet. Tiki was easily capable of believing that it was I, the man giving him bad news, who was responsible for the bad news. Prosecutors, defense attorneys, judges, juries, parole officers, jail guards—he couldn't quite sort it out. We were *fooling* him.

He was very tense for a moment, dangerous, then he relaxed and said, "Almost exercise time."

I passed him my package of cigarettes. The guard watched us through the window.

"What do you say, Tiki? It's up to you."

Stupidity made him sullen and terse. He was angered by language: words that somehow represented things, people, thoughts, laws, the world and all that it contained.

"Shit," he said finally. "Do it."

"I'll make the deal," I said. "Has your mother been here to see you?"

"I got to exercise now," he said, and he got up from the table and walked across the room. The guard unlocked and opened the door, and Tiki was returned to the jail population in time for his exercise period, his next meal, a couple hours of community TV, a night's sleep, breakfast . . . He would almost certainly earn that teardrop at Raiford.

*   *   *

Candace was preparing to leave when I arrived back at the office. She had spent much of seven hours grooming herself for this moment, quitting time, when real life commenced. She had once again converted herself from woman to magazine illustration.

"Candace," I said, "who was that brunette waiting here at noon?"

"Evelyn? A friend of mine. She was waiting for us to go to lunch."

"She's very attractive."

"Isn't she?"

"Is she married?"

"Was. Twice."

"Kids?"

"Two."

"Oh."

"Do you want me to fix you up? Evie loves to party. Boy, does she!"

"Never mind."

Candace grinned, shot out one hip and, in an imitation of Mae West, nasally said, "Hey, sailor, why don't you let me show you a good time?"

"Good night, Candace."

"*Buenos noches, Señor Pendejo.*"

Judge Samuelson was still in his office. He invited me inside, and poured out a couple of Scotch whiskeys.

"I'm thinking about quitting my law practice," I said. "It's about time," the judge said.

"*Et tu,* Levi? I'm taking a beating from every quarter today."

"Cheers."

We drank.

"Do you like cashews, Daniel?"

"I do, yes."

I watched him take a large can of cashews from a walnut cabinet, shake portions into two wooden bowls, and place the bowls on his old oak desk. The judge had decorated his office with fine antiques and semi-antiques and objects that would eventually be regarded as antiques. His room looked like an executive's office; mine like the back storage space of a used-furniture shop.

"I understand why you couldn't attend the wedding," he said. "But, you know, I received the impression that Martina missed your presence. She often glanced around the church in a way that made me suspect that she was looking for you."

"You tell the most courteous lies, Levi."

The judge poured generous splashes of Scotch into our glasses. He was a tall man, a few inches taller than my six-two, lean and very fit for a man in his late seventies. He was in his shirtsleeves now at the end of the day—a tailored shirt of the kind he ordered by the dozen from a shop in London's Jermyn Street. He wore both a belt and suspenders. White hair, a recently grown white mustache, a rosy complexion, and a deep rich voice that was sometimes gentle and sometimes snapped with authority. He was a former Michigan appeals court judge, and occasionally let you know it.

I said, "Nestor Naranjo was taunting me about Italy and Anton Arbaleste today."

"What does Nestor know about that?"

"More than I like. Phil Karras has been shooting off his mouth, telling everything he knows and a lot he doesn't know. He says that he saw me kill Arbaleste, which is true.

Nestor has talked to the Italian federal police. He's poking around in Italy."

"Nestor has no jurisdiction in Italy."

"He knows that, but he's still snooping."

"Well, Phil Karras . . . I hear he's gone half mad."

"Phil also says that I killed his wife and, it isn't clear, maybe killed Samantha, too. But who's going to listen to a crazy man?"

We ate cashews, sipped Scotch, contemplated Phil's treachery and Nestor's meddling, and thought about how the ugly past had a way of circling back to haunt the present and future.

"More whiskey?"

"No thanks, Judge."

I was light-headed, a bit woozy, but the judge appeared perfectly normal. A healthy liver, a strong heart, and a good mind at seventy-nine. He had once confided that he feared his body would outlast his mind. Now the old wooden wall clock chimed six times, and the judge turned a belch into a polite hissing.

"Levi," I said, "I'm clearing out my files. I've got to get away for a while. Will you take over anything that I can't clear up before leaving? Nothing more than a couple consultations and a couple court appearances."

"Your clients might not appreciate my taking over."

"They'll have to settle for inferior representation," I said. My clients would be proud and pleased to walk into court at the side of this patrician old man, a former judge, a former officer in the American Bar Association, and an eloquent advocate. Tom Petrie called him the *faux* Jew. He had been born Arnold Elsworth Crowcroft. During the Korean War, a soldier named Levi Samuelson had lost his life while saving the judge's, and after the war Levi had taken on the soldier's name and many of his obligations. He remained gentile in all but name.

"It's mostly plea bargain stuff," I said. "Anyway, people think we're law partners because we share the same offices."

"All right," he said. "I have plenty of time."

Levi carried a light caseload, and filled in his schedule by preparing defenses and writing appeals for famous histori-cal legal conflicts. He had recently finished writing a brief in what he called the *Sir Walter Raleigh* v. *Queen Elizabeth I* affair. He allowed himself to now and then defy history and win, though in this instance Raleigh had lost his head in Levi's case as in life.

"What are you working on now?" I asked him.

"I'm defending Charles I against Cromwell's gang."

I finished my drink and stood up before he could begin telling me about it.

"Where are you going?"

"Home."

"I mean, you said you had to get away."

"I thought I'd go sailing. Cruise the islands for the summer."

He frowned and half closed one eye. "Are you that good with a boat?"

"No, but every good sailor was once a poor sailor."

"That or a dead sailor."

"Thanks for the beer and nuts," I said. "And for taking any of my cases that might be left over."

He stopped me when I reached the door. "Daniel," he said quietly. "You're an adult. You have responsibilities. You're too old to run away to the circus or the sea."

"No, I'm not," I said. "See you later, Judge."

FOUR

The entire society page of the *Bell Harbor Record* had been devoted to the "glamorous Slocombe-Karras nuptials." There were photographs of the happily smiling bride and groom, and a gushy text that extolled their many accomplishments: Ellis Slocombe was a "celebrated" portrait painter, heir to the talent and tradition of John Singer Sargent; Martina Karras, an internationally syndicated cartoonist, a favorite of the "cognoscenti," had received many prestigious awards. Both were "movers and shakers." A photo of Martina showed her wearing a ghastly dress of white satin and silk and lace, with a six-yard-long train, a gauzy veil, and a tiara, and holding a bouquet while surrounded by flower girls. Martina, the thirty-four-year-old virgin princess. The groom was "devastatingly handsome" in his morning suit and top hat. I looked for a hint of the satirical in Martina's veil-fogged smile, but couldn't find it. This was the sort of society news that, a year ago, would have convulsed her with laughter. We might have spent half a morning mocking the pretensions and mimicking the silly prose. How could she have changed so much so quickly? It was like learning that your most trusted friend had all along been a spy for the other side.

*   *   *

Tuesday morning I phoned Candace and told her that I would not be coming into the office that day, and then went down to the Bell Harbor Marina. Herman, the dockmaster, was dozing in his shack at the end of the central pier. I let him sleep.

My boat, *Roamer,* was berthed midway down one of the narrow branching piers. She was a thirty-foot cutter with a long keel, lots of teak—teak bowsprit, toe rails, and grab rails; teak stripping inlaid into the fiberglass deck; teak hatch covers and cockpit combings—and a graceful sheer. She was not fast. You wouldn't race her unless you enjoyed finishing at the back of the fleet. But she was stiff and stable, tough, and capable of long passages in a variety of seas and weathers. Capable too, of forgiving the errors of a green helmsman.

I had considered buying a bigger and more comfortable boat, one that I could call a yacht without embarrassment, but instead had purchased the six-year-old *Roamer* and then invested a lot of money in her: new sails and winches, new standing and running rigging, jib roller furling gear, bow and stern pulpits, lifelines, and a compass as big as a cantaloupe. And I'd had the little marine diesel overhauled. She was almost ready to sail. We would go where we took each other, if I had the nerve.

After a while a boat takes on a personality, ceases being a thing and acquires life, becomes a *she. Roamer,* tightly restrained by her spring lines, seemed impatient to go. This narrow berth, this small harbor in a small bay, was like a boat prison. Pelicans and seagulls shat on her deck. Barnacles and silky beards of moss grew on her bottom. Now she lifted and rocked a little to the incoming tide. Her halyards chimed against the aluminum mast. She was a seductress, all right, but so far I had been a reluctant lover.

She dipped beneath my weight as I stepped aboard. The cockpit was small. Water weighs about eight and one-third pounds per gallon. You don't want a big cockpit filled with water in heavy weather. I unlocked the hatch, slid it back, removed the boards, and went down the ladder into the cabin. The bronze-rimmed portlights needed polishing; the wood of the cabinets, table, and trim was dull; the mattresses on both the port and starboard berths were damp and smelled of mildew. There was a galley niche with its compact ice box and stove, lockers, head, and chart table. A marine radio, a shortwave radio, and a global positioning receiver were secured to shelves above the chart table. Forward, through a curtain, was a double V-berth (another damp mattress), and stowage for sails, anchor and chain, odds and ends. The square foredeck hatch above the V-berth was made of tinted Plexiglas so that some light entered the cramped space. The entire cabin, fore and aft, received fresh air from portlights and ventilators that could be closed in bad weather.

I sat on the starboard berth. Well, hell. Might as well go. Hate my new profession, lost my girl, cops inquiring into my past, own a boat that disapproves of me.

Herman was spin casting from the end of the pier

when I emerged from the cabin. He was a big guy, a former NFL lineman who had gone to fat since retirement. He had lost his money somewhere along the way and now lived off his pension and what he earned from the dockmaster job.

"See it all the time," he said to me.

"See what, Herm?"

"See boat owners come down here and stare at their boats, tinker with their boats, dreaming. They dream, but they never go, do they?"

"Most don't."

"They polish the brightwork and bronze, they look out past the breakwater to the blue sea, dreaming. A lot of them don't take their boats out two weekends a year. Sailing gets in the way of dreaming. They scrub off birdshit and dream."

"Kiss my ass," I said.

He laughed, a sound like the grinding of a car's gears. "I see your girl got married."

"Yeah."

"Married a stud who can keep her smiling."

Herman had spent half of his life in locker rooms and on playing fields, indulging in the rough and rude banter of athletes. He was not trying to offend me. We were, from his point of view, just killing time and having fun.

"You think you might go sailing someday?"

"In two weeks," I said, knowing that now I was committed, that by God I was through dreaming.

Herman freed the lines while I started *Roamer*'s engine, and then I motored across the bay to a small boatyard on Bell Harbor's southern promontory. The yard had a lot of work waiting at this time of year, but the owner, Morris Wheeler, agreed to sneak *Roamer* to the top of his list. I asked that they haul the boat, scrub her beneath the waterline, and apply coats of antifouling paint; check out everything, *everything,* from the forestay turnbuckle to the rudder bearings; then check again, and replace any part that looked as though it might possibly fail in heavy weather. And I told Morris to fit a reliable self-steering apparatus.

He wrote it all down in a little notebook. "Where are you going?" he asked.

"God knows," I said. "I don't."

FIVE

Two weeks later, a few of my friends gathered at the marina to see me off. Tom Petrie was there, and Judge Samuelson, Candace, Herman, some others, and they presented me with a satellite telephone unit, an expensive object and one that I was not sure I wanted aboard my boat. We shared a magnum of champagne. Petrie proposed a mocking toast—something about wooden boats and iron men, plastic boats and plastic men—and finally I was free to go. I motored away from the pier to the somewhat derisive cheers of the group; they expected me to return within the week.

I motored past Martina's lighthouse and through the breakwater and straight west until I was about four miles offshore, and then I shut off the diesel and raised the mainsail, staysail, and jib. It was a bright blue day with a fair wind out of the northwest, puffy cirrus clouds that occasionally dimmed the sun, and docile three-foot swells. Half a dozen raucous gulls, mistaking *Roamer* for a fishing boat, followed for a mile or two before turning back. There was something wrong with the self-steering gear, and so I sat in the cockpit at the tiller all day, and at night anchored in Flamingo Bay between Sanibel and Pine Islands. There, with town and car lights all around, I ate a cheese sandwich and drank a can of beer. It was not a quiet or pleasant anchorage; I could hear car traffic from Sanibel and loud music from St. James on Pine Island. That night, between eight and eleven, I received three calls on my cell phone. The third was from Petrie.

He said, "'Alone, alone, all, all alone, alone on a wide wide sea!'" Tom had given me a paperback copy of *The Rime of the Ancient Mariner*, and had apparently kept a copy for himself.

"Why are you people bothering me?" I said.

"I'm not the first to call?"

"No, the last."

"I tried the new satellite phone, but nothing happened."

"It isn't switched on."

"'I fear thee, ancient Mariner!'"

"Tom, for Christ's sake—"

"'I fear thee and thy glittering eye . . .'"

"Are you drunk?"

"Stimulated merely." Petrie recited more lines from Coleridge in a deep, stagy voice. "'I looked upon the rotting sea, And drew my eyes away; I look'd upon the rotting deck, And there the dead men lay.'"

I turned off the phone before Tom could go any deeper into his prepared list of ominous quotations, hesitated a moment, and then tossed the cell phone overboard. The satellite phone would have followed except that it was a gift, and an expensive one at that, but I could at least deep-six the batteries.

I left Flamingo Bay at dawn. It was a day much like

the previous one—clear and blue, with scudding clouds and faceted green swells—and *Roamer* danced south on an ideal beam reach at about five knots. In the early afternoon I managed to repair the self-steering gear. Now I was not forced to sit at the tiller hour after hour; I could move around, attend to chores, study the charts, read, go down into the cabin to prepare a meal. The coastline, hazy in the distance, was always in view; and I was never out of sight of other boats: commercial and sport fishing boats, sail yachts, freighters, and one gigantic cruise ship that looked like—and was—an ugly floating hotel.

That night I anchored off the little island of Chokoloskee; the following night among a cluster of cays in Florida Bay. The dark swarmed with vampirish mosquitos and so, despite the heat, I was forced to sleep below in the closed-up cabin. There were no lights visible from my anchorage; no sounds that did not belong—only owls, splashing fish, night birds, wind blowing through the mangroves.

I had intended to stop at Alice Town in the Bimini islands, some forty miles east of Miami, but everything was going well and so I sailed on, and two days later made the tricky passage between Berry Island and Bonds Cay into the North East Providence Channel. I continued east until I was well clear of long, narrow Eleuthera Island, and then I altered course to the southeast. Now I had a long, open run to the Virgin Islands—my tentative destination. I marked a thousand-mile-long passage on my small-scale chart. There were islands to starboard all the way: Eleuthera, Cat Island, San Salvador, Crooked Island and Acklins Island, Mayaguana, the Turks and Caicos Islands. I could, if necessary, duck into a port at the first sign of heavy weather. It was now hurricane season, though the really big storms usually didn't arrive in the Caribbean until late summer and early autumn.

Still, those many islands to the southwest were a comfort. I marked "bolt-holes" on my big-scale charts.

The weather was mostly good. There were occasional squalls that I rode out with shortened sail, and I saw great smokey waterspouts on the horizon. Generally, the southwest trade wind was steady and the seas moderate. I gained confidence in myself and in the boat. Navigation was simple with the global positioning system; I knew exactly where I was at all times. The self-steering apparatus was my mechanical day-and-night helmsman. I was often idle but never bored.

It was like Sunday sailing much of the time, but now and then a big ship scared me. They were fast and relatively quiet, and appeared out of nowhere. Great steel monsters—tankers, cruise ships, container cargo ships, freighters—that plowed the seas with a terrifying indifference. Their computers cared nothing for a little sailboat. I saw their arrays of lights at night. Some passed within a mile or two. One day a freighter came so close that I could see figures on the bridge and hear the throbbing of engines and the churning of the screws. Its bow wave knocked *Roamer* on her side, and her mast was nearly horizontal for a few seconds. The ship had not deviated. I had to count on luck during these encounters.

My skin tanned to the color of teak, my hair turned crispy and bronze-tipped, calluses formed on my hands and feet, I lost weight. I lived slowly, minute by minute and, paradoxically, time passed quickly. My sleep, though never more than two or three hours without interruption, was tranquil, my dreams original.

I was strangely affected by the solitude. It freed me from the incessant babble of modern civilization: hectoring voices on the radio, brainless TV bombast by talking heads, office and social chatter, telephone jabber, voices buying and voices selling, voices persuading and voices bullying, voices that had become internalized without my awareness. I don't mean that before I suffered from hallucinations—"hearing voices"—but that the bogus opinions and values and ideas and formulations of modern mass society had gradually and insidiously colonized my mind. It's almost impossible, these days, to avoid invasions of these alien brain worms. But then, after sailing alone for weeks, severed from all of that white noise, the voices were reduced to one, my own; the thoughts, bold or banal, were mine, too.

The trade wind died early in the morning on my twenty-third day out of Bell Harbor. I motored east for several hours, passing over the deepest part of the Puerto Rican Trench, then cut the engine, furled the sails, and prepared to wait for a return of wind. Big ocean swells continued rolling in during the rest of the day, but they ceased near sunset, and *Roamer* was becalmed on a sea that slowly heaved and subsided with a jellylike viscosity.

SIX

Roamer drifted westward at about half a knot. The deepest part of the Puerto Rican Trench was miles away now, but there was still more than five miles of water beneath the keel. That realization could make one dizzy. How long would it take for a body to sink down through the cold blackness to the bottom? Hours, maybe, although you would not reach bottom intact; things would be eating you all the way down.

The next morning I rigged a cockpit awning with the spare jib. There was not a breath of wind. The bleached sky was empty of clouds. It was early July, *Roamer* was well below the Tropic of Cancer, and shade on deck was essential. At noon a thermometer below in the airless cabin read 116 degrees. I spent my time in the cockpit, in the awning's shade, sipping water and numbly waiting for a breeze. It was too hot to eat. Too hot to sleep. Too hot to read or think or write in the log. Sharks were a concern, and I was spooked by the five vertical miles beneath the keel, but finally I put the accommodation ladder over the side and went swimming. After the first cool shock the sea felt like warm syrup, though still refreshing, and I could dive down ten or twelve feet and find a cooler layer of water. After that first time, I often dove overboard and swam for a few minutes, staying close to the boat, close to the ladder, not exactly afraid but very wary. Sharks, I think, were a metaphor for my general unease. Thought of them had not prevented me from swimming elsewhere at sea.

Late in the afternoon I found that my eyes were sore and felt gritty, as if there were sand beneath the lids. Light—the light overhead and the light glittering on the sea—had caused a condition like snow blindness, and that had been aggravated by salt water. It was not a severe case; my vision was affected only by a fogginess on the periphery, but I could expect it to get worse if I did not take care. I went below and rummaged through the lockers until I found a pair of sunglasses with very dark lenses.

There was not as much ship traffic as one might expect just eighty-five miles off a major port like San Juan. Occasionally I saw a freighter appear, as if rising out of the sea, and I watched as it proceeded along the horizon before gradually sinking out of sight. First the superstructure arose, masts and stacks and radar gear, then the deck houses and bridge, and finally the hull; and she vanished beneath the earth's curvature in reverse order. None came close.

The sea all around continued to heave and settle, rise here and subside there, restless liquid mounds and depressions that did not appear to move horizontally. The trade wind had died far out in the Atlantic, and the normal roll of swells had halted. The water had a faint rusty tinge from the profusion of plankton—what is sometimes called the Red Tide.

Now and then objects drifted past on the gentle current: patches of yellow weed; jellyfish; a dead seabird, probably a petrel; pieces of trash—shore trash and ship's trash—the mostly submerged trunk of a big tree. I would not like to collide with that tree or one like it at six knots. But mostly the sea was empty, desolate.

I ran the diesel engine long enough to fully recharge the batteries. Burning fuel caused an alien stink out on the sea. The smell lingered in my nostrils for hours.

At dusk I turned on *Roamer*'s lights, port and starboard, fore and aft, and a bright masthead light that could be seen for miles.

At nine o'clock I got a can of beef barley soup from the galley and ate it while sitting in the cockpit. It did not require heating. I spooned it out of the can while listening to a weather report on my transistor radio. The high-pressure system was expected to remain stationary for a few more days. San Juan could expect a temperature in the high 90s again tomorrow. A meteor shower would be visible tonight in the western sky. I switched off the radio, poured a few ounces of whiskey in a tin cup, splashed in a little warm water, and drank it with my first cigarette since morning coffee. (Kate was swimming for her life as I sipped my whiskey and smoked.)

It cooled a bit. At midnight I determined that the air temperature was seven degrees cooler than my blood.

I had chocked boat cushions into the cockpit, and it was fairly comfortable, although there wasn't room to stretch out. I dozed, awakened to scan the horizon for lights, dozed again. It was too hot, and I was too anxious, to sleep for more than twenty minutes at a time. The source of my anxiety was a mystery to me. It wasn't just my fear of being run down by a big ship. I had been able to sleep through other nights at sea since leaving Bell Harbor. But these were new conditions: no wind, an absence of ocean swells, the sultry heat, the sky raining meteors, and the sea flashing with bioluminescence.

Roamer was wreathed with an eerie green light. Each little splash of water foamed green. Any fish that swam through the plankton-rich sea created arcs of light. Small animals, probably shrimp, glowed like a constellation of stars thirty feet down. I heard fish splash out in the darkness. Once I awakened to find a flying fish flapping on deck. I returned him to his perilous element. And I saw one great flash, bigger than a man, as big as a big shark, rise up through the dark water to the surface, then turn and just as steeply descend. The stern light attracted hundreds of two-inch-long fish that swarmed about in a frenzy. And all the time, above and to the west, the sky rained meteorites. I saw none for periods, then there might be ten, a dozen, more, arcing across the sky like sparks, like "falling stars." Earth was passing through a meteor belt. I switched off the boat lights so that I could better observe the show. There was only a thin slice of moon, but the Milky Way was so dense with stars and "stardust" that the night was as bright as a false dawn.

After half an hour, I turned the boat lights on, drank another whiskey, and went to sleep. This was my deepest sleep of the night. There were dreams. In one, the last, I heard a cry like the mewing of a kitten or seagull, and saw an image of the flying fish flapping on deck. The fish was making cat sounds, bird sounds, and this seemed so ominous a sign that I abruptly awakened.

It was almost midnight. The night had not changed much: it was slightly cooler and the constellations had changed position. I got up, stretched my cramped muscles, walked to the bow pulpit, and urinated over the side.

I heard the mewing sound again, except that it was a bit louder now, more like a far-off a cappella singing. I was still groggy from sleep; I had recently drunk three ounces of whiskey; and long solitude has a way of stimulating the imagination. There were no soprano mermaids or sirens out there, no one at all.

I returned to the cockpit and tried to get comfortable. Again the night was almost totally silent. There was just the gentle creaking of the boat, the occasional slap of water against the hull, and beyond that a silence that itself seemed to vibrate. An airliner, lights flashing, descended toward Puerto Rico, but I heard nothing. The plane was too high for sound to carry down to me.

I went below to get a bottle of water, and when I returned to the deck I noticed an object off the starboard beam. I didn't recognize it at first: it might have been a bag of trash jettisoned from a distant ship; a dead or injured animal, a shark or squid or dolphin; debris of some sort. Whatever, a ring of phosphorescence spread out from the pale core. Then I recognized the human form and for an instant assumed that it was a corpse, a floater. Alive? Impossible. We were eighty-five miles from land. The movement of its limbs, the feeble thrashing, were a result of the current. Closer now, and I heard harsh breathing that turned to whimpers on the exhalations. She was naked, very pale, corpse-white in that dark, jellied sea, and her skin and hair sparkled with plankton. Very close now, she lifted a hand, an arm, a pale face that exhaustion had tautened into a death mask. Her fingernails scratched at the hull.

For an instant I was paralyzed. I didn't want to touch it—her. But then I moved a few feet along the deck, leaned down, and grasped her cold right wrist. Her eyes were huge, accusing. Green sparkles on her skin and in her hair. She went slack then, heavy. Her eyes closed and she expelled a long, rasping breath. Many survivors collapse at the moment of rescue. They let down when it seems certain that the ordeal has ended. Some die. I knew that I couldn't relax my grip; I had to find the strength and leverage to haul her dead weight aboard. And I experienced one of those time-compressed visual flashes and saw her nude body sinking down through a light-speckled blackness, luminous herself in the dark, turning, arching, limbs writhing in the currents, falling slowly through five miles of sea to the silty creature-crawling bottom.

I tightly gripped her wrist with both of my hands, bent my knees and back, sucked in a breath, and hauled her out of the water and over the lifelines and rail to the deck. Then I dragged her down the narrow aisle between the rail and cabin to the open foredeck. She did not move. I turned her over. I could not tell if she was still breathing. There were welts all over her body, breasts and belly, arms and legs—jellyfish stings. Jellyfish toxins can kill. Her skin, except for the welts, was a gray-white, bloodless, and icy cold to the touch. Blood retreats from the skin in hypothermia, neglecting the extremities in order to preserve the vital organs. I found a pulse in her wrist. It was fast and irregular, arrhythmic. Low blood pressure? High? And she was probably badly dehydrated.

I went back to the cockpit for my water bottle, hesitated: would a splash of whiskey act as a stimulant or depressant? No whiskey. When I returned to the foredeck, her eyes were open. I kneeled.

"You're safe now," I said. "You'll be all right." It was the kind of thing you told the dying.

I lifted her head and upper body with my right arm, held the water bottle to her lips with my left. She was able to drink a little.

"I'd like to get you below into the cabin. Do you think you can walk a few yards?"

She did not reply, though her eyes remained open, staring up at me with what I took to be hope and fear.

I went down into the cabin and removed my first-aid kit from its brackets. There were hypodermics and ampoules of epinephrine, a powerful heart stimulant. The drug might strengthen and stabilize her heartbeat. And it might, I guessed, kill her. Roll the dice. I fitted an ampoule into the hypodermic, got a bottle of ammonia and some rags from a locker, and returned to the deck.

Her eyes were closed, but she opened them when I touched her. She watched my face as I knotted a cloth around her arm above the elbow. I had difficulty finding a vein, more difficulty getting the needle in, and then I squeezed the plunger. I remembered that I had failed to first swab her skin with a disinfectant. I removed the tourniquet.

"They say," I told her, "that ammonia is an antidote for jellyfish poisoning." I vaguely recalled hearing that. Or maybe it was an antidote for the venom injected by a stingray. I soaked a rag in ammonia and began to gently bathe the swollen streaky welts. She lay passively, staring up over my shoulder toward the stars.

"I've got to turn you over now," I said. Then, "Wait."

I went aft for three of the boat cushions, returned, and spread them out on the deck next to her.

"Can you turn over?" She couldn't.

I rolled her over onto her stomach and bathed the welts on her back, legs, and buttocks. She had been badly stung. After bathing her wounds, I rolled her over onto the cushions. Her body was slack, boneless, it seemed. Perhaps she had been paralyzed by the jellyfish poison.

I could not tell much about her except that she was young. Her face looked old with exhaustion and pain, but her body was that of a healthy young woman.

"You should drink more water," I said.

I lifted her head and held the water bottle to her lips. She drank a few ounces with difficulty, then turned her face aside.

"What's your name?"

She looked at me blankly. Perhaps she didn't know English. Her eyes were bloodshot, and the lids swollen and crusty from salt water. And then she moved; she reached out and weakly clasped my hand.

"When you're a little stronger," I said, "we'll go below and put you in a berth."

Wrap her in a blanket, bring her body temperature up to normal, rehydrate her, look through my medical books to see what else I might do. I didn't know if she had been helped by the drug injection and ammonia bath, but she seemed stronger now. Probably her recovery was due more to her youth and natural recuperative powers than my clumsy first aid. At least I hadn't killed her.

"More water?"

"Yes."

"She can talk! Soon she'll be talking and walking like an ordinary nereid."

She politely tried to smile.

SEVEN

Tubes of dust-freckled light slanted in through the port-holes and illuminated the woman in the port berth. She was wrapped mummylike in a red wool blanket. Her lips and the flesh around her eyes were puffy. Her salt-lank hair, dry now, was a dull brown that might, when clean, be a rich chestnut. She was awake. Her eyes were hazel, green with a brown fringe around the irises.

"How do you feel?" I asked her.

"Who are you?"

"You look much better now."

"Better than what?"

"You looked sixty last night, but today more like forty."

"Am I forty years old?"

"You don't know how old you are?"

"I don't think I'm forty."

"No. Maybe thirty."

Her voice was hoarse, perhaps strained by hours of shouting, calling for help.

"Who are you?" she asked.

"My name is Daniel Shaw."

"I mean, who *are* you?"

"Dan Shaw. Your new shipmate."

"What's my name?"

"You tell me."

"Katherine? Kate, maybe. It seems to me . . ."

She had arrived late last night nearly as naked as it is possible to be. Naked except for a platinum wedding band that she now twisted and pulled, unconsciously trying to remove it as we talked.

"What is this? Where am I?"

"You're aboard my sailboat."

"How did I get here?"

"You don't remember?"

"Something. The sea . . ."

Her coloring had improved. She had obviously spent time in the sun recently, and her tan was a honey brown, and the fine—almost invisible—hairs on her forearms were bleached white.

"Are you hungry, Kate?"

"I'm very thirsty."

I went to the galley sink and, working the hand pump, filled an eight-ounce plastic cup with water. She drank that thirstily, spilling a little, and held out the cup for more. She drank three cupfuls, then lay back on the bunk.

"What is your husband's name? Where is he?"

"Am I married?"

"You're wearing a wedding ring."

She lifted her left hand and gazed at the ring.

I was sure there had been a boating accident of some sort. The weather had been good for weeks, few squalls, no real storms, but there are many ways of losing a boat and crew. Fire was always a danger. Being run down by a big ship was a possibility. A stuck valve on a through-the-hull fitting could jam and sink a yacht by reversing the flow of water. Flush the toilet and watch the Atlantic rush in.

"Have I been here long?"

"About nine hours now. It was near midnight when you found us. Me and my boat. You're a powerful swimmer, Kate."

"I *swam* here? Is that why I ache so badly?"

"Fatigue, and you have a lot of nasty welts on your body, jellyfish stings. And I'm afraid I bruised you while dragging you aboard."

"Thank you," she said with a grave, formal courtesy.

"For bruising you?"

"For saving my life."

"You saved your own life, really."

I guessed that she came from a privileged background. There was evidence of that in her diction and emotional restraint.

"There are things," she said, "that I can't remember."

"What's your most recent memory?"

"Waking up here."

"Before that? Before me and the boat?"

She was silent, thinking, twisting her wedding band.

"Do you remember being in the sea?"

She shook her head.

"Well, tell me your most recent memory."

She thought deeply, and then said, "I am riding my horse."

"Where?"

"I don't know, but I am a young girl and it is springtime."

I could detect a mild southern accent beneath the hoarseness of her voice, a certain lilt.

"My horse's name is . . . Rusty."

"And what is your name?"

"I don't remember."

"How old are you in this memory?"

"Fifteen. My hair is long, and I'm riding fast through hilly country. It's very green."

"And before that? After that?"

"There are images, like in a dream, but . . ."

"Don't press, it will all come back."

"Who did you say you are?"

"Dan Shaw."

"Did I know you . . . before?"

"No."

"I am so very confused."

"You need rest."

"I have amnesia, don't I?"

"You suffered an enormous shock of some kind, followed by many hours alone in the sea. Your mind, your body, are exhausted. Temporarily burned out, maybe."

"It's all there," she said, "but sort of misfiled."

Her face was puffy, her eyes dulled by fatigue and the lids inflamed and crusted, but I could see in the symmetry of her features that she would be pretty when she recovered. "Go to sleep now," I said.

"I'd like to shower when I wake up. I'm salt-sticky. Does this little boat have a shower?"

"Yes, but I'm low on fresh water."

"Is there enough for me to take a sponge bath?"

"Sure."

"Wash my hair?"

"If you can bathe and wash your hair with one bucket of water."

"Two buckets?" she asked. "Please?"

"All right."

"What about clothes? This blanket won't serve for all occasions."

"There are clothes in the lockers. All too big for you, of course."

"I'll make do."

Vertical frown lines appeared between her eyebrows.

"Never mind. Don't force it."

"I changed my mind. I don't want to sleep. Go away while I wash."

I got my compact medical encyclopedia from the book locker and carried it up on deck.

Roamer drifted through a vast blue desert. There were no clouds, no ships on the horizon, and the sky and the sky-reflecting sea were almost exactly the same cerulean. We were suspended in a luminous blue that was without definition or dimension.

To give her privacy, I went forward to the bows, away from the open hatch and portlights. She moved around below in the cabin. I heard water being pumped from the tank.

The medical encyclopedia informed me that comprehensive amnesia, without brain trauma or brain deterioration of some kind—head injury, senile dementia, tumor, the Korsakoff's psychosis of a chronic alcoholic, etc.—was very rare. Some memory loss could be expected to result from an accident or violent event. Recall of the event itself and a short period preceding the event might never be recovered. However, claims of comprehensive temporary or long-term memory loss due to psychological causes (blocking, repression) should be viewed with skepticism.

Kate emerged from the hatch and, moving delicately, like an invalid, stepped down into the cockpit. She wore a denim shirt of mine that fit her like a baggy sheath. Kate was a tall woman, maybe five nine, but even so the shirt fell to mid-thigh. Smiling a little, she lifted the front so that I could see part of a snake-eating eagle. In looking for something to wear, she had gone through the locker where flags were kept—signaling pennants and flags of the countries one might sooner or later visit—and had fashioned a sort of diaper from the Mexican flag. It is red, green, and white, and has an illustration of a fierce eagle clutching a snake in its talons.

"That's a scary symbolism," I said.

I went aft and sat down with her in the cockpit. Bruises and welts marred her long, smooth, gold-tanned legs. Her hair was darkly wet and spiky.

"It hurts to sit," she said. "I have jellyfish stings on my derriere."

"I know. I bathed them in ammonia."

"Thank you so much," she said with a small, wry smile. Then: "Small boat, isn't it?"

"A good size for a single-handed sailor."

"Is that what you are?"

"At present."

"Daniel Shaw, solo mariner."

"Yes."

"Are you some kind of seagoing hermit?"

"For now, and *Roamer* is my seagoing cave."

"Do you have a destination?"

"Not really. But St. Croix in the Virgin Islands is marked on my chart. How do you feel?"

"Mentally? Remote. Not here—nowhere."

"Maybe you shouldn't talk much. Your voice is very hoarse."

"Even hermits should never advise a woman not to talk."

She had a way of directly engaging my glance and holding it. She compelled my attention. Few are so insistent about imposing eye contact. Her eyes were a paler green in the bright sunlight, and the pupils had contracted to black pinpoints.

"Why aren't we going anywhere?" she asked.

"No wind."

"I can see that, but don't you have an engine?"

"A little marine diesel, but there isn't much fuel left. Enough to keep the batteries charged. As soon as we get a breeze I'll sail into San Juan. Sorry for the delay."

"San Juan, Puerto Rico?"

"Yes. Where did you think you were?"

"Don't you have a radio?"

"A marine radio, sure. But it went on the blink five hundred miles back. I spilled a cup of coffee on it."

"An ordinary radio?"

"A little transistor radio I've been using to get weather reports. I had a shortwave radio, too, but the marine environment is hell on electronics." I decided not to tell her that I had deep-sixed my cell phone and the batteries to a satellite phone.

She smiled then. It was her first full smile, and it was charming despite her puffy lips and swollen eyelids.

"No fuel, no marine radio, not much fresh water, no wind. Maybe I should dive back into the sea and swim for Puerto Rico."

"My GPS unit works fine."

"So you know where we are and where we aren't," she said with a gentle mockery.

"I don't have much patience with modern technology. People take satellite phones to the top of Everest. Satellite phones, computers so they can send out newsletters and e-mail. Cell phones in the wilderness. Why? So people can chat with friends? Call nine-one-one? That sort of thing ruins the adventure, spoils the solitude."

"I'm afraid that I've spoiled your solitude."

"Well, no, nymphs from the sea are welcome."

"Then you're not going to throw me back?"

"You're a keeper."

"Have you been looking through that medical book? Do you plan to give me another ammonia bath?"

"You're pretty chirpy for a woman who looked half dead last night."

"That ammonia was not a good idea. Ammonia can burn the skin."

"I looked up amnesia in the book."

"And?"

"I got the impression that amnesia is chiefly a plot device for romantic novels and TV dramas."

"You don't believe me?"

"I'm sorry I can't motor you into port or radio for a helicopter. People will be worried about you."

"Will they? Who are these people?"

"You have to tell yourself that."

"It's very strange," she said. "Like a dream, not knowing where one is, who one is, whom one is talking to. It makes me feel . . . insubstantial. Like a ghost nymph."

"The pilot book for this section of the Caribbean says prolonged calms are rare. We'll get a breeze soon."

There was a black smudge on the southern horizon, though the ship itself was not visible. We were silent for a time, watching the smoke move toward San Juan.

"It isn't credible," Kate said. "But it apparently happened. You plucked me naked from the sea. Do you know what the Chinese say about saving another's life?"

"Everyone knows. Anyway, I didn't save your life, not really. You saved it."

"The Chinese say that if you save another person's life, you then become responsible for that person."

"Very well. Responsibility accepted."

"Once you swab a woman's behind with ammonia . . ."

"Right, freedom is gone. Are you hungry, Kate?"

"I changed my mind again—the female's prerogative. I'll go below and sleep. I'm tired, and I ache all over."

"I can arrange the cushions into a bed here or on the foredeck. It's terrifically hot down in the cabin."

"I don't mind the heat. I'm actually chilled. Can you believe that? Let's see if I can remember where the hatch is."

I helped her stand, and watched as she uncertainly descended the ladder.

EIGHT

Kate slept for six hours. I heard her moving around late in the afternoon, lockers being opened and closed, the sound of the water pump, the hiss of a propane gas burner, and then, moving stiffly, she came up on deck bearing a tray that contained two cups of instant coffee and a pile of soda crackers.

"I know it's awfully hot for coffee . . ."

"I'll fix us a real meal," I said.

"Later."

We sat in the shade of the cockpit awning. It was six thirty, hot and bright and blue, and the sea was still unnaturally smooth.

"Has your memory returned?"

"No. Well, bits and pieces, fragments."

"Tell me a fragment or two."

"These crackers are soggy. Like paste."

"The salt attracts moisture from the air."

"Oh," she said, smiling faintly.

A small tern arrowed toward us out of the south, slowed and fluttered, and landed on the mast's upper spreader. It was not the sort of bird you see far from land. No storm had blown it out to sea. Feathers ruffled, beak half open, it perched on the spreader for ten minutes, and then flew off—not south, toward land, but farther out into open water.

"Poor baby," she said.

"Kate, how did you end up in the sea alone and eighty-five miles from land?"

"I don't remember."

"Come on. Were you dropped from an airplane, expelled from a submarine, fell off a cruise ship?"

"Not now," she said. "I can't, now. Tell me about yourself. What about you?"

"Starting where?"

"Anywhere."

"Well, I was in the army for twelve years, in the CID."

"Which is?"

"Criminal Investigation Division. Now I'm a criminal defense lawyer. A night law school graduate. I've been a member of the Florida bar for a few months."

"Two occupations that contain the word 'criminal.'"

"I learned that I'm not temperamentally suited to practicing law. And then my fiancée got married to a rich artist. There were other problems."

"And so you sailed off into the sunset."

"Sunrise. Sunrise sounds more like a fresh start."

"And one night in the middle of the ocean a swimmer arrives to disturb your solitude."

"Yes, a naked long-distance swimmer. It must have been terrible for you out there, Kate."

"It was a miracle, wasn't it? I don't mean in a religious sense—God selecting me to live while millions died elsewhere."

"I know what you mean. My little boat in this vast patch of ocean."

"Stationary, no wind."

"Drifting a little, but not so fast and far that you couldn't reach it in a long, hard swim. It was an amazing feat of endurance."

"Mostly I just treaded water, floated, drifted with the currents. It required all I had, and then some."

"The surface water is eighty-two degrees."

"It seemed very cold after an hour or two."

"Sure. You lost a lot of body heat."

"I willed myself to fight. I thought—I *knew*—that I was going to die, but I couldn't stop fighting. I fought and fought until I couldn't fight anymore, until my mind and body were finished, and then I kept fighting on some resource I didn't know I had."

"And how did you get into the sea, Kate? What happened?"

"I don't remember that."

Kate seemed to lack what psychologists call "affect" and the rest of us call emotion. Her range of emotions seemed narrow. Even her rare smiles were measured, provisional. Of course, the hoarseness of her voice prevented much range in the expression of emotion. But I was puzzled by her reticence in discussing the event that had cast her naked and alone into the sea. Why didn't she feel more, reveal more of her suffering? I supposed it was possible that her many hours in the sea had temporarily burned emotion out of her. So long alone, living on adrenaline, might have exhausted her capacity to feel.

"Who are you, Kate? Really?"

"Don't bully me," she said.

Later I went below, opened a can of lentil soup, put it on a burner, opened a canned Danish ham, and made two sandwiches while the soup warmed.

Kate was hungry now; she finished both her bowl of soup and her sandwich. It was full night when we finished.

I switched off *Roamer*'s lights and rolled back the cockpit awning, and we sat together in darkness, looking up at the stars and planets and the bright powdery swath of the Milky Way. Meteorites arced across the sky tonight, but there were fewer of them, none very bright. I pointed out certain stars that were important to navigators in the old days, and told her how mariners established their positions on the great oceans with nothing more than a sextant, a chronometer, and mathematical tables. Whole constellations were mirrored on the surface of the sea, and there was a green flash and glitter of phosphorescence below. No breeze, hardly any sound, just the occasional creak of gear or the slap of a wavelet against the hull.

"Care for a drink?" I asked her.

"What do you have?"

"Scotch, gin, a few bottles of wine."

"No ice?"

"No ice."

"Just a glass of wine, red, if you have it."

I went below, got a couple of not very clean glasses from a cabinet, poured a glass of wine for Kate and a large whiskey for myself.

She refused a cigarette. I lit one and blew smoke toward the stars. A ship's lights appeared above the southwestern horizon. It did not seem to be heading our way, but I took the precaution of switching on *Roamer*'s array of lights.

"You have an accent," I said.

"Everyone has an accent."

"Yours sounds as though you might be from one of the Carolinas, maybe Virginia."

"A po' white trash accent?" she asked lightly. "Or the accent of the gentry?"

"You dissimulate, Kate."

"You mean I lie. Tell me about your ex-fiancée, Mr. Shaw."

"Martina? Well, Martina was—is—a cartoonist. A serious cartoonist, if that makes sense."

"Martina Karras? The one who does the strip about all the swampland creatures?"

"Yes."

"It's a very earnest cartoon. Why did she abandon you?"

Martina had abandoned me because I had killed two men: one out at her lighthouse reef, her home, while she slept; and the other in Italy during a period when I was involved with another woman.

"She ran from me like a scalded cat," I told Kate, "and for good cause."

"What cause?"

"Maybe I'll tell you about it someday."

"Do you miss her?"

"Not since I plucked you from the sea *en déshabillé* . . ."

"*En déshabillé*, indeed! The naked jellyfish-maimed hag from the sea."

"I like hags. I've always liked hags."

"My God," she said, "I still can't believe in you and your little boat. The lights—when I saw the lights, I cried. Oh, white lights, red lights, green lights. Your boat was lit up like a Christmas tree. I was so afraid that the lights would vanish before I could reach them. And then they did! They did vanish."

"I had turned out the lights for a while so I could look at the stars."

"Nighttime was much worse than the daylight hours. At first, I really didn't believe it when I saw the lights. I was sure that I was hallucinating. I had hallucinated before that. And the jellyfish—my God, do they sting!"

"They can kill."

"They half paralyzed me. My hands and feet are still numb."

"The jellyfish toxins. The numbness should pass. At least there were no sharks."

"Oh, but there were sharks, four or five of them. They swarmed around me at night for—I'm not sure—ten minutes, and then they went away. I was sure they were going to eat me."

"Most likely they were curious porpoises."

"Sharks, porpoises—I was horrified."

Now the emotion was returning; now she was again feeling the isolation and terror.

"What time did I reach the boat?" she asked.

"Around midnight."

She closed her eyes and moved her lips as she silently counted, and then she opened her eyes and said, "I was in the sea for twenty-six and a half hours."

"That's a long time."

"You don't believe me?"

"It's possible," I said. "I heard of an American marine who fell off the deck of an aircraft carrier in the Arabian Sea. He was in the water for two days before he was finally picked up by a fishing boat from Pakistan."

"Maybe I'm half as tough as that marine."

"Do you want another glass of wine?"

"No. This one made me feel sick."

"You're still dehydrated. I'll go down and get some water."

"No, I'll get it. I'm tired. I want to rest."

"Goodnight, Kate."

"Goodnight," she said, and she stiffly went down the ladder into the cabin.

I was awakened several hours later by her hoarse, sleep-thickened voice urgently calling out, but I couldn't understand the words.

"Kate?" I called. "Kate?"

She was quiet then. She had been dreaming.

NINE

I slept on deck. There was no breeze during the night and none blowing when I awakened. It was dead calm, with the water as smooth as you could ever expect to see on the open ocean. Glassy smooth, empty of waves and ripples, just a slow oceanic heaving that you perceived only by the boat's sluggish responses.

It had been a hot night. It was hot both day and night, and by noon the sun burned a hole in the fabric of sky and bleached away color halfway down to the horizon.

Kate came up on deck at seven. She still wore the absurd flag diaper, but had exchanged the denim shirt for a faded blue tennis jersey. She carried a tray containing two cups of coffee, a jar of raspberry preserves, and a round loaf of sweet brown bread. The bread came from a vacuum can and so was fresh.

"You promised me a wind," she said.

"And I shall deliver. Eventually."

"'Day after day, day after day, we stuck, nor breath nor motion; as idle as a painted ship upon a painted ocean.'"

"You found my copy of *The Rime of the Ancient Mariner*."

She passed me a round of bread smeared with raspberry preserves.

The jellyfish stings on her thighs were healing well. Kate moved freely now, without pain, and most of the swelling was gone from her face. Her eyes were clear. Beauty was emerging from that crusty mask.

"I saw a fish just now," she said. "He darted out from under the boat and darted back again."

"I noticed some fish this morning. They like the shade beneath the boat, and they feed on the weeds and tiny shellfish."

"You have a foul bottom, Shaw."

"*Roamer* does."

"Shall we catch a fish and eat him?"

"They're too small."

"The one I saw just now wasn't small."

She bit into a slice of bread, sipped her coffee, and when she lowered the cup flecks of raspberry were visible at the corners of her mouth. She licked one spot away, then the other.

I said, "I see that you finally managed to remove your wedding band."

"Finally. I used cooking oil to make my finger slippery."

"What did you do with the ring?"

"I threw it out a porthole this morning."

"Was that a symbolic divorce?"

Kate often parried my questions with questions of her own. "Doesn't the Ancient Mariner tell his story at a wedding party? '. . . And is that Woman all her crew? Is that a Death? And are there two? Is Death that woman's mate?'"

There was a tiny scar at the corner of her mouth, a glossy crescent that dimpled when she smiled. And there was another scar which interrupted the line of her left eyebrow. Small flaws that charmed.

We finished breakfast. No ships or airplanes were visible. I looked over the side and saw leaning columns of sunlight penetrate far down through galleries of color. Light slowed in water, was refracted.

"It's going to be scorching later," I said. "I'll put the ladder overboard. Will you be afraid to go into the sea?"

"I'll know when the moment comes. But I don't think so."

"Right. Get back on the horse what throwed yuh."

"Go into the sea what almost killed yuh."

We swam once or twice an hour during the long hot afternoon. She showed no fear of the sea. The sapphire water was cool, caressing, sensual on the skin. We swam together, then sat in the cockpit until the heat became overwhelming, and again dove overboard. Kate got my face mask and dived down beneath *Roamer* and swam along the mossy keel, surprising the bright little fish, and then she surfaced, laughing. We were suspended within a blue crystal globe.

We rested beneath the cockpit awning and chatted. Kate did not volunteer any information about her ordeal, nor did I press her. I didn't want to be responsible for ruining her relaxed, impish mood.

She went below at twilight and did not return to deck until after dark.

"I dreamed," she said.

"What did you dream?"

She started to speak, halted, shook her head. The dream had altered her mood. She was again the pensive, inward Kate.

It was still dead calm. We occasionally saw ship's lights on the horizon and aircraft lights overhead. The air had a scorched taste and a sour smell from the algae bloom.

"Hungry?" I asked.

"No."

An English-language radio station in San Juan gave weather forecasts at five minutes past the hour. I tuned in at ten, early enough to receive the news. Violence in the Middle East. Violence in Africa. Protesters had marched against Puerto Rico's commonwealth status with the U.S.; they demanded independence. A scandal in the Puerto Rican legislature. A woman missing at sea.

Katherine Adams-Cardinal, twenty-nine, an American citizen resident in the Dominican Republic, had been reported missing at sea by her husband, César Cardinal. The incident occurred aboard the yacht *Zodiaco* after it had completed its voyage north through the Mona Passage between the Dominican Republic and Puerto Rico, and was an estimated thirty-five miles northeast of the city of Aguadilla. Mr. Cardinal, a diplomat accredited to the Dominican Republic's embassy in Washington, reported that his wife had been drinking, and had gone alone to the afterdeck for fresh air. He stated that he became concerned when she did not return after twenty minutes, and went to look for her. When he was unable to find Mrs. Adams-Cardinal, he ordered the ship to turn back, and then alerted the crew and guests, who conducted a search of the large motor yacht. She was not found. Mr. Cardinal alerted the Puerto Rican Coast Guard and provided it with *Zodiaco*'s estimated position at the time Mrs. Adams-Cardinal vanished, and the course it had then been following. The *Zodiaco* continued to search until daylight, when Coast Guard boats and helicopters arrived to assist.

Mr. Cardinal said that his wife had been depressed for some time, but rejected suggestions that she might have committed suicide. "She has too much to live for," he asserted. "She would not abandon our son and me." The Coast Guard is continuing the search.

"She had been drinking," Kate said bitterly. "She had been depressed. Mr. Cardinal did not believe she had committed suicide."

"Were you drinking?"

"Yes. We all were. But I wasn't drunk."

"Depressed?"

"Depressed, angry, rebellious—yes! My marriage was a failure. I was going to leave him."

"Did you jump overboard, Kate?"

"No."

"An accident, then? You fell?"

"My God, I didn't jump or fall overboard! I was thrown like a sack of garbage into the sea by my husband."

"Will you tell me about it now?"

"The bastard! Oh, Jesus!"

"Kate?"

"Get me something strong to drink. Whiskey.

And turn off all the boat lights. I'll tell you about it in the dark."

*   *   *

First, Kate said, you should know a little about the couple involved and the state of their union, which, three nights ago, culminated in an attempted murder.

Katherine Adams was a fifth-generation Virginian, though not an *old* Virginian—your family had to live in the state before and during the Civil War to qualify for the reverential *old*. It was even better if you could claim an ancestor who had fought with Lee. But Kate's great-great-great-grandfather, Nathan, was a Pennsylvanian who had fought with the Union against Lee; he lost an arm, but discovered country that he liked. After the war he sold his big farm in Pennsylvania and moved his family to Virginia. Land was cheap in the Confederate South after the war, and labor—former slaves—could be hired for little more than simple food and a few pennies. His new farm prospered, and so he bought another, and then another. His son and grandson also prospered, and bought more land, always more land—they were land-hungry farmers and shrewd businessmen. And they understood that politics and business go together like a hand in a glove. The male Adamses became involved first in state and then national politics: there was almost always a Congressman Adams in the house. Still, they were farmers foremost. Just plain old farmers, then rich farmers, and ultimately gentleman farmers with smooth hands and manure-free shoes. It was the gentleman farmers, Kate's grandfather and father, who began selling the land. Times had changed, America had changed. Washington, D.C., had boomed during World War II, and afterward you could make a lot more money selling or developing land than you could growing crops and tending herds.

The family owned a lot of land in northeast Virginia, land along the Potomac, more land to the west but still within easy driving distance of the capital. Kate's grandfather formed a land company, a real estate company, and a construction company, opened a bank, and closed down the farms. Houses sprouted in croplands and pasturelands. Villages gradually formed to serve the new residents. One, naturally, was named Adams. Her grandfather, Kate said dryly, had built a "brand-new ancestral home" on three hundred acres in the Virginia horse country.

"So you're rich," I said.

"Many people would think us rich. But the real, modern rich know better."

It was almost midnight now, and still very hot. We saw ship lights moving from the north-northwest toward San Juan, but the vessel would not pass close to us. I did not switch on *Roamer*'s array of lights.

I said, "I've met a few of the very rich recently. They're an insular tribe."

"Not as insular as they'd like to be. They share the same horrors as everyone else—foul air and water, crowding, crime, terrorism, all of that."

"Well, they still have their remote palaces and secluded hideaways. They can buy escape. I'm glad you aren't filthy rich."

"Why are you glad?"

"A huge amount of money is a complication."

"Complicating what, exactly?"

"Our relationship."

"Do we have a relationship?"

"We must. We sleep a yard apart and pee in the same basin."

César Cardinal was the elder son of an old and powerful family of the Dominican Republic. They had always been among the island's ruling elite. A family legend claimed that an ancestor had fought with Cortés during the conquest of Mexico. Another, so they boasted, had sailed with Columbus. They had an insane pride. They regarded themselves as little gods and goddesses. The Cardinals talked of their pure Spanish blood, uncontaminated through the generations, untainted by Indian or Negro or mongrel elements, blood exalted by just wars and Christian sacrifice. They were absolutely mad, Kate said, but amiable enough if they regarded you as a near equal.

César served with the Dominican Republic's embassy in Washington. No one quite knew what his duties were. His title was "Special Envoy." During daylight hours he could be found on the tennis court or golf course or polo field; at night, he either gambled or attended important parties given by the various embassies.

All the women of the Washington-Virginia area loved César. Young women, the debs and sub-debs, middle-aged women, old women with lizard skin—they were all stunned stupid by César Cardinal. There was gossip about his many brief and dangerous affairs. He enjoyed risk. He liked to provoke fate with his choice of partners—the higher the official, the more intently he targeted the wife. Those were the rumors.

He was handsome, more than movie-star hand-some, young-god handsome, physically perfect, but that wasn't all. He was very bright, too, quick and witty, with excellent manners and a sympathy that seemed sincere. He was a rogue, no one doubted that, but of course a reputation for roguery was attractive to women, and the aura of danger surrounding him was a provocation. He never boasted. His friends, male and female, boasted for him, lied for him, maybe. He had, years ago, been shot at by a jealous husband. He had driven race cars, fought bulls in Colombia, climbed Aconcagua solo and without oxygen. All as an amateur, naturally: aristocrats did not have jobs or serious professions; they didn't *work*.

"So," I said, "you fell in love with him, and he with you."

"He selected me."

"Why you? Money?"

"There were for richer women he could have had with a finger snap."

"Because of your beauty?"

"I'm not beautiful. He *liked* me. We had fun together. He was thirty years old, it was time for him to marry, have kids, and he selected me out of the lineup. Look, I was crazy in love with the man. Being with César—it was living at a higher pitch in a new world. The world changed when you looked at it through his eyes. He felt affection for me. I knew that. Maybe I understood that he wasn't deeply in love with me, whatever that means. But I didn't care. It simply seemed that I couldn't live without him."

"Couldn't live with him, eventually—he tried to kill you."

"Yes."

"You sound as though you still love him."

"In part, of course. Love can't be turned on and off like a water tap."

Kate's residual love and her former near worship of the man were evident in her description. She had lost herself in him. That kind of love is more than blind, it's delusional, and she had made her husband sound almost mythic in the telling. The Demon Lover. No doubt César was handsome, charming, dashing, all of that and more; but Kate's was a special view—a special creation—and had to be regarded skeptically.

"You sound tired," I said.

"I am."

"Why don't you sleep now?"

"I will, yes."

She went down into the cabin. I sat in darkness for half an hour, finishing my drink, and then I switched on all of the boat lights, went below, and crawled into my berth. I listened to Kate's breathing. I believed that she was awake. Sometimes you can sense another's consciousness in a small dark place. I thought about going to her, comforting her, holding her, making love to her. But I remained still. I feared not so much that she would reject me, but worse, that she might submit out of gratitude and loneliness.

TEN

Next morning there was a brownish smear around the horizon and a haze in the air. Several days of virtually motionless air had caused a buildup of pollution. It was produced in the world's industrial centers and generously distributed to more pristine locales by the jet streams. This smog would be carried to some other area when the trade wind resumed.

The sea remained smooth, hardly wrinkled, and there were few clouds. Today we saw more ship traffic in the hazy distance. *Roamer* had been slowly drifting for days, and perhaps her drift had taken her closer to the sea lanes.

Kate and I sat beneath the cockpit awning, sipping water and nibbling at pieces of brown bread. All of the puffiness was gone from her face now; her eyes were clear, and the jellyfish welts on her arms and legs had faded to a faint pink. There would be no scarring.

So, Kate said, seven years ago she and César Cardinal were married in a big outdoor ceremony at the family's Virginia estate. There were hundreds of guests from all over the world; many members of the Washington diplomatic community attended, and of course César's family and friends from Latin and Caribbean America were represented. It was beautiful. Spring, with the cherry trees in blossom, a bright warm day—just beautiful. She'd wept with happiness. She became Katherine Adams-Cardinal.

Their life was wonderful at first, perfect, for a couple of years. They usually spent the springs and autumns in the Washington-Virginia area; the summers at Newport or Martha's Vineyard; and winters in the Dominican Republic. It was a fast, exciting life, rather frantic, really: travel, parties, gambling excursions to Las Vegas or Monte Carlo; risky sports, new people, always new people, and some of them not very nice. César had an almost superhuman energy; he always had to be doing something, going somewhere, planning a new adventure. Naturally, he dominated every gathering. He swept people along, often against their own interests. He was like a spoiled king.

César was, as far as she knew, faithful to her until she became pregnant in their second year of marriage. His affairs were not serious. A weekend liaison in New York; a Las Vegas hooker, and at least a couple of times he and a woman guest had vanished to a bedroom during a party. Those were the infidelities she knew about. No doubt there had been others.

César could not understand her anger, her humiliation, her tears. Those women meant nothing to him. They were merely physiological necessities. Kate was late in her pregnancy. She knew he was a highly sexed man, she knew and appreciated that, and that he was incapable of abstinence, not always able to resist the temptation of other women. It was skin only, friction only, not the fusion of souls that *they* had. Her Puritan American background caused her to behave stridently, foolishly. If she had been raised in the island culture, the Hispanic culture, she would understand: there, wives knew and understood how men were made, were tolerant because they were loved, and were content in raising their children and involving themselves in female things. "I love you madly, Kate. You know that."

Her son was born almost two years to the date of their marriage. César was ecstatic; he'd feared that their newborn would be female. Next a girl, that was fine; but the firstborn had to be a boy.

Her life changed with the birth of their son, but his did not. He was the same old reckless and manic César. It seemed that nothing could halt his mad plunge into life. He wanted to devour the world. Kate had a baby, César had a life—ten lives—to live. At times he vanished for weeks. He returned very tired, but affectionate, and he played delightedly with his son, but a few days later he became bored again and again was off to France or Mexico City or Bogotá. Once, while playing polo in the Dominican Republic, he fell off his mount and seriously fractured his left arm, but he was so busy, he had so many balls in the air, that he neglected to visit a doctor for several days. He was told that he had come very close to losing his arm to an infection. He was not chastened. He did not slow down. He himself removed the cast two weeks ahead of schedule.

During the last part of Kate's story a cargo ship, en route to San Juan, had risen above the horizon in the northwest. It slowed, changed course, and angled in toward *Roamer.* We saw seamen standing at the rail. The ship finally altered course and increased speed. The bridge officer had determined that we were not flying distress flags, not in peril.

"Your César," I said, "sounds like a charming guy."

"Of course he's charming. Isn't that what I've been telling you? I didn't marry a dull, witless man, I didn't marry a fool."

"A weak man, then?"

"Is he?" She was now defending herself by defending César. She had married him, after all, had his son, and stayed with him up to the instant when he had thrown her into the sea. "To a large extent his vices are the vices of his class and generation and culture. Gambling, whoring, taking enormous risks—they're *virtues* in his milieu. César is loved and admired by many people. Is he weak? That's not the word."

"And murder? Is murder admired in his milieu?"

Her smile was uneven. "It might be acceptable to kill a mistress, but a wife, a mother—no."

"Murdering a wife is stepping over the line?"

Again the wry, uneven smile. "Murdering a wife— unless she's caught cheating—is considered excessive."

"Were you caught cheating?"

"I never cheated. But listen: even though murdering a wife might be taboo, it would probably be justified eventually. César's friends and family would defend him. Murdering or attempting to murder a wife—well, she was a bitch, wasn't she, never one of us, a schemer and a gringa besides, and we don't know everything, so maybe she deserved it. Anyway, it never happened, it's all lies."

"Nice people."

"I like many of them."

"Even those who will turn against you?"

"They'll be forced to choose."

"So you like people whom you expect will condone your husband's attempt to kill you?"

"It won't be that clear to them, will it? It will be confused, blurry, emotional. Most will simply refuse to believe it. It isn't a rational process. People defend family and friends. And isn't loyalty a virtue?"

"Not if it's unjust."

She laughed. "It's probably just as well you gave up your criminal defense practice."

"You're right."

"God, it's hot. I'm broiled. Let's swim."

We swam for half an hour. Today we ventured farther from the boat, a hundred feet or so, and remained there for a time, treading water.

"It's lovely," Kate said.

"We'll be getting a breeze tonight."

"How do you know?"

"See those puffy little clouds coming in from the east?"

"Yes. Popcorn clouds."

"The trade wind picked up out in the Atlantic. It's on its way. We'll head in to San Juan as soon as it arrives."

"I don't want to go to San Juan."

"No?"

"I've been thinking. It seems to me that the only advantage I have is that César believes I'm dead."

"You might have a bigger advantage by reporting his attempted murder and your terrible ordeal."

"You heard that radio report. Mrs. Adams-Cardinal

was drinking, she was depressed, she was perhaps suicidal. By now César and the others have told their version of events. The depressed lush leaped overboard."

We swam in toward *Roamer.* Kate was a strong and elegant swimmer. Her strokes and kick appeared leisurely, but I was unable to keep up. It was not difficult to imagine her surviving a full day at sea.

We took our places in the shade of the cockpit awning. Kate looked about twenty now, with her face healed, with her sleeked-back hair and water-beaded skin.

I said, "You have the facts on your side. There's one big obvious lie—the false report to the Coast Guard. César reported you missing at least forty miles from the true position. That's why we never saw any search planes or boats."

"But the false report can be explained as a navigational error, a natural mistake in the confusion of the moment."

"Who will believe him?"

"Who will believe the claims of a hysterical, drunken woman with mental problems?"

"I will," I said.

"You see, César—his family—have my son. They'll never give him up to me, never."

"The cruise. Tell me about that, Kate."

They had gone cruising on a one-hundred-and-forty-foot motor yacht named *Zodiaco.* César had invited three couples: the Dickeys, the Solomons, and the Maldonados, friends of César's, or business contacts—it was often hard to distinguish between the two. They all knew each other pretty well, it seemed, but all were strangers to Kate. She felt like an outsider, excluded from references and jokes and people's names, snubbed, a little, maybe. She had not wanted to go on this cruise. She had resisted. Their marriage was breaking up; she had previously told César that she was leaving and taking Antonio with her. César begged her to reconsider. Their marriage, their family, their life together—seven years!—was far too precious—sacred!—to dissolve so casually. No, it was intolerable. Please, Kate, please come on the cruise with me, it's a chance to restore our love, re-create what we had before. César could be very persuasive.

"How many were in the *Zodiaco*'s crew?"

"There were five. An engineer, two deckhands, a cook, and a steward."

"And the captain."

"No, the captain was scheduled to join us in San Juan."

"Whose yacht is it?"

"It was chartered from a company in Santo Domingo."

"Well, who was responsible for taking the yacht from Santo Domingo to San Juan?"

"César. César was captain, first mate, bosun. He is anything he says he is."

"One-hundred-and-forty-foot yachts are worth a great deal of money, and it's hard to believe that a charter company would let it out without providing their own captain all the way. The insurance company wouldn't tolerate it."

"Maybe you don't understand the Dominican Republic, places like that. Second world, third world . . . The few rich and powerful people down there are all cousins in blood or in regard. *Primos.* César is a *primo* of the charter company's owner. In fact, I think he has some money invested in the company."

"All right. You were headed to San Juan to pick up a captain. Then where?"

"I'm not sure. The Virgin Islands, St. Maarten, St. Kitts, Guadeloupe, maybe. It was a loose itinerary. The yacht had been leased for a month."

"Go on. You left Santo Domingo . . ."

"We sailed from Santo Domingo in mid-morning and cruised east along the coast, and then in the afternoon turned north. At one point I could see the coast on my left, and an island on my right."

"You were traversing the Mona Passage. How fast could the *Zodiaco* go?"

"I don't know. But we seemed to be moving fairly slowly. When we cleared the Mona Passage, the yacht was stopped so that we could swim. The currents were strong there. But we swam and sat out on the deck."

"Drinks served?"

"Drinks with a late lunch. Will you stop interrupting?"

"Sorry."

At twilight they resumed cruising at a moderate speed. They could see lights from a city on the west coast of Puerto Rico. Someone said it was Aguadilla. They sailed north for a time, perhaps half an hour, and then turned east.

"We all went below to our cabins to bathe in fresh water, relax, and dress for dinner. At eight we gathered in the saloon for cocktails. It was awkward for me, but everyone else seemed to be having great fun."

"Tense atmosphere?"

"As usual, César and I had been fighting. Not openly, no shouts and tears, just our own kind of clandestine warfare. Insult and smile, insult and turn away. I was furious. I didn't like his guests. I felt trapped among . . . not enemies, exactly—but certainly not sympathetic people. I missed my son. I regretted my weakness for going on the cruise."

"How much did you drink in the saloon?"

"Three gin and tonics."

"And at lunch?"

"A glass of wine."

"So there you are in the saloon with your husband and the Dickeys and the Solomons and the Maldonados. Music playing, the steward passing out drinks and canapés. You were isolated?"

"I felt isolated. Maybe I isolated myself. But I hated it, being trapped on that boat with people I didn't know and didn't much like."

"So you went up on deck for fresh air."

"Not then. Later, halfway through dinner."

"Wine with dinner?"

"One glass. Why do you insist on counting my drinks?"

"Others will. So you went up on deck for fresh air."

"I went up on deck to escape them, all of them."

"Who was in command of the ship at that time, Kate?"

"One of the sailors, I suppose."

"You went up on deck—aft?"

"The big open rear deck, yes."

"It's night. You—what?—you went to the stern rail, looked down at the wake, looked up at the stars, tried to relax."

She had been alone for only ten or fifteen minutes when César appeared. He embraced her. He smelled of whiskey and suntan oil. His skin was warm. She had not returned his embrace. He kissed her cheek, her neck, held her tightly, and whispered something about the pity of it. And then he picked her up, as a man picks up his bride before crossing the threshold, and he threw her over the railing.

"That sounds spontaneous," I said. "A sudden impulse."

"No. It was as cold and cynical as can be. Listen. Earlier in the day he took my engagement ring. I'd removed it when I went swimming, placed it in my jewelry box in our cabin. The wedding ring, which you saw, was too tight; I couldn't take it off. I noticed that the engagement ring was missing when I dressed for dinner. I said, 'César, my ring has been stolen.' I believed it had been stolen by a crewman while we were up on deck. César just shrugged, said it would show up. But he took it. He didn't want that ring on the bottom of the sea."

"An expensive ring?"

"Platinum, with a five-carat white diamond. César bought it for me when we became engaged. What César gives, César takes. No, he didn't want me wearing that ring when I drowned."

"So now you're in the water, Kate, in the turbulence of the wake. Lucky the screw didn't chew you up. You surface, the yacht is moving away. César is standing at the stern rail, looking back at you. You scream."

"This is hard," she said. "I'm hot and I'm tired. Let's swim now and wait until tonight for the rest. What do we have to eat?"

"The same old canned stuff."

"Why don't you catch a fish?"

"I will, by God."

At dusk I got out my spinning rod, attached a small rubber squid that looked remarkably lifelike moving through the water, and began casting from the stern. On the third cast I saw a shadow swiftly move out from beneath the boat, and my rod bent double, and line whined out through the reel.

"It's the great fish!" Kate cried, laughing. "The leviathan!"

It wasn't a very big fish, maybe seven or eight pounds, but it fought like a giant, a god of fishes.

Kate, laughing, dancing back and forth along the deck, yelled, "Catch him! Don't lose him! He got away, you dope. No, there he is!"

At last, with luck, I got the fish up on deck where it flapped wearily and worked its gills. It was a dorado, dome-headed and chunky, and as it struggled, dying, its skin rippled with a delicate gold and iridescent blues and greens. Kate was disturbed by the fish's dying beauty, and she retreated to the foredeck.

I killed the fish with a hammerthump on the head, and then got out my filleting knife. The dorado had been feasting on the small fish that lived beneath *Roamer*. I found some of them in its stomach, along with Kate's wedding band.

ELEVEN

The dorado is a delicious fish, as good as any, and Kate had no difficulty in eating her share. Pity fades with a sharp appetite. I grilled the fillets on my charcoal brazier, and with them we had boiled rice, a can of lima beans, and a bottle of warm-to-hot chardonnay. "It was good," Kate said.

"She said it was good."

"She said it was good and indeed it was good."

"What are you going to do with the ring now that it has been magically restored to you?"

"Strange, isn't it, that you found it in the fish? A metaphysical statement of some kind? Meaning: it isn't that easy to get rid of the son of a bitch."

"Where did you go to school, Kate?"

"Wellesley."

"Studies?"

"Nonspecific. The genteel ladies' curriculum. I'm really well prepared to do nothing."

"I've noticed that you know your way around a sailboat."

"Sure, I'm from the lesson-taking class. Piano lessons,

ballet lessons, riding lessons, tennis lessons, ski lessons, sailing lessons . . . We think leisure requires instruction. A student and a boss. The one thing we won't tolerate is spontaneity."

Individual stars appeared, then clusters, then constellations, and soon we were able to see a great hemisphere of the galaxy. With night the water began sparkling and flashing, swarming with secret life.

"So, Kate," I said, "the son of a bitch threw you over the stern rail. There you are, in the turbulence of the wake. César is watching you recede. You scream."

"Not then. I was too shocked to scream, and I was choking on water. I screamed later, when I understood that the yacht was not going to turn and come back for me. Until then, I thought it was some horrible joke. César is a prankster. Or I thought it might even be an accident—he had picked me up and lost his balance and . . ."

"You swam after the *Zodiaco*?"

"No. I removed my clothes; they were dragging me down. Shoes, skirt, blouse, a blazer. I took off everything except my pants and bra. I don't know when or how I lost my underwear."

"And César waited until you were out of sight and your shouts couldn't be heard, and he went below and said . . . ?"

"God knows. Woman overboard. Kate is gone. But I'm sure he convinced them it was a suicide or accident. César is an actor. He can act any part—lover, husband, father, diplomat, entrepreneur, genius. For a long time he convinced me in each of his roles. But then I got to know him, finally. I knew him, all right, and it was over. He persuaded—coerced—me to go on that cruise. He intended to kill me."

"Why?"

"Why! What kind of question is that? 'Tell me, Kate, why did the poor fellow want to kill you? Couldn't he take it anymore?'"

"Easy."

"Shall I list my defects? I was not always kind to his friends and his dogs. I was never as submissive as he demanded and deserved. I was cheeky—that was it, I was cheeky, and I disapproved of his whores and the way he gambled away my money, which, by the way, he called 'Kate's dowry.' Every penny he could seize was dowry."

"I was only suggesting that he had a motive. Was it the money?"

"I stopped giving him money," she said. "I stopped paying his debts."

"You told me that you weren't really rich."

"Not rich in relative terms. But rich enough to keep him at the gaming tables for a good while."

"César inherits if you die?"

"César and my son."

"Well, you're alive."

"Freaky luck, isn't it? And I want to stay alive. I just can't reappear with my story now. He'll kill me. No, more likely, one of his friends will kill me. And he has my son."

"Where is the boy?"

"In the Dominican Republic, with his grandparents, his aunts and uncles, his cousins, his nanny, the lackeys."

"What will César do now?"

"He'll cancel the cruise and return to Santo Domingo. He has my son. He has—he thinks he has—my money and property."

"And what will he say when you reappear with your story?"

"He'll continue lying. Katherine was drunk, depressed, lost, suicidal, the poor woman, but thank God she survived. Now we must all try to understand her and help her, free her from her painful delusions."

"The guests, the Dickeys and Solomons and Maldonados—do you think they might have been complicit in César's plan to kill you?"

"No."

"A hundred-and-forty-foot yacht is big in one way, not so big in another. What if a crew member saw César throw you overboard?"

"He would keep his mouth shut. He wouldn't dare oppose César. And working on the *Zodiaco* is a very good job for a poor boy."

"I infer that César tried to murder you for your estate. But isn't the Cardinal family rich?"

"They were, a generation ago, but now they're deeply in debt. And they won't sell anything, they won't cut back, they refuse to do the things necessary to restore their wealth. César is the elder son, the one elected to recoup the family fortunes, marry the rich wife. But he's a habitual gambler, a careless businessman, and a mad spender."

"Okay. You want your son. How are you going to get the boy out of the Dominican Republic?"

"You're a lawyer. You tell me."

"You seem to understand the situation. The courts? Which court? U.S. or Dominican Republic, either or both? Forget it. You'll be tied up in litigation for years, damn near forever. Your son will shave every day by the time you next see him. Foreign country, prominent and powerful family, corrupt courts and government . . . What are you going to do, Kate?"

"I don't know."

"I can help you."

"You've already helped me."

"I might have an idea or two."

"You might be out of your league."

"Want a drink?"

"No. I'm exhausted. I need to sleep."

"There are angles," I said.

She leaned close, kissed my cheek, and stood up. "Shaw? Thanks. You're a nice guy."

"I'm not, really. Not at all."

She stepped to the hatch.

"We'll snatch the kid," I said.

She went down into the cabin. I turned on the boat lights, poured myself a whiskey, leaned back, and regarded the clockwork turning of the constellations.

TWELVE

I awakened at dawn and lay supine on my berth, aware of new sounds and smells and sensations. And movement: *Roamer* was very slowly lifting and settling. Wavelets splashed against the hull. Above, I heard the creak and whir of rotating ventilator caps. The air was definitely cooler now, and smelled fresh.

Careful not to wake Kate in the other bunk, I got out of bed and went up on deck. Puffball cirrus clouds streamed across the sky. There was not yet much of a breeze at sea level, and it blew intermittently; the widely spaced foot-high waves could hardly be called ocean swells. But it was coming; the trade wind was blowing again, and within an hour or so we could be under way.

Kate came up on deck. She looked around, sniffed the air, and smiled at me.

"Where do you want to go?" I asked her.

"Can I just get lost for a while?"

"I know a place."

"Take me there."

"It's at least seven hundred miles from here, seven or eight days sailing even with a steady wind. And we're low on food and fresh water."

"Let's go. We'll eat rope and drink dew."

Within an hour everything was stowed that needed stowing, all sails were set, and we were under way, sailing on a broad reach, starboard tack, heading northwest. The wind was desultory for a time, then stiffened, and *Roamer*—"a bone in her teeth"—rocked along at about five knots. Now and then she surfed down a following swell. The sea, rougher now, flashing white, had taken on an opaque gray-blue color. Kate and I sat together on the high side of the cockpit. Cool spray, a sensation of power and speed, taut sails—we were exhilarated.

I told her about Finn. I had served three years in the army with a man named Finn T. Cooley. He had been a sergeant, a good one, in my CID unit, and when his tour was up he returned to Boston and joined the fire department there. We exchanged Christmas cards yearly, phoned occasionally, and one summer he stopped off in Bell Harbor for a few days while returning from a Caribbean vacation. Finn spoke with a strong Boston accent: "I pocked the cah not fah from the bah." In the late nineties he and seven of his firehouse chums went together to purchase lottery tickets. One of the tickets came through. Their winnings amounted to forty-three million dollars after taxes.

Finn succeeded in persuading six of his partners to invest in a little Bahamian resort he had discovered on his Caribbean travels. Woeful Cay was remote, far off the tourist track, but a pretty little island which contained a charmingly shabby resort hotel that could be converted into a moneymaker. And if not? If not, they each had a useful tax deduction and, more important, they had an ideal semiprivate vacation spot for their annual family vacations. Why invest in a Florida condo or Hawaiian time-share when they could own a piece of pristine Woeful Cay? Fishing, boating, and diving for the active; sitting on white sand beaches and sucking up piña coladas for the others. Plenty of healthy activities for the kids, too. His partners referred to the resort as Finn's Folly, but they invested their money, continued investing, and began spending a part of each winter on the island.

"And that's where we're going?" Kate asked. "To Finn's Folly on Woeful Cay?"

"Not exactly. Finn, with the consent of the Bahamian government, changed the name to Treasure Island. It's still Woeful Cay on marine charts and in atlases, but Treasure Island in advertising brochures, and the Folly is now called the Tahitian Village Resort. And Drowned-Man Bay is now Crystal Lagoon."

She laughed. "Actually, I prefer Finn's Folly and Woeful Cay. Can you find that little island?"

"As long as my GPS doesn't conk out."

I drew pencil lines on the chart: west a few hundred miles, passing between Silver Bank and Cabo Frances Viejo of the Dominican Republic; west and a little north for another few hundred miles, keeping well south of the Turks and Caicos Islands; sailing the passage between Great Inagua and Little Inagua islands; west and north then to the Bahamas and the hundred-mile chain of little islands strung out below Great Exuma. They had names like Man-of-War Cay, Nurse Cay, Raccoon Cay, The Brothers, Ragged Island, and our destination, Woeful Cay, which was roughly two thirds of the way down the chain. There was shoal water along the way, reefs like the *Mira Por Vos* and others unnamed; you did not want to stray far off course. And weather was always a concern. But we were lucky: except for a few rain squalls and some choppy seas, the weather remained fine all the way to Woeful Cay and Finn's Folly.

It was easy sailing. The self-steering gear kept *Roamer* on course. The wind was generally moderate and steady, and it was rarely necessary to change or reef the sails. Nothing cracked, snapped, ripped, tore, broke, fell, quit. We saw freighters, tankers, a few grand yachts, but none came close. *Roamer* sailed on day and night. We took turns napping during the daylight hours, and sat together in the cockpit much of the night, sometimes talking but more often silent. Kate worried about her son.

"When did you last see your boy?" I asked.

"The day we left Santo Domingo on the cruise."

"Not a long time. Haven't you been away as long before?"

"Not often. But how long will it be before I have him back?"

"He's safe and well cared for, isn't he? His grandparents, all those uncles and aunts and cousins."

"Yes. But I miss him, and I know he misses me."

"Sure. We'll get him back. But the thing is to do it once and do it right. A coup de main—a sudden strike."

"You sound like a movie guerrilla commander," she said.

"Stay out of the courts, stay out of the newspapers, remain dead for a while. Better a few weeks' wait to get your son back than a few years."

"I hope you know what you're doing."

"I have resources at my disposal," I said, trying to sound like her movie guerrilla commander, "both human and matériel."

We sometimes saw isolated squalls on the horizon, but they all missed us until, on the fifth day, I saw that a black howler and *Roamer* promised convergence. Kate rushed below to fetch soap and shampoo, and when she returned I disconnected the self-steering apparatus, and went forward to lower all sail and secure the forward hatch. The air ahead of us smoked with mist and rain. There was no lightning. Kate had closed the main hatch by the time I returned to the cockpit. We abruptly passed from sunlight to a smoky darkness. The wind and rain were not very powerful on the fringe of the squall, but soon we were immersed in the deluge. Swirling gusts of wind and confused seas knocked *Roamer* about; she rocked and rolled as Kate and I stripped off our clothes, soaped up, and let the cold hard-driving rain wash us clean. Kate shampooed her hair, and passed me the bottle. We hurried to wash thoroughly before the tempest passed. The squall moved on as swiftly as it had come, and we found ourselves standing wet and naked in sunlight. There was no need to speak. I opened the hatch and we went down into the cabin.

Our position on the charts changed continuously, but time seemed to remain static; it was all one long day and night, one fine dream that was lucid minute by minute but would, we knew, condense and partially fade when we reached the world.

Woeful Cay was flat, and we didn't see the tops of its palms appear until we were almost on the reef. There was no diesel fuel left and so I had to sail *Roamer* through the cut and into the little yacht basin. We passed within a few feet of an anchored sport-fishing boat, and a red-faced porcine clown—drink in hand—shouted at me.

"Watch where the fuck you're going, cowboy!"

PART II
Angles

THIRTEEN

Finn liked to say that he had improved on nature. What was the average tropical island, anyway? Sand, stones, palms, thorny shrubs, insects, rodents. Big deal. Finn hired a horticulturalist who had imported exotic flowering trees and shrubbery—hibiscus, frangipani, jacaranda, etc.—and created the "botanical gardens" and "rain forest," and supervised the construction of a rocky waterfall and pool that cycled seawater. Flowering pink and white bougainvillea vines climbed the walls of the housekeeping cottages. There were seven cottages tucked away in the ferny rain forest, whitewashed plaster Hansel and Gretel buildings with what appeared to be palm frond roofs. No. The cottages were roofed by brown overlapping plastic palm fronds fabricated by a small company in Florida. You had the look and novelty of palm frond roofs, Finn said, without the insect infestations and rot.

There was not much that Finn could do to improve the reef waters except assign romantic names to natural features: there was the Grotto, Pirates Cove, the Amphitheater, and my favorite, Seahorse Pastures. Finn had a gift for PR and an understanding that you really couldn't go too far in naming things for tourists. "In these hands I have apples," he would say, holding up two empty palms. "They look alike. They *are* alike, exactly the same. But this one is just an apple, and the other is a Golden Delicious."

The island, shaped like a boomerang, was a little more than a mile and a half long and no more than two hundred yards wide at its broadest point. There was not much fresh water, and so cisterns had been built to collect rainwater; in a drought, water was shipped in from a neighboring island. The yacht basin was located at the south end; a "native village" (where the hotel employees lived) lay in the north, close to the dirt airstrip and electrical generators. It was a pretty little island, made lush by the horticulturalist and not much harmed by Finn's tourist humbug and topographical fakery.

The main building was a long two-story frame building painted a pale yellow with white trim. It had overhanging roof eaves, dovecotes, and hurricane shutters on all the windows. There were sixteen rooms upstairs, eight in front, eight in back, with a pair of outside stairways and a wood-railed walkway girdling the second floor. The lodge, at least, had a Bahamian look. Downstairs was the reception area, offices, shops, a bar and lounge, a big rectangular dining room, and a game room for kids.

The desk clerk, a slender black girl who pretended not to notice that Kate wore a flag diaper (this time, the Haitian flag), told me that Finn was presently at Georgetown on Great Exuma, but would return this evening.

I registered as Mr. and Mrs. Daniel Shaw, accepted

the key to cottage number five, and Kate and I went back outside and down a flagstone walk past the swimming pool and tennis court to a flowery wood on the east side of the island.

The cottage had a bedroom, a bath, a Pullman-type kitchen, and a big living room with cane furniture and bamboo matting on the floor and white-washed plaster walls hung with amateurish watercolor paintings. Kate went to a cane sofa and watched me open all of the sash windows and the doors between rooms.

"The desk clerk," she said, "mentioned a minibar."

"I don't see it."

"Try that cabinet."

Inside the cabinet was a small refrigerator and wire shelves that contained glasses and packets of snack foods and rows of miniature bottles of spirits. I got out two bottles of beer and two frosted glasses, carried them to a low table that separated the sofa from a wicker chair, sat down, and poured out the beer.

"There's a clothing shop in the lodge," I said. "I'll give you my credit card."

"You don't like the way I dress?"

"I like the way you undress."

She drank her glass of beer. "Cold," she said. "It makes my eyes ache."

"This is the life," I said.

"Finn's Folly."

"Woeful Cay."

I got two more bottles of beer from the refrigerator, and a couple bags of salted peanuts.

"The room is moving," Kate said.

"You've only had one beer."

"No, I mean, this room, everything, seems to be pitching and rolling. It's making me dizzy."

"You haven't got your land legs yet."

"Ah, that's it. I'm still navigating on sea legs."

"Are you all right, Kate?"

"I'm very tired."

"Not depressed?"

"Maybe a little."

"You miss your boy."

"I miss my son, I miss my husband—what he was or what I thought he was. I miss myself. I gave up one life for another, and now I have neither. It's as though I really had died during that day and night in the sea." She laughed briefly, without humor. "That's awfully pretentious, isn't it?"

"A little, maybe."

"It's like most of me has evaporated."

"You appear quite healthy to me."

"You didn't know me before."

"Time," I said. "Give it time."

"Time," Kate said, rising, "a shower, and a long nap."

"I'm sure Finn has a satellite telephone at the lodge. Tonight I'll summon the cavalry."

"Do that," she said, and she went into the bedroom.

*   *   *

The bar and lounge had only a few customers at seven o'clock, with a few more in the dining room annex. The bartender explained that this was the slow season, business wouldn't pick up until autumn, though some budget travelers could be expected during the hot months. A waitress brought a gin and tonic to my table.

There were stuffed fish on the walls and photographs of boats and triumphant fishermen who posed squinty-eyed at the weighing station. Wood blade fans turned slowly overhead, without much effect, since the room was air-conditioned. There were no rugs on the hardwood floor, no plastic or formica, and the employees were not wearing the sort of humiliating uniforms standard in most resort hotels. Finn had managed to restrain his imagination here. The dining room was similar but more formal, and the tables were set with white tablecloths and good silver and glassware.

I was on my second drink when Finn came grinning into the room. Neither of us had given in to the fashion of males embracing; we shook hands in an old-style power grip—cartilage popping—and then sat down at the table.

"So you finally did it," he said.

"Did what?"

"Married Martina."

"Well, no, actually I didn't."

"When I saw Mr. and Mrs. Daniel Shaw signed in the register I assumed—"

"A natural assumption, Finn. But Martina recently married another guy."

"Then that must be your wife I saw in the boutique. She's beautiful."

"We aren't married," I said. "But I did sign in as Mr. and Mrs."

Finn described himself as midway between short and tall, halfway between handsome and ugly, not quite bright and not quite dumb. His suntanned face was deeply lined for a man his age, thirty-eight, and he was losing his hair; but his blue eyes were bright and he had the kind of teeth that can crack a Brazil nut.

"Still smoking, I see," Finn said, taking a cigarette from my package.

"You, too."

"When I was a fireman people would disapprove of my smoking. Smoke outside, Finn. Thank you for not smoking, Finn. That filthy habit is going to kill you, Finn. This was when I was regularly eating smoke on the job. I'd cough up these huge gobs of black mucus, and half an hour later people would lecture me about cigarette smoke."

"So, how is it going, Finn?"

"Good. Very good. I love it here, even in the hot months, the hurricane season."

"The books showing black yet?"

"This place will never show a profit. But our losses haven't been too bad during the last couple of years, and I figure this year or the next we might break even. Even—I'll take that."

"It's tough to show a profit when some cottages and rooms are occupied gratis by your partners during the high season."

"We get paying customers, too, mostly firemen and cops from the Northeast. A pretty good crowd. Now you can stop being polite. Talk of business is putting you to sleep. What about you? What are you up to?"

"Jesus. It's a long and complicated story. Can we get together for a private talk later?"

"Sure."

"Do you have a satellite phone?"

"Two of them."

"I'd like to make a call to Bell Harbor tonight."

"I'm told you came in on a yacht."

"Kate and I sailed here from Puerto Rico."

"That's her name. Kate."

"She hasn't got her passport with her."

"You don't need a passport in the Bahamas."

"We'll be going to the States soon. Will you watch out for my boat?"

"How long will you be gone?"

"I'm not sure."

"Best to haul your boat, then, especially now when we're heading into hurricane season. This island hasn't been hit direct by a hurricane for a while, but they've come close, and then the wind and tides can be nasty. We'll haul your boat, scrape the bottom, and put on some antifouling paint."

"Good. Do that."

Finn abruptly got to his feet. I turned, and saw Kate walking barefoot across the room. She wore a pleated white skirt and a blue-and-white-striped blouse, and was carrying two packages tied with pink ribbons. She placed the packages on the table.

"Kate," I said, "this is Finn Cooley. Finn, Kate."

He showed her his incandescent grin, and took her hand as if it were a wounded bird. "Lovely," he said, "but deeply flawed if you keep company with this bum."

She smiled. "Dan's my savior."

"That's blasphemy, Kate—Kate what?"

"Kate Incognita for the present."

"A woman of mystery."

"An unshod woman." She turned to me. "I'm going back to buy some shoes. And then we'll eat. I'm starving."

"This is the place for a starving mystery woman," Finn said. "We've got fish in the kitchen that are still flapping."

Finn watched her walk out of the lounge, then he sat down, took another of my cigarettes, and said, "The late and very much lamented Katherine Adams-Cardinal. May she rest in peace."

"How did you know?"

"I saw her picture on the television in Georgetown last light. She's in all the news broadcasts from Miami."

"I was afraid of that."

"You don't have to worry about this island. We don't have newspapers, and the satellite TV system has been down for weeks."

"It's a very strange story, Finn."

"I know it is. It has to be. And you will tell me all about it, won't you, Shaw?"

"I found her ninety miles off the north coast of Puerto Rico. Or rather she found me, my boat. She was swimming."

"Incredible."

"It's true, Finn."

"Oh, I believe it, but it's still incredible."

"I'll tell you all about it later."

"Yes," he said, "you will."

*   *   *

Rations had been meager and unappetizing during our sail, and so Kate and I were ravenous. She ordered a pair of rock lobster tails, I asked for their biggest steak. They came with salads, potatoes, creamed corn, and a crusty half loaf of bread. We had cheesecake for dessert, and coffee and a cognac afterward.

"I'll talk with Finn now," I said.

"What do you want me to do?"

"Wait in the lounge or cottage."

"The cottage."

"We're going to have to change your looks, Kate."

"I'll cut my hair short and color it. What do you think—blond or red?"

"Black."

"Black hair dyes are awful. They look like soot, there's no luster. Red, then, cut short and maybe teased or curled. Will that do? I'll see if they have hair dyes in the shop."

"We'll have to keep you pretty much out of sight for a while."

"What did Finn tell you about the news broadcasts?"

"Just that they showed a photograph of you, and there was a short videotaped interview with your husband. The same stuff—she was drinking, she was depressed, she simply vanished, a terrible tragedy. He—César—must now pull himself together and live solely for the child."

"The son of a bitch! I'm surprised that the story is still alive after ten days."

"I'm not. It's got all the ingredients loved by trash TV."

"You're going to help me, aren't you, Dan? You will keep promise. You will get my son back for me, won't you?"

"Piece of cake," I said.

FOURTEEN

"Tom," I said, "it's me."

"'I fear thee, Ancient Mariner!'"

It was nine thirty, and Tom was at his home north of Bell Harbor. His voice was clear over Finn's satellite telephone. Finn himself was leaning back in a leather-upholstered swivel chair, his feet up on the desk, a cigarette in one hand and a flyswatter in the other.

"We need to talk," I said.

"Where the hell are you?"

"At the Tahitian Village Resort on Treasure Island."

"Where?"

"At Finn's place on Woeful Cay. You met Finn, remember?"

"You know, pal, some people have been worried about you."

"I'm touched."

"I didn't say that I was worried. The sentimental old judge was worried. Candace was worried. Your creditors were worried. A few vicious felons were worried."

"Martina?"

"Probably not. Listen, I tried to reach you a dozen

times on your satellite phone. It was a gift, remember, so that you could do things like order a pizza delivered or call the Coast Guard when the boat was sinking. Did we forget to instruct you on the location and function of the on-off switch?"

"I lost the batteries."

"How can you lose batteries?"

"I'm using Finn's satellite telephone. Is there someone there with you? I heard voices."

"It's the TV."

"I thought you despised TV."

"Nah. I love TV. I love the endless parade of plastic pseudo-people, the lies and slanders, the stupefying banality. Don't ever say that I despise TV."

"Seen anything of special interest on TV lately?"

"I think we've about exhausted the subject."

"Seen anything about a woman who was lost at sea off the north coast of Puerto Rico?"

He was silent for a moment, then he said, "Yes, in fact I did."

"How safe are these satellite phones?"

"You have to ask? Nothing is safe these days. Big Brother always watches and listens. We are all humble subjects of the Corporate State. And yet—incompetence still rules, bud. It will be six months before a clerk gets around to reading the transcript of this conversation, and then he probably won't know English very well."

"You're a windy guy, Tom."

"It's your dime."

"She's with me."

"Katherine Adams-Cardinas?"

"Adams-Cardinal. Her husband tried to kill her, threw her overboard from a yacht. I picked her up."

"Interesting," he said after a pause. "Implausible."

"She intends to remain dead for a while."

"Yes."

"He'll be going after her money."

"And there's a lot of it, according to reports."

"She wants to get her five-year-old son away from him. The kid's in the Dominican Republic. She's afraid."

"She wants legal representation?"

"That, too."

"I hope *you* haven't been giving her legal advice."

"She wants her husband to believe she's dead until she can get the boy back. I thought we'd snatch him."

"We, huh?"

"I'm going to take her to Bell Harbor. Can she stay at your place?"

"I've seen photos of her. The answer is yes."

"All right. Now, when can Leroy pick us up at Georgetown on Great Exuma?"

"I can't speak for Leroy's schedule. But his Beech-craft is temporarily down for engine repairs, and I'm not sure he'll be willing to fly over all that open water in the Cessna."

"Since when has Leroy worried about flying a single-engine aircraft over open water?"

"Leroy's been a little strange, lately. Un-Leroy. He looks over his shoulder a lot. He waits to see if you die before he eats his portion of food. He wears an occult charm of some sort on a rawhide string around his neck."

"He'll be no more than a hundred miles from land

on any stretch of the flight. Florida to Bimini, down to Andros, fly the length of Andros Island—there are four good airports along the way in case of an emergency—and then across to Great Exuma."

"Don't tell me, tell Leroy."

"You tell him, and get back to me."

"*Ja wohl.*"

"We've got to smuggle her into the country, Tom. No customs, no big airport, no chance of anyone identifying her."

"I can see that."

"This might be interesting."

"I can see that. But will it also be profitable?"

"Could be."

"Is she lovely, your Katie?"

"You bet."

"Are you a pair?"

"A unit."

"Yeah. You're so lucky with love."

"This time I am."

"You know," he said, "I can sympathize with Leroy. I'm forty, and the world is beginning to seem a dangerous place. It might be that Raven Ahriman took something out of me. Ditto Anton Arbaleste."

"You'll be fine once we get under way."

"Why do I have the feeling, Ancient Mariner, that you have just hung your albatross—named Kate—around *my* neck?" He abruptly broke the connection.

Finn, his feet still up on the desk, the flyswatter held aloft, poised to strike, said, "That the lawyer I met two years ago?"

I nodded.

"A good lawyer, I think you told me."

"Very good."

"But not a very likable guy."

"I like him half of the time."

"Dan, maybe Kate ought to stay here with me while you and your lawyer pal go about your intrigue. She'll be safe here, anonymous. Bored, maybe, but safe."

"I'll ask her."

The flyswatter swiftly arced down and slapped on the desk blotter. A damaged fly limped away toward the In-Out basket.

"They aren't like northern flies," Finn said. "They're slow buggers."

* * *

Kate was in the cottage's living room, reading an old copy of *Vogue* that she had found among the stacks of magazines and paperback books hidden away in a closet. There was a half-full glass of whiskey on the coffee table.

"Did your call go through?"

"Yes."

"And?"

"The game is afoot, as Sherlock Holmes liked to say."

I went to the minibar. Earlier, there had been four bottles of Scotch lined up on a shelf, but now only one of the miniatures remained. I left her the last Scotch, and poured some gin over ice.

I said, "Finn suggested that you stay here for a while. This place is remote, quiet. You'll be safe here from reporters and scammers and your husband. Do you really think your husband might try to harm you?"

"He tried to murder me not long ago. That's a concern, don't you think? César takes chances, crazy chances sometimes. That's what makes César César. Don't think of him as your ordinary prudent male."

Kate did not appear drunk. She was composed, there was no slurring of speech or loss of coordination, and her eyes were without that telltale glassy shine. She could hold her liquor. That is, she had acquired a tolerance to alcohol if she could drink three Scotches—a little more than five ounces—and not show the effects.

"Coming to bed?" I asked.

"Not yet. There are things I want to think about."

"Wake me when you come in."

"Okay."

But she didn't wake me; she slept that night on the sofa, and awakened me after the hotel restaurant had delivered two breakfasts of coffee, orange juice, eggs, ham, fried potatoes, and bread.

She asked me if I cared for a shot of brandy in my coffee.

"Kate, do you have a problem with alcohol?"

"No, but I have a problem with people who ask me questions like that."

FIFTEEN

Later that morning I phoned Petrie at his office in Bell Harbor: Leroy Karpe, Tom said, would arrive at the Great Exuma airport in his Cessna 180 by noon tomorrow.

"Leroy expects you to be punctual."

"We'll be there."

"Leroy expects you to pay the charter fee before takeoff."

"He'll have to take a check."

"Get this, pal: *The Miami Herald* reports that César Cardinal found a suicide note from his wife among her possessions. He's back in the Dominican Republic now, but says he went through the things she'd left aboard the *Zodiaco*, and found a handwritten note tucked away in her writing kit."

"What exactly is a writing kit?"

"In this instance, according to the reporter, her writing kit is a compact eighteenth-century marquetry box, not much bigger than a laptop, which contained monogrammed stationery and envelopes, a Mont Blanc pen, and even sealing wax and her personal signet stamp. The rich like those kinds of toys."

"Did the *Herald* publish the note?"

"Better than that, they published a photograph of the note on the front page above the fold."

"Tom, what did the note say?"

"Quote: 'The sea whispered me through the night, and very plainly before daybreak, lisped to me the low and delicious word Death; and again Death—ever Death, Death, Death.' End quote."

I asked him to read it again, slowly, so that I could write it down.

"And that's all?" I said.

"That's plenty."

"Was the note signed?"

"No, but it's in her hand, according to her husband and other family members. She writes a fine, old-fashioned script, Palmer method, almost calligraphy."

"A strange suicide note, don't you think?"

"Is it? Not if you assume that the lady was highly emotional at the time, deranged. Suicides often are deranged, you know."

"It could be a forgery."

"Yeah? Is that the sort of prose a forger would use?"

"There's an explanation. Wait until you meet her, Tom."

"I can't wait."

"Do you think Leroy will be able to dodge a customs stop?"

"Our boy will certainly try. He managed to dodge the feds often enough during his delinquent youth."

"All right. I'll see you day after tomorrow."

"Alas," he said, and he broke the connection.

I spent most of the day preparing *Roamer* for storage, and at three the boat was hauled out and moved to an open space near the boatyard's steel shed. I carried two duffel bags of personal items to the cottage.

Kate was reading an old paperback copy of *Le Rouge et le Noir*. I was not surprised that, with her education, she could read French, only how that particular book had found its devious way to Woeful Cay. When I got a can of Coke from the minibar, I saw that she hadn't had anything alcoholic to drink that day, unless she had walked over to the hotel bar while I was gone. I felt like a rat for checking up on her, counting bottles, observing her behavior for signs of drinking.

"Good book," I said.

"You've read it?"

"In English translation."

"It's much better in French."

"Sure, everything's better in French, from snails to Stendhal."

She dog-eared a page, closed the book, and set it aside. "I bought a swimming suit on your credit card."

"Have you baptized it?"

"I was waiting for you."

"I've got my snorkeling gear in one of those duffels. Let's go diving before we lose the good light."

"Let's."

"Crystal Lagoon, Seahorse Pastures, or the Amphitheater?"

"The Amphitheater, by all means."

The Amphitheater was an irregular patch of white sand surrounded by pink coral walls. It was about forty feet in diameter, fifteen feet deep at low tide, and well protected from ocean swells by the coral and some off-shore reefs. The water was warm and nearly as clear as the air. Each grain of sand, each mossy weed, was sharply defined. Kate had no difficulty diving to the bottom and remaining there for a minute or so. She was beautiful in her new bikini, lithe and graceful, and her long hair streamed away in the gentle currents. There were sponges and sea fans on the bottom, sinuously weaving snake grass, animals that looked like plants and plants that looked like animals, starfish, sea cucumbers, and sea slugs like giant snails without shells. And we saw brightly colored tropical fish, mullets, snappers and grunts, conchs in their whorled shells, the heads of moray eels poking out of their coral lairs, schools of small fish that flashed silver and moved in perfect synchronization, and the always curious barracuda— they observed us with cynical disdain. And there were printed signs staked out here and there on the bottom, forbidding spearfishing, the molesting of animals, the taking of souvenirs, damaging the coral. *Do Not Touch! Enjoy Without Destruction!*

We left the water when the good light failed, stretched out on the hot sand, and kissed. Her lips were cool and salty. It started out playful, and soon became intense, and then we got up and walked barefoot to the cottage.

✻   ✻   ✻

That night, during dinner at the lodges restaurant, I said, "'The sea whispered me through the night, and very plainly before daybreak, lisped the low and delicious word Death; and again Death—ever Death, Death, Death.'"

Kate crossed her knife and fork on the plate, folded her hands, and rested her chin on them. "A quiz? Walt Whitman? Yes, Whitman." She closed her eyes. "'High and clear I shoot my voice over the waves; Surely you must know who is here, is here; You must know who I am, my love.'"

"That's from a poem?"

"'Out of the Cradle Endlessly Rocking.'"

"Well, Kate, that death, ever death, death, death part is what is being called your suicide note. A photo of it was published in a Miami newspaper. Your husband said he found it among your possessions."

She laughed. "Not really! Poor César, he didn't recognize the Whitman poem."

"Neither did the newspaper's editors, apparently."

"It makes César look the fool."

"Maybe not."

"Come on. César made a big mistake producing those verses as a suicide note. It's a blunder. I write down all kinds of things, parts of poems that interest me, musical notation, stray thoughts, epigrams and aphorisms, a daily journal. Was this note written in verse?"

"I don't know. It was read to me over the phone."

"Probably not. I usually break down verse into prose. I read a thing three or four times, then try to transcribe it from memory. It rarely comes out exactly right. And I suspect that César had to trim the page, cut it or tear it, to make it look like a suicide note."

"By now that note is in all the newspapers and is being shown on TV."

"César of course knew that I spent an hour or so every day writing. So he went through my papers and found something that he was sure would make me look sick and suicidal. A few lines from a Whitman poem. Who, for God's sake, would say farewell to life with a poem?"

"Not many, maybe, but a few. And poem or not, it will probably convince some people."

"But not you."

"Not me."

"Because it's all rubbish."

"César has been at bat ever since you were reported missing. Your turn will come."

"Yes, but when?"

"I'm sorry I brought this up during dinner."

"This nonsense won't ruin my meal."

And it didn't ruin her meal; she ate like a wolverine, and had my dessert as well as her own. She drank moderately, a whiskey sour before dinner, and wine with her food. She did not want a brandy with her coffee.

When we got back to the cottage, Kate asked me to cut her hair. She intended to dye it afterward.

"Letting me cut your hair is not a good idea."

"Just cut it short. It will grow back."

"It might be better to have one of the women at the hotel come over to cut it."

"Cut," she said.

I took the comb and scissors and hacked away for several minutes. Kate laughed when she saw the damage in a mirror. "Keep cutting, but try to layer it."

I continued cutting until she informed me that it was past time to cease.

"Sorry," I said.

She took the box of hair dye I had bought in the

hotel shop into the bathroom. The dye was called Crimson Sunset, and was a pretty color on the model who had posed for the box illustration and instructional folder, but on Kate it came out carroty, similar to the orange you saw on clowns' wigs. She combed her bright spikey hair while it was still wet, and then turned so that I could view the result from every angle.

I said, "It gives you a sort of . . . gamine look."

She laughed. "I'm too big for the gamine look."

"Really, you have a certain elfin street-urchin appeal now."

"It's hideous. My hair looks like orange crabgrass."

"Are you going to cry?"

She laughed. "I don't think so."

"Actually, Kate, your new hairstyle has a goofy charm. And it serves the purpose. No one would expect Katherine Adams-Cardinal to look like a stoned punk rocker. With the right makeup . . ."

"Shit," she said, but she was smiling. "I need a drink."

SIXTEEN

Finn, after his first year of isolation on Woeful Cay, had taken flying lessons, obtained his license, and bought a four-seat airplane that he had fitted with pontoons. Not many of the thousand islands in the Bahamas had landing strips, but all were accessible from the sea. It was a short flight. We flew north over a string of small cays, above a sea mottled a dozen shades of green. Surf creamed over the reefs and along the windward shores.

Finn landed in a big harbor at Great Exuma, taxied to a position among some anchored yachts, cut the engine, and threw his anchor over the side. Next he inflated a little raft, fixed an outboard engine at the stern, and the three of us buzzed into a little sandy beach tucked away among some rock slabs. He remained in the raft while Kate and I stepped ashore.

"You'll find a cab outside the yacht club," he said. "Or you can phone for one."

"Thanks, Finn," I said.

"You," he said to Kate, "really ought to stay with me on Woeful. I can give you jewels and unqualified affection."

She smiled. "I have to say no, though it's a decision I'll regret all my life."

"You," he said to me, "for years you promised to visit me, and finally when you do, it's just for a few days."

"I'll be back."

"Sure. I'm holding your boat hostage. Give me a push, will you?"

I shoved the inflatable off the beach. He started the outboard, ran it in reverse for a moment, then swung around and headed back toward his airplane.

"A good guy," Kate said.

"Finn T. Cooley. I always felt, in the army, that Finn was the officer and I was the non-com."

We ate breakfast in the yacht club's restaurant. No one asked if we were members. Halfway through the meal, Kate abruptly got up and left the table. I watched as she hurriedly zigzagged through the tables and off into the section that contained the restrooms. She was gone for fifteen minutes. I ate her eggs before they got cold, finished the bacon, and drank her coffee. Kate was very pale when she returned, and there was a film of perspiration on her face and neck.

"Sorry," she said.

"Are you okay?"

"I'm in a panic."

"Don't be. We'll get your son back. Everything will be all right."

"It isn't that. I'm scared that I'm pregnant."

"But maybe not?"

"I've been through this once. I'm pretty sure."

"Not a happy occasion?"

"Damn. You'd think I would have miscarried during that long, awful swim."

"I ate your food," I said. "Shall I order another plate?"

"God, no. Let's get out of here."

We took a taxi to the airport and waited in the lounge. Kate's illness seemed to pass. Leroy arrived promptly at noon. We walked out on the hot tarmac and waited by the Cessna as it was refueled.

"You're late," I said to Leroy, though he was exactly on time. It was necessary to keep Leroy off balance.

"I am *not* late."

"Leroy Karpe, this is Kate Adams."

He was shy around women. They were creatures from a world he did not understand or much inhabit. Leroy had his machines. Machines were predictable, and there was always a logical explanation when something went wrong. Machines did not weep or talk back or betray you with another machine.

"Mr. Karpe," Kate said.

"Ma'am." He briefly removed his greasy baseball cap.

Karpe's new face was at last taking form. He had received a terrible beating a couple years earlier, been in a coma for a week, and since then the cosmetic surgeons and dentists had been working to reconstruct his features. The scar tissue was not so apparent now. His new nose had taken shape. One eye still looked a little lower than the other, the jaw was slightly askew, but the dentists had created a fine new smile—rarely employed—that was far superior to the uneven gray smile he had originally been given by nature. He looked half mad. But then, even before the beating, Leroy had the sort of face you saw on wanted posters.

It was a long flight to Bell Harbor. The Bahamian Sea is gorgeous, but I had seen it from the air many times, and I was tired, and so I dozed most of the time. Kate tried to engage Leroy in conversation, but he was a yes-ma'am, no-ma'am, I-don't-know sort of guy. She became quiet, and all I heard after were voices on the radio and, later, Leroy speaking to the controllers. We were not diverted to another airport. No government authority was waiting for us at the Bell Harbor airstrip. Leroy had simply been fulfilling his charter, flying a pair of American citizens home from a vacation in the Bahamas.

"Was it this easy getting in during the old drug-running days, Karpe?" I asked.

"Sometimes," he said. "Other times I dirtied my pants." He drove us to Petrie's house in his double-cab extended-bed pickup truck.

*   *   *

"So this," Tom Petrie said, "is your gift from the sea."

Petrie owned a house in a small upscale community known to its inhabitants as Venetia. Each lot was big, at least a couple of acres, with plenty of room for tennis courts and swimming pools and guest cottages. And each house fronted on one of a network of canals (lined with yachts and half choked by water hyacinth) that gave egress to the sea. Owners were constrained by a strict code of covenants, and the streets and canals were regularly patrolled by security personnel (most of them retired cops) that Petrie called the Mobile Geriatric Strike Force. The Venetia Home Owners Association mightily disapproved of Thomas Petrie and quietly conspired against him, though warily, in fear of his reputation as an absolutely ruthless mad-dog lawyer. "I am grit," Petrie would say, "in the machinery of Utopia."

He had invited a neighbor over to meet Kate. Natalie Coleman was a divorcee that Tom had once dated, and their rancorous romantic relationship had somehow survived into chaste amity. She was petite, with tiny hands and feet, big eyes, and a terribly sincere manner. Nat was one of those women who were always telling you how direct and truthful they are. "That's just the way I am, and if anyone doesn't . . ."

"You poor thing," Natalie said to Kate when they were introduced.

Old Judge Samuelson, lean and very tall, imposing in an immaculate white three-piece suit, gently took Kate's hand, and surprised us all by saying, "I knew your grandfather Prescon well. I regarded him as a friend, and I hope we may be friends as well."

Petrie, rebelling against the judge's courtly ways, shook Kate's hand vigorously, and said, "You like barbecued pig testes, Katie?"

"Moderately well," she said.

"Don't let this rogue put you off stride, Mrs. Adams-Cardinal," the judge said.

"It's just Adams now," she told him.

Kate was not easily put off stride. She remained relaxed and skeptical, made no effort to charm the men, and was definitely cool to Natalie.

A portable bar had been set up in the shade of a great

live oak that trailed tattered shrouds of Spanish moss. Nearby was a smoking barbecue unit. Leroy Karpe had designated himself bartender and *chef de maison.*

We lined up for drinks, and carried them to a large round table set on a flagstone terrace. The swimming pool was on the lawn directly below us; the tennis court on an elevated patch of land to our right; and Tom's Bertram cabin cruiser was tied at a dock on the bright green water of the canal. Kate remarked on the unusual color, and Tom told us that the Association, disapproving of nature's ugly palette, had recently taken to dyeing the canals a bright yellow-green. It didn't seem to harm the fish, crabs, or eels, though it did temporarily stain the feathers of water birds.

"Even Utopia requires cosmetic assistance," he said. Natalie sympathetically looked at Kate. "It must have been horrible," she said.

But Petrie cut her off: "We aren't going to discuss that," he said.

"The Chicago River," the judge said, "is dyed a shade similar to that canal every Saint Patrick's Day. It's the same dye, I'm told, as that used by survivors at sea, to attract the eye of searchers."

We contemplated that.

"Speaking of dyes," Natalie said, "what did you use on your hair, Katherine?"

"Ask Dan. He bought it."

"It's called Crimson Sunset," I said.

"He cut my hair, too. Chopped it off, I should say."

"Nonthenth," I said. "I thtyled your hair."

"Having trouble with your esses?" Natalie asked.

"Yeth."

"Homophobic bigotry isn't funny."

"No thit."

There were clouds of pungent smoke coming from the barbecue grill. Leroy was laying slabs of pork baby-back ribs above the coals.

"Where did you know my grandfather?" Kate asked the judge.

"At Georgetown University. I received my LL.B. at Michigan, but went to Georgetown to study for my LL.D. Sorry. LL.B. is a Bachelor of Laws, LL.D. a doctorate."

"No thit," Petrie said.

"Pres," the judge went on, "your grandfather, was in a couple of my classes."

"But my grandfather wasn't a lawyer."

"That's right, but he took some law courses. Even then he intended to go into politics, and most politicians like to have a background in law. Prescott didn't want the degree, but he thought it useful to acquaint himself with that labyrinthine discipline."

"Were you close friends?"

"Yes, for two years. There was a group of five of us who chummed around together. Drank together, played sports, attended parties, got into mischief."

"Did you know my grandmother?"

"I met Emily at some debutante parties. She was the beauty of the season. Everyone fell in love with her. But she and Pres—well, here you are, Katherine."

"I don't recall my grandfather speaking of you."

"Did he ever mention a Chub?"

"Why, yes, I believe he did."

"I'm Chub. Short for Chubby, which I was not. The opposite, in fact."

"Did you know my father and mother?"

"No. We lost touch, your grandfather and I. You know how it is. You write, you telephone, but less and less frequently. And you say to yourself, I really ought to get in touch with old Pres. Friendships slip away."

"Chub," Petrie said. "Pres. God of patricians, save me. I suppose there was a Winkie in the group, a Bertie, and maybe a couple of Dickies."

Judge Samuelson smiled. "There was, in fact, a Dickie."

"He had freckles and big ears," Petrie said. "He stammered under pressure, did Dickie, and he married a first cousin and went off to Wall Street."

"Shit!" Leroy yelled.

We all turned: Leroy was frantically licking the burned fingers of his right hand.

"And were you a debutante?" Natalie asked Kate.

"I recall that I was."

"My, an authentic Virginia debutante."

Kate smiled.

"And you danced and danced your way through the nineteenth century."

"We boogied."

"It seems," the judge said, "that girls don't come out in the old stylish way anymore."

"Because," Petrie said, "ideally a babe had to be suspected of virginity to make her debut. That was important in the old flesh marketplace. What you want to know now—does she have AIDS? Syphilis, gonorrhea, herpes?"

"What do we have here?" Kate asked. "An actual misogynist?"

"A misogynist manqué," the judge said. "Tom is a disappointed romantic."

"I have tried for years," Natalie said, "to persuade Tom to see a health professional."

"She means a psychotherapist or New Age mystic," Petrie said.

"But Tom believes that there is still, even now, a stigma attached to seeking psychological or spiritual help."

"He believes," Petrie said, "that if he did need help—which he does not—he would rather consult an old-fashioned reader of chicken entrails or caster of bones than one of Nat's cocksure health professionals."

"I consulted a psychiatrist a year ago," Kate said.

"Good for you," Nat said.

"I was unhappy with my marriage, my life, and I thought that perhaps . . ."

"Did the shrink advise you to be sexier?" Petrie asked.

"How did you know? He did, in fact. Dr. Parsons told me that I should be more adventurous sexually."

"Sure," Tom said. "That's known as the slut solution to marital discord."

"But he really didn't want me to talk about the present. It was my childhood that interested him. I had a deliriously happy childhood. No child was ever happier. But Dr. Parsons didn't believe me. He *knew* that the source of my problems lay in repressed childhood horrors. He suggested that I had been sexually abused by my father. Or maybe my uncle." She smiled.

Petrie laughed. He hated psychiatrists and psychologists—"smarmy frauds"—and tried to destroy them personally and professionally whenever the prosecution brought one to the witness stand during one of his trials.

"There are unethical members of every profession," Natalie said. "In the law, for example. Isn't that so, Tom?"

"Have you had psychotherapy?" Kate asked her.

"Yes, and through it I discovered a new self and a new world."

"Nat," Petrie said, "is a Columbus of the psyche. She sailed out looking for self-realization and returned with clichés."

"For Christ's sake," Leroy shouted, "someone set the table and bring out the potato salad and other crap!"

Kate's "psychiatric history"—new to me—would surely give credence to her husband's assertion that she had been depressed and suicidal that night on the *Zodiaco*. Despite Natalie's claim, there is still a stigma attached to mental health issues, both in the courts and in public opinion.

The glass of wine Kate had taken before the meal was still half full when she finished.

"Ladies," Petrie said, "please excuse these brutes for twenty minutes. I want to show them the new dacklefritt I bought for my boat."

"Oh, a dacklefritt," Kate said. "Of course. The brutes are excused."

Halfway down the lawn I turned: Natalie, leaning over the table, was speaking to Kate in an urgent manner. No doubt she was trying to lever out information. But Kate, I expected, would parry and evade the questions until finally, if necessary, she would become rude. And I knew that Kate could be very rude.

* * *

Tom Petrie was a grimly serious boater two or three weeks a year; the rest of the time his forty-eight-foot Bertram cabin cruiser floated at his dock on the canal, with the underwater section of the hull cultivating barnacles and marine weeds.

The four of us went down into the saloon. Petrie ran the blowers for a while, switched on the air-conditioning, and rigged the center table.

"Anyone want a drink, there's the bar. No ice."

Acquittal was originally a salty boat that over the years had been converted, inside, into what now looked like a plush motel suite. There were many amenities, concealed and unconcealed, but the hull had not been compromised and the engines were well maintained. Tom did not believe in nautical austerity. "People like you," he'd once told me, "think that suffering is an essential part of going to sea."

He and the judge sat on the port sofa; Leroy and I opposite them on the starboard side. A dim aqueous light filtered in through the ports. *Acquittal* rocked a little as a powerboat passed up the canal.

"Talk," Petrie said.

I told them what I knew, starting with the night Kate had arrived naked and exhausted, through all she had subsequently told me, plus what I had surmised.

"Do you believe that she was in the sea for a little more than twenty-six hours?"

"Yes," I said.

"Extremely implausible, pal."

"She's a very strong swimmer. Anyway, her time line

is the same as her husband's and the guests and crew."

"As they say in detective stories: did she jump or was she pushed?"

"I believe her story."

"Sure you do. You're in love. This stuff about receiving psychiatric help worries me."

"Me, too."

"What about the suicide note?"

I told them about Kate's habit of regularly writing down things that interested her.

"The so-called suicide note is part of a poem by Walt Whitman called 'Out of the Cradle Endlessly Rocking.'"

"An appropriate passage for a suicide note."

"Selected by from many pages."

"What's the point here?" Leroy impatiently asked.

"Is this too nuanced for you, Leroy? Too abstract?"

"Fuck you, Tom."

"You see, Leroy, there's a difference between a woman being thrown overboard by her husband, and jumping overboard. The difference between a murder attempt and a suicide attempt."

"Bullshit. It's simple. The lady wants her kid. We'll get her kid for her."

"Look at it this way," the judge said. "It would not be right to take the boy away from his father— for all we know a good and affectionate father— and give him to a mother who may have grave emotional problems."

"What is this? A meeting of some social services committee?"

We studied Leroy. His wit did not usually take the form of irony.

"The kid should be with his mom," Leroy said stubbornly. "And she isn't crazy. Can't you jerks tell when someone's crazy?"

"We aren't," Levi said, "talking about crazy or insane or any of those judgmental words. One can be troubled without being crazy."

"And, Leroy," I said, "one can be crazy without being troubled."

The judge and Petrie smiled, but my reference to Leroy himself passed him by.

He said, "I'll fly down to the Dominican Republic and look around."

"No," I said.

"No yourself. I'm going down there."

"Hold off, Leroy, until we can get more information. Judge?"

"I have friends in the State Department. Formerly in the State Department—they've all retired now, but they have connections. César Cardinal was and still is a Dominican Republic diplomat, accredited to the D.R. embassy. My friends can tell me about this aspect of his life at least."

"And Kate?" Petrie asked.

"I'll make inquiries about her, too. Both of them, separately and as a couple."

"All right. Now you guys shoo—I want to talk privately with the Ancient Mariner."

They ascended the ladder to the deck, the judge stiffly, Leroy obviously furious—not a novel emotion for him.

"Money," Petrie said.

I went to the bar and poured a couple ounces of

whiskey in a squat crystal glass with a gilded rim and gilded Petrie monogram.

"Coin of the realm. Filthy lucre. Moolah, buddy."

"Tom, why, for Christ's sake, did you invite Natalie here today?"

"I thought your Kate might relax if there was another woman present."

"That was dumb."

"Nat is not usually so bitchy."

"Tom, Jesus, the idea is to conceal Kate's identity for as long as possible. Remember?"

"Nat can keep her mouth shut."

"No, she can't. Not for long."

"All right. I'm rebuked. Now, money."

"Kate can afford your fees."

"Because, even though you—and no doubt our altruistic judge—will elect to volunteer your services, Leroy and I expect fair compensation for services rendered."

"Don't talk to me about money. Speak to Kate."

"I shall. Fine, now let's return to the festivities."

"Wait. You really can't be serious about sending Leroy down to the D.R. to snoop around."

"Why not? He knows Spanish. He's familiar with the Latino culture. And he's not half as dumb as you think he is."

"A ringing endorsement."

"I never said his judgment was impeccable, but Leroy listens to me."

"No, he doesn't. Leroy only listens to his inner chaos."

"We've previously covered your antipathy to Leroy."

"I can't figure it. Is Leroy actually your illegitimate retarded brother?"

"You know," Petrie said, "you embody a conundrum that has baffled humanity since the beginning. To wit: why don't boring people bore themselves?"

"Is this boring?" I asked, and I threw my whiskey into his face.

I expected a fight, but Petrie just laughed and began wiping the whiskey from his face with a shirt sleeve. He blinked his eyes, rubbed his nose. Tom had a bad temper, and he was as tough as he needed to be, but he seemed genuinely amused now. Still, I was certain that there would be a payback eventually; Tom might now and then forget an obligation, but he never forgot a grievance.

"Why did you do that?" he asked me.

"I wanted to."

"It was boring."

"You can be a nasty shit, Tom."

"Sure. But you always knew that."

"I'm sorry."

"There it is! Boring people have to ruin everything by apologizing."

He turned off the air-conditioning, followed me to the deck, and locked up. We stepped off onto the pier and walked toward the others.

SEVENTEEN

I went to the office the next morning. Candace was glad to see me.

"Oh, Mr. Shaw," she said. "You're alive!"

"Knock wood, Candace."

"We heard you were alive, but not everyone believed it. Martina was very glad to hear you weren't missing anymore."

"How do you know that?"

"I talked to her on the phone not ten minutes ago. She has an appointment to see Judge Samuelson at eleven."

"She probably intends to file for a divorce."

"Prolly not," Candace said.

There was a stack of correspondence on my desk. Bills, solicitations, e-mail printouts, phone messages, advertisements; letters from people I hardly knew and some from people I didn't know at all; a note, posted from Raiford prison, threatening my life—another disappointed client. I divided the material into two stacks: one batch to be answered, the other to be thrown into the trash. Then I divided the remaining stack into two parts, fussed with it for a while, then tossed it all out.

So Martina had an appointment with the judge. No doubt it concerned old litigation over the lighthouse. I had half forgotten what she looked like. You can remember the faces of your entire third-grade class, but after a couple of months it becomes hard to visualize your lost love. Martina and Kate. They were not at all alike. Of course, one I had chased, the other had rather spookily arrived at my boat in the middle of the night. I had chosen Martina. Katherine Adams was—what? Fate?

Later I heard female voices in the outer office: Candace and Martina, chatting in a friendly way. Then, next door, I heard the judge's mellifluous courtroom baritone and Martina's thinner tones. I went to the door separating my office from Levi's, and pressed my ear against the panel. Polite small talk first, then business, but although I could pick up a word or phrase now and then, the gist of their conversation was lost to me.

It was a short meeting. After twenty minutes Levi's voice changed again, turned social rather than business-formal, and a chair scraped. Martina laughed, the judge spoke.

Candace, her eyes closed, arms folded over her breast, was doing her deep-breathing exercises.

"I'm leaving, Candace."

"Okay." She did not open her eyes.

"Forever."

"Okay."

I went out the door and down the hallway to

the elevators. There were two of them, and I pressed buttons that sent them both down to the ground floor.

Soon a door closed behind me, footsteps tapped down the hall, and I smelled a familiar perfume. I aggressively pushed more buttons. Busy man, impatient man.

"Hello, Dan," Martina said.

I turned. Surprise. "Why, Martina! How are you?"

"Fine."

It was the same face that I could not completely recall not long ago, but there was something new in it, a slightly different expression, a more confident smile.

An elevator arrived, we entered it, and each of us tried to think of something to say as it descended.

Then: "I heard you have a new friend."

"A woman," I said.

"That's what I meant."

"Of course."

"Who is she? Where did you meet her?"

"Yes, by God," I said, "I got me a real woman. And how was your widely advertised honeymoon in Paris?"

The elevator reached the ground floor, the doors hissed open, and Martina, exiting, smiled at me over her shoulder and said, "I never knew that it could be like that."

I laughed, followed Martina through the revolving door, and watched her jauntily stride down the sidewalk. Shoulders back, head high, hair bouncing, she was a woman who knew exactly where she was going and how long it would take to get there. Martina was confidently proceeding from A to B to C and on through the alphabet to the end.

Later I drove out to Petrie's house. Kate was sunning in a lounge chair by the pool. There was no one else around except the Nicaraguan housekeeper and the Guatemalan gardener.

I walked down the lawn, halted on the pool apron, and repeated Julius Caesar's vain words: *"Veni, vidi, vici."*

Kate looked up at me, laughed, and said, "You came, you saw, but don't be too sure about the conquered part."

There was a pitcher of lemonade on the table, the ice mostly melted, a fashion magazine, a portable radio, and a brown bottle of suntan lotion. Kate's skin was oily and smelled of the lotion, a spicy coconut, and her eyes were concealed by dark sunglasses.

I sat at the table. It was quiet except for the *snip-snip-snip* of the gardener's shears as he worked at a flower patch near the house. Nearly all of the green dye had faded from the canal and the water had returned to its usual opaque mud brown. Three cattle egrets stalked insects along the opposite bank.

I said, "Manatees have been seen in this canal."

"Oh?"

"And a pair of dolphins, once. But dolphins can't stay long in fresh water. And alligators have been sighted."

"My, alligators. What else?"

"A few years ago a corpse was discovered floating down the canal. A woman, a tourist from up north somewhere. A handyman was charged with the murder, but they didn't have enough evidence, and the charges were eventually dropped."

"Those handymen," Kate said.

"Do you want a drink?"

"No."

"Sure?"

"I'm pregnant."

"No doubt about it?"

"I bought a home pregnancy test kit this morning. I'm pregnant."

"What are you going to do?"

"I don't know. Here's something else: I heard on the radio that there's going to be a memorial service for me on Sunday."

"In the Dominican Republic?"

"Virginia. My family and friends—I don't know how long I can do this, play lost at sea, dead, while people who love me grieve."

"You decide. We can call a press conference anytime you choose."

"Is a press conference really necessary?"

"I'm afraid so."

"Couldn't I just make an announcement? Issue a press release?"

"Won't do, Kate. This is a pretty big story, and it's going to get bigger."

"I can't wait. My son believes I'm dead."

"Maybe not. César might not have told him. Anyway, he's only five years old and won't understand."

"That's a great comfort."

It is not always easy to read facial expressions; one can sometimes be confused with another: fear with bafflement, anger with disappointment. But Kate, in her misery, showed no expression at all; her face— eyes closed, lips slightly parted—resembled the sort of frozen plaster mask that sculptors make. She did not want to talk. She coiled within herself.

Later I saw Petrie and Judge Samuelson walking

down the lawn, followed by a woman carrying a tray of drinks. Tom had removed his jacket and tie, but the judge remained formal in his elegantly cut three-piece suit, club tie, and old English-lasted brogans.

"K-K-Katie," Petrie called out. "B-b-beautiful K-K-Katie." And then, as they arrived, "And ugly, ugly S-S-Shaw."

"Pay no attention." Judge Samuelson said. He frequently found it necessary to remedy Petrie's rudeness.

"Thank you, Nita," Petrie said, after the woman had placed the four drinks on the patio table. "Four more in half an hour, if you please."

We three sat down at the table; Kate remained on the chaise longue.

"Guess what?" Tom said. "I received a telephone call from Leroy this afternoon."

"Leroy's learned how to use a telephone, has he?" I said.

"A call from the Dominican Republic."

"You sent him down there?"

"He went on his own. And today he phoned. I didn't send him, he didn't ask permission, he just went. You think Leroy's just a psycho swampbilly, Shaw, but the man doesn't sit around brooding and intellectualizing, he acts."

"That's the problem."

"No two-bit Hamlet, he."

"Jesus, Tom, can't you get him out of there?"

"I'll suggest that he come back the next time he calls."

"Why don't *you* phone *him*?"

"He said he was checking out of his Santo Domingo hotel, going to a place called Mil Flores."

"Mil Flores," Kate said, "is where my husband's family have beach property. They go there every year in summer."

"Peachy," Petrie said. "Our bloodhound has the scent." The drinks were tall gin and tonics. I sipped mine, watching Petrie as he went through the cigar ritual, biting off the tip, striking a match, and revolving his cigar in the flame.

I said, "Kate's family intends to hold a memorial service for her in two days."

"Yeah?"

"Tom?"

He bit down on his cigar and critically studied me through the writhing smoke.

"She wants to come out in the open. Now."

"The lady is articulate," he said. "And on my lucid days I am able to understand simple words."

Kate got up from the chaise longue, spread a bath towel over her shoulders, and came to the table.

"Right," Petrie said, implying by his tone that it was all wrong. "Kate, phone your relatives this evening. Tell them that you're alive and well, but wish to remain out of sight for a few more days. Ask them to keep the secret."

"That's a secret that won't last long," I said.

"It will leak out pretty quick. But we might have a couple of days. We're a bit ahead of this César Cardinal now, let's stay ahead."

"But my son," Kate said. "My family."

"Think about it. And when the news does come

out, that you're accusing your husband of trying to murder you, all of the pressure will be on him. He might crack."

"You don't know César."

Tom reached out and patted her thigh. "You'll be hugging and weeping all over your boy in four or five days."

"This is crazy," she said.

"And I want to talk to your lawyer up in Virginia, Kate. I want to know all the details of your financial situation. Investments, property, assets shared with your husband, everything. Technically, of course, he can't touch a penny with you presumed dead. But this César isn't your ordinary timid citizen."

"César and Tony are the beneficiaries of my will."

"That all goes into probate. Did you ever give César power of attorney?"

"No. But listen, I'm sure he has control of all the money and property in the Dominican Republic. It won't matter what the law is in this country."

"Well, I want your permission to speak to your lawyer. He'll want to talk to you, have you introduce me to him, get your okay."

"All right."

"César is going to steal some, maybe a lot, but we want to protect as much money and property as we can, and pronto."

She nodded.

"Can you buy your son back?"

"You mean . . ."

"Settle a large sum of money on César in exchange for custody of your son."

"Impossible. César loves Antonio, he's crazy about him."

"Done. You've hired me. I am now serving as your legal counsel. Co-counsel, as far as your Virginia lawyer is concerned."

"This is going too fast," Kate said.

"Good. Too fast is maybe just fast enough."

"I want time to think."

"Sure you do. You've got an hour, and then I want to phone your lawyer, and you'll want to phone your family." Kate looked at the judge. She trusted Levi. Everyone trusted Levi. They trusted his credentials—former superior court and appellate court judge—and they trusted his wise, solemn aspect and his old-fashioned manners, his kind gaze and gentle voice.

The judge smoothed his mustache, first the right wing, then the left, with a bony forefinger six inches long. There was a low rumbling in his throat. We were about to hear from the bench.

"I'm not sure," he told Kate. "I'm never as cocksure as Tom here. But it seems to me that there are only two possible courses of action: the strictly orthodox legal option, open and public, trusting to the courts; or Tom and Dan's . . . guerrilla action. With the latter, you have the prospect of a speedy and conclusive resolution; with the other . . . The courts are slow, so very slow, and though they generally get it right in the end, it often takes years."

"On the one hand," Petrie said scornfully. "On the other hand . . ."

It seriously pained the judge to be placed in the position of influencing Kate's decision. You could imagine him in the old days, taking six months to write a labyrinthine opinion on a relatively simple matter. But she had asked.

"The clean way," he said finally. "The legal way. The courts. I believe you should inform your family of your survival immediately, Katherine, and inform the world soon after. I do believe that kidnapping your son is absolutely the wrong course of action."

Petrie was furious. He nodded half a dozen times (nods that expressed his disagreement), chewed on his cigar, rolled his eyes. Tom had a Napoleonic confidence. If you couldn't attack a flank you attacked the center. His Waterloos were always the result of unreasonable fate, official malevolence, or incompetent associates.

"I can compromise," he said through clenched teeth. "Let's do it this way. We'll have a good meal, relax afterward for an hour, and then, Kate, me, and Shaw will jump into my car and drive straight through to Virginia. Interstates all the way; 76 north, cut east on 10 to 95, then buzz up through coastal Georgia, South Carolina, North Carolina, and into Virginia."

"I don't know."

"You can't get on an airplane without being identified. And there'll be just a short delay in informing your family. Inform them in person tomorrow morning. You're not much more than nine hundred miles from home."

"Let me think."

"Conduct your resurrection in home territory. Hold your press conference in home territory. Expose that son of a bitch, César. Tell your story among sympathetic family and friends. It's the best way, believe me."

"How long until we reach my home?"

"We'll be there by seven thirty, eight, tomorrow morning."

"All right," she said. "Yes." And she smiled.

"Good. And now I'll commence preparing some of my famous chow. Chicken marengo, perhaps, delicately sauced. New potatoes, peas, and salad stuff from my garden. A crisp white burgundy. Yes. I'll have Nita send out more drinks while I perform my culinary magic. Yes? Yes."

Tom regarded himself as a great cook. He believed that he cooked as well as he lawyered. But he didn't; he was a mediocre cook who thought that he could bully food into tasting good.

EIGHTEEN

Kate was cheerful when we left Bell Harbor in Petrie's Mercedes. She was eager to see her family, eager to clear up the mystery of her "loss" at sea and subsequent absence. She seemed to believe that a simple announcement to the media would resolve the conflict—murder or suicide—and lead to having Antonio returned to her custody.

Traffic thinned out on 95 north of Jacksonville. We were beyond Savannah by midnight, and reached the South Carolina border fifteen minutes later. It rained off and on in the Carolinas; hard downpours when the clouds were reined with lightning, steady drizzles, and periods of clearing prior to the next rain. Tires swished on the wet pavement. Trucks shot up long rooster tails of water. Petrie did not adjust his speed to the varying conditions; he bulled on; that was his way. By two the traffic was mostly trucks, brightly lighted eighteen-wheelers that Petrie called dreadnaughts. "Watch me smoke that dreadnaught ahead." He passed all the dreadnaughts and all the cars; the speedometer needle rarely fell below eighty-five.

Kate had brought a pillow and blanket from the house, and when we were halfway through South Carolina she announced that she was going to sleep.

"Kate," Petrie said, "I want your permission to hire a good Washington public relations firm."

"Public relations? Why?"

"We need to get your story out. César has been spinning for almost two weeks now."

"I don't think so."

"There are a lot of slurs and slanders that should be publicly refuted."

"You mean that we must now slur and slander César."

"That's what I mean."

"No."

"I don't think you understand the happy malice of the tabloid press and the cable news channels. They've already implied that you're an unstable, suicidal, rich lush. Wait until you reappear. Wait until you hear the inventions, the speculations, the outright lies."

"Doesn't the truth count?"

"Nah," Petrie said. "Not unless it's more sensational than the lies."

"I can't believe that."

"Get the fairy dust out of your eyes, honey."

"But why, for God's sake, should this incident, involving only a few people—why should this receive so much attention?"

"Let me count the ways. Because you're young and rich and beautiful, from a politically and socially prominent family, and you claim your husband threw you into the Atlantic Ocean in the middle of the night. Because the Ancient Mariner here plucked you dripping and jellyfish-stung out of the drink. Because you and the Ancient Mariner apparently—it will look like that—went on a pleasure cruise to a romantic Bahamian isle, and you didn't reappear for twelve days. Because your husband is a handsome, dashing diplomat and adventurer, and *he* says you jumped. This is a gift from the gods of sleaze for the tabloids and cable TV. They'll entertain the masses and make millions peddling sewer gas."

"Let them," Kate said irritably. "Who cares? No one who counts for anything will pay the slightest attention. The people you're talking about, media and public, are worthy of nothing more than contempt."

"That is a truly aristocratic attitude," Petrie said. He, too, was becoming annoyed. The speedometer needle was rising past ninety-five now, and ahead a dreadnaught was looming. He waited until he had passed the truck before continuing. "Yeah, allow the rabble their cheap entertainments. Let the *canaille* bark and drool. Fuck the vox populi. But, baby, there is no longer—if there ever was—an aristocracy to support that attitude. This is the twenty-first century. We're all riffraff now."

"I'm glad I'm not as cynical as you."

"Lots of people tell me that," Petrie said cheerfully.

Kate wrapped herself in the blanket and coiled up on the backseat.

"Sweet dreams," Petrie said.

I had stopped myself from intervening in their clash of wills. He had been rough with Kate. But I knew that Petrie had been lawyering, working for his new client in his usual aggressive way, and he was ten times the lawyer I could ever be.

We stopped for gas outside of Fayetteville. Petrie had his thermos filled with coffee and bought several candy bars, and we were back on the highway by three. He caught up with and passed several dreadnaughts, and then exuberantly pounded my knee with his fist.

"Don't you love a long drive at night?"

"Not especially," I said.

"Rain, speed, the sweep of your headlights, other headlights, red taillights, dreadnaughts, hallelujah."

I looked at the speedometer; we were going ninety, too fast for the conditions, and in trouble if clocked by a highway patrol car. I knew that he would only speed up if I told him to slow down.

"We're in this little steel capsule," he said. "Moving through the night, through time, through time and space. Our capsule is going ninety. The planet is rapidly revolving on its axis, and is also hurtling around the sun, which is hurtling through the galaxy, and the galaxy is hurtling through the universe. Doesn't it make you think?"

"No."

"The universe—finite or infinite?"

"Both," I said.

"Brilliant! You sound like an astrophysicist. Is there life elsewhere in the universe?"

"Yes."

"Like us?"

"Yes, except they're inside out."

"Maybe we're the ones inside out."

"No, they are."

"Have you ever been abducted by aliens?"

"Just once."

"Did they impregnate you?"

"No. They commanded me to mate with an inside-out alien."

"Did you?"

"I was scared."

"Did you?"

"There was nowhere to run."

"Did you?"

"Yes."

"Was she pretty?"

"I don't know. She was inside-out."

"How was the sex?"

"I don't want to talk about it."

"Will the court instruct this witness to answer the question?"

"The sex was pretty good," I said.

"I am appalled," Petrie said. Then, "Is Kate still asleep?"

"She seems to be."

"What do you think?"

"We don't have much control over this, Tom. It's all loose ends, contradictions, complications."

"What's with her Pollyanna viewpoint? The media will crucify her if she doesn't fight back."

"She's been through an awful lot. Imagine those twenty-six hours at sea. She misses her son, she's half crazed by her husband's action. I don't think she's able to accept what's still ahead."

"Sure. Do you want to drive?"

"Pull over."

"No," he said. "You drive like my old granny. I'll drive."

NINETEEN

It was still dark when Kate awakened. We were ten or fifteen miles south of Fredericksburg. She drank a cup of coffee from the thermos, then leaned forward, staring ahead through the windshield. She smelled of coffee and sleep and, faintly, of the sandalwood-scented soap she used.

"Did you dream?" I asked her.

"Yes. I was in the sea again. I'm always in the sea in my dreams."

"Not very pleasant."

"I'm awake now."

Awake, and quietly happy to again be nearing her home country.

The rain had ceased and the land was obscured by a thick white fog that the headlights could hardly penetrate. Cars and trucks suddenly loomed out of the fog, passed with an eerie hissing, and vanished behind us. Petrie drove at a reasonable speed now.

"I think . . ." Kate said. "Yes, take the next exit."

We left the Interstate, and Kate guided us onto a good secondary highway that angled northwest through patchy woods and fields layered in a seething fog that resembled a surf-spumed sea. I was trying to find our position on a Virginia map. Everywhere I looked there were places made famous by Civil War battles: Manassas, Wilderness, Brandy Station . . .

We reached a town and Kate told Petrie to turn off onto a blacktop road that slanted north for a few miles before hooking to the west. It was hard to keep one's sense of direction in the fog; I was soon lost, but Kate knew exactly where we were and where we were going.

We passed through a one-stoplight hamlet, and then were out in the country again. It was growing light now. Details emerged out of the fog. We went by a newly cut wood scattered with tree stumps and debris, and it was easy, in the distorted perspective, to imagine the stumps as soldiers—Union or Rebel—advancing toward death through the foamy white light.

Petrie, too, was thinking about that war. "Any of your people fight?" he asked me.

"One. He was a poor farmer, too old at the time, but he accepted three hundred dollars to substitute for the local rich man."

"What?"

"It was standard practice on the Union side," I said. "You could buy your way out by paying three hundred dollars to a man who would fight in your place."

This was the sort of fact that delighted Thomas Petrie.

Kate said, "My great-great-great-grandfather was quite well-to-do in those times. He didn't buy his way out, though; he enlisted and paid his own company of soldiers and became commander."

Petrie could not believe his good luck in discovering yet another ugly fact about the grossly unjust ways of human society. You could buy another man to die in your place; you could rent a company of soldiers and commission yourself its lead officer.

"And," Kate said, "A law was passed in the South exempting the owners of twenty or more slaves from the fighting."

Petrie laughed. "This, friends, is truly class warfare."

"There were draft riots in the North," I said.

"My ancestors would have walked barefoot a thousand miles if they'd known they could earn three hundred dollars losing limbs for the other side."

We entered a town that was different from the farm communities behind. It was the sort of place that strives to combine history and commerce, with history losing badly. Now, in the early morning, the empty streets had the feeling of a mall or theme park. We saw art galleries and artsy-craftsy stores, gift shops, antique shops, sidewalk cafes, fancy boutiques, a wax museum, and there was a bronze equestrian statue of a noble Confederate officer in the town square. You could hire a horse and buggy in Haywood, have your photo taken in Civil War attire, eat a crepe, buy a forged antique, but fail to find a place to buy a screwdriver or toaster.

A few miles beyond town Kate said, "The road forks ahead. Go left."

It was bright now as sunlight illuminated the fog. Blurs of sunlight pierced through to the ground. We drove down a two-lane blacktop that had many right-angle turns. The surveyors back then hadn't wanted to cut directly across a farmer's cropland, and so the road had been plotted to conform to property lines. We passed hilly fields, farmhouses and barns, with here and there a mist-swathed tree that looked like a puff of cotton candy in the sunrise.

"Turn here," Kate said.

Petrie eased off onto a narrow pebbled drive, crossed a cattle guard, and then we waited while Kate got out to open a white board gate.

"Home?" I asked, when she returned to the car.

"Home."

The land was not quite hilly here, but undulating, and about equally divided between pastureland and woods. The fog had burned away except for patches in the hollows and a great mist snake that crawled down a creek bed. I identified oaks and chestnuts, syca-mores, cedars, and a row of poplars following a fence line. The road was bordered by a white plank fence, and there were similar fences dividing the land into large squares and rectangles in which horses, frisky in the morning cool, ran around and around. Ahead, there was a wooden arch, another cattle guard, and a heavy timber gate that was counterbalanced so that it swung open fairly easily.

The drive curved through a dense wood of several acres, and then entered the compound, a large open space, mostly lawn, with buildings spaced around the perimeter. There was a stable with a peaked hayloft above, equipment sheds, several small frame structures (guest houses or perhaps employee quarters), what looked like a chapel, and, on raised ground to the west, facing the sunrise, the main house. It was big, as I had expected, but unimposing except for the size. There was a porte cochere in front, and a fan of steps, narrowing as they climbed, led to the double front doors. The house was rectangular, with a row of windows on the second floor, and bigger, irregularly shaped leaded windows downstairs. Several stone chimneys protruded above the long-eaved roof.

Petrie followed the drive and halted the car beneath the porte cochere.

"Safely delivered," he said.

Kate's cheeks were flushed, her eyes shined, and she jumped out of the car, ran to the steps, then pivoted and hurriedly returned.

"Come *on*," she cried.

I said, "You go, Kate. This is a private occasion."

"No, no, don't be stupid. "They'll all want to meet you and thank you."

"Later," I said.

"Please. Won't you come in?"

"We'll see you in a few hours."

"Dopes. All right, then."

"Where's the nearest good motel?" Petrie asked.

"Stay in one of the guest houses. There are three. If one is occupied, try another. They shouldn't be locked." She turned, ran up the steps, opened a door, and vanished inside.

The guest house we selected was older than the main house, and had sash windows and slightly warped hardwood floors and floral wallpaper in every room except the kitchen. But it was comfortably furnished, and more than big enough for the two of us, with a living room, dining room, kitchen, three upstairs bedrooms, and screened porches in front and back.

"Okay," Petrie said when we were inside. "Now we've got work to do."

"You've got work," I said, and I went up the stairway and down the hall to a bedroom that looked over the grassy courtyard.

I had just fallen asleep when Petrie rapped loudly on the door, and then, without waiting for a response, he entered the room. He was smoking a cigar.

"I talked to Kate's lawyer just now," he said. "We're going to meet here tomorrow."

"Good."

Petrie's hair was wet. He had showered, shaved, put on a clean shirt, and now looked completely rested.

"You're smoking a cigar at eight in the morning? That's disgusting."

"Barlow—that's the lawyer's name—received a phone call from César Cardinal last night. It seems that César is flying up here to attend Kate's memorial service tomorrow."

"The man has gall."

"The loving, bereaved husband—why shouldn't he be with his wife's family at this somber time?"

"Because he tried to kill his wife."

"Oh, that. And after the service, he wishes to have a confidential chat with Barlow. Wants to know specifics about the will and other financial affairs, we may presume."

"Is he bringing Tony with?"

"Barlow didn't know. Didn't ask."

"This might work out perfectly, Tom. If he brings the boy here . . ."

"Which surely would be the decent thing for him to do. Allow the tyke to attend his late mom's memorial service, visit again mom's side of the family."

"When will César arrive?"

Petrie grinned on both sides of his cigar. "His plane is scheduled to arrive at Reagan International tomorrow morning at eleven forty-five. Just about the time that Kate should be concluding her press conference, during which she will accuse her husband of . . . well, you know all that."

"Has a press conference been scheduled?"

"Not yet. Got to talk to Katie first."

"Listen," I said, "you know, don't you, that I'm not going to any press conferences."

"Oh, yes, you are—you must. You, my friend, are the laconic, not very bright captain who saved our Kate."

"Get out. I'm tired."

"There's more."

"Save it."

"Kate's pregnant."

"I know that, but how do you know?"

"She stayed at my place, remember? My housekeeper found the pregnancy test kit in the trash. She told me. You aren't the papa, are you, by any chance?"

"Of course not. I've only known her a little more than two weeks."

"César?"

"Yes, César. Go now, will you? Get out."

"There's still more. I phoned my office. Leroy called there not half an hour ago. He's in jail down in the Dominican Republic."

"Good. What's the charge?"

"Not sure. Bum rap, he says."

"Leave him in jail."

"Yes. I thought I would do just that. Sleep well, Bunky."

TWENTY

I awakened at six with a sore molar and a lump the size of
a golf ball on my jaw. Petrie emptied an ice cube tray into
a dish towel and gave it to me to hold against the swelling.
He observed that the abscess gave that side of my face a
hint of character, while the other side contradicted it.

"Cocktails at seven," he said. "Dinner at eight."

"Who's going to be there?"

"Small group. Katie, her mother, her sister Eleanor
and Eleanor's husband—another sister's flying in from
California, will arrive tomorrow—and Kate's bachelor
uncle, Warren. Warren, who may or may not be gay,
was an investment banker in New York when Kate's
father died of cancer three years ago. He, Warren, quit
his job to come here and stand in as paterfamilias. Plus
a pair of close friends and neighbors, a Mr. and Mrs.
Stanley Hope. Seven, plus you and me. I'll help you
with the arithmetic; that makes nine."

"Have you talked to Kate?"

"Briefly."

"And?"

"She seemed frightened to hear that César is coming,
will arrive tomorrow. But that's not all. She's changed

her mind once again. Kate has decided against holding a press conference, and has vetoed even issuing a press release that accuses César and contradicts César's bullshit story. She intends to stand mute. Will not, no, besmirch the reputation of the father of her son, the father of her fetus. Let the world gnash its teeth and rend its garments. Screw the media, screw the curious public—that's my interpretation of her attitude. She is good, our Katie. We can only marvel as we watch her turning all of her cheeks."

"My tooth is really sore," I said.

"Serves you right."

"You can be a mean shit, Tom."

"Indeed."

"Maybe Kate is right in keeping silent. What good would it do for her son, her kids, to someday hear that their father tried to murder their mother?"

"She's silent *now,* tenderheart, but she's already told a lot of people about being chucked overboard by her dear hubby. And then, afterward, she demanded that they keep her secret."

"It will leak out fast."

"No kidding."

"I think I'll skip the dinner."

"They're waiting. Get dressed."

Kate, smiling, met us at the door, and we followed her through a foyer and into a big room with what real estate agents call a cathedral ceiling—you could look up forty feet to the age-blackened roof timbers. There were stone fireplaces at both the north and south walls. The room appeared underfurnished because of the big space, and was in a style that Petrie had described as "nouveau colonial," but most of the furniture looked to me like actual antiques or very good copies of pieces from the Colonial period.

Petrie went off to the bar, and Kate guided me around the room, introducing me to everyone.

Her mother was an attractive woman of about fifty, tall, like Kate, with the same mouth and eyes and the light, almost teasing manner that her daughter displayed in her carefree moods.

"I'm so glad," she said, "to have the chance of personally thanking you for saving my daughter."

"Your daughter," I said, "swam around the ocean for twenty-six hours. All I did was put down my Scotch and haul her up on deck."

"And bathe her derrière with ammonia. Why ammonia?"

"I was running low on whiskey."

Smiling, she said, "Yes, both whiskey and ammonia are famous remedies for jellyfish stings. Just liberally apply one or the other to the affected area and watch for blisters."

"You two can stop discussing my ass now," Kate said.

"Katherine is going to take you away. But we must have a talk."

"Yes," I said, "but not tonight. I can't stay for dinner."

"I understand. Your poor tooth."

Then, serious now, she said, "What do you think of a man who throws his wife into the sea in the middle of the night?"

"No, Mother," Kate said. "We aren't going to talk about that anymore."

"I think," I said to Mrs. Adams, "the same thing you think."

Mr. and Mrs. Hope, neighbors and longtime family friends, were in their late fifties, an amiable couple who chatted easily, thanked me for saving Kate, and expressed the hope that my abscess would soon improve. Mr. Hope, a yachtsman who often sailed on the Chesapeake, appeared disappointed when, in reply to his questions, I told him the make and dimensions of the slow *Roamer.* He was a racing sailor.

Kate's sister, Eleanor, two years younger than Kate and easily as attractive, told me that she had somehow got the impression that "the brave captain" was an old man. She said that she was glad that I was not old, and could clearly tell that her sister was even more glad. Her husband, Rob, a Philadelphia architect, did not say much, but wisely nodded his head in agreement to all that we said. As we parted, they both thanked me for saving Kate, and advised me to seek dental care for my tooth.

Kate's uncle, Warren, was as tall as the judge, maybe six-six, and two hundred and fifty pounds. He, like Mr. Hope and Rob, wore a tuxedo. His shaved head was darkly suntanned, and he wore a Vandyke beard and aviator-style glasses. His voice was low and gravelly. Uncle Warren looked more like a retired pro wrestler than a retired investment banker, and he skeptically studied me as we shook hands.

"What the hell were you doing out there in the middle of the sea in your little boat?" he asked in a half-jolly, half-accusing way.

"Waiting for wind," I said.

"Damned fine for Katherine that you were. What do you do, Shaw, besides float around on the big puddle?"

"Dan's a lawyer," Kate said.

"What sort?"

"Criminal defense," I said.

"Do well at it?"

"No," I said.

Kate smiled at me. Her uncle was behaving as though I had come to plead for his niece's hand, a permission that, it appeared, he was inclined to deny.

I submitted to his interrogation for a while longer, then Kate rescued me, took my hand, and led me toward one of the big fireplaces.

"Is he going to have me horsewhipped?" I asked.

She laughed. "He's a dear, really. When my father died he immediately moved back here to take care of us all. He's still taking care of us. That, he says, is his vocation."

"Your hair looks good," I said.

"I darkened it. But it sill looks like crabgrass, and I still look like a tart."

"Kate, I think I'd better go now."

"Does your jaw hurt?"

"Not too bad, but I feel rotten. I can't eat anything solid, anyway."

We walked to the door and stepped outside. It was a soft, humid night perfumed by night-blooming flowers and disturbed, briefly, by the insane whining yelps of coyotes. "Have coyotes spread this far east?" I asked.

"Oh, yes, and they're rascals. We have to watch out for them when the mares foal."

"Apologize for my absence to the others, will you?"

"Of course. They'll understand. I hope you'll feel better for the—I guess you could call it a party."

"Tom mentioned it. People coming in from all over to see you."

"Most were coming for the memorial service, and now are going to attend a party."

"Good night," I said, and I kissed her.

"Dan, wait. I stupidly told people about what César did to me. It was a mistake. I don't want the world to know about that. I don't want my son—my children—to even hear that their father tried to kill me."

"All right," I said.

"It would be so ugly to have it known."

"It was an ugly thing."

"Yes, but—"

"People know about it now. The news will get out."

"Yes, but it will never be confirmed, it will remain just a rumor, gossip."

"Okay."

"Good night."

"Good night, Kate."

I started across the dew-wet lawn. The door closed behind me. Far to the west I heard the yammering of coyotes as they hunted rabbits or deer fawns or newborn foals.

TWENTY-ONE

Kate's mother arranged for me to see a dentist in a nearby town late Sunday morning. Dr. Pratt examined my tooth, said that it had to come out, but not until the infection had been eliminated. He wrote a prescription for pain pills and an antibiotic, told me to stay away from alcohol, to rest, and to see a dentist when the antibiotic treatment was completed. I thanked him and apologized for taking up a part of his Sunday.

"You liberated me from church services this morning," he said. "And you're paying my greens fees this afternoon. Thank *you*."

The town pharmacy was open. I had the prescriptions filled, and drove Petrie's car back to the Adams place.

Petrie had tossed a Federal Express mailer on my bed. It was from the judge and carried a windy report on what he had been able to learn about César Cardinal and the Cardinal family. I dropped it in a dresser drawer, stripped to my shorts, and got into bed.

Twenty minutes later I got up and took two more blankets from a closet shelf. I had a fever from the infection and was both sweating and trembling with chills, and my fever dreams carried me off to the deep and lonely sea near the Puerto Rican Trench. In one demented dream, I hauled Kate up on *Roamer*'s deck, but then saw that it was not Kate, not a woman at all, but a great silvery fish that thrashed wildly, destroying my boat.

I thought I had locked my bedroom door, but the latch was defective, and Petrie walked in at a little before six o'clock. My fever had broken.

"Rise and shine, Rip," he said. "Family and guests are now gathering in the sacred grove. The faithful darkies are cooking up a fine repast; the antagonist has arrived; the melodrama is about to commence."

"What's he like?" I asked.

"César? I haven't been introduced. But he looks like an actor whose name I forget, one who generally played a mambo dance instructor. His brother's with him. He looks like an actor, too, a guy who played a thug in lots of old noir films."

"The boy?"

"No Tony. César was smart enough to leave the kid at home in the D.R."

"Who all is out there?"

"Get out of bed. I'll brief you while you dress. Wear a suit and tie. Everyone out there is elegantly attired. Not like at our own down-home swamplands 'possum and 'coon barbecues, where anything more than a dirty undershirt is regarded as class insolence."

"Why are you so chirpy?" I said.

"I may be falling in love."

"With whom?"

"Kate's sister."

"She's married."

"Not Eleanor. Barbara. The young one."

"Is Kate out there?"

"I didn't see her. She might be a prisoner in the tower."

"This is very strange."

"You mean the fact that a memorial service has turned into a festive occasion? That the would-be murderer who came to mourn stays to celebrate?"

"It's all crazy."

"For Christ's sake, Shaw, will you get the hell out of bed before they've drunk all the whiskey and eaten all the 'possum?"

The party was being held on an expanse of lawn and gardens behind the house. There were shade trees here and there, a screened gazebo that looked like a giant birdcage, a swimming pool and tennis courts at the far end of the grounds, and a stone barbecue big enough to cook for the thirty-five or forty people present plus forty surprise drop-ins. Petrie's "darkies"—the catering crew—were working around the smoky barbecue unit, setting a long white-clothed buffet table, and manning a portable bar. Tables, some with striped awnings advertising Pernod and Cinsano, were arranged on a flagstone terrace near the fringe of woods. I did not see Kate among the crowd.

Petrie cut me loose at the bar; he said he had to hunt down Barlow, Kate's Washington lawyer.

I got a tonic water from a bartender, and watched César Cardinal circulate through the groups of people. He was completely at ease. You might have assumed that he was the host. By now he had to know that Kate had accused him of trying to kill her, and kill her in a particularly horrible way, and yet he smiled and moved about with a perverse innocence. Some of those he approached were very cold, but he didn't appear to notice or, more likely, he was indifferent to their hostility.

I hadn't expected César to fully match the image that Kate had created during our days on the boat, and he didn't. We are all more or less biased in our view of lovers. One woman's Romeo is another's Caligula. Normally acute perceptions fail when profound emotions are engaged. Freud wrote that romantic love was a form of insanity.

César was about five ten or eleven, lean and fit-looking, with an erect posture and easy carriage. Some women would surely find him attractive, but he was not the Adonis that Kate had described to me. No doubt he had changed some since her first powerful impressions. He was in his late thirties now, and his dark hair was receding at the temples and was a bit fuzzy in front. I supposed that his enormous confidence—arrogance, rather—compelled interest more than his appearance. His casual arrogance and his reputation: César the lover, the gambler, the rebel, the daredevil. The dangerous man.

"The man's a piece of work, isn't he?"

I turned; Kate's uncle, Warren, wearing a white dinner jacket, and with his head freshly shaved and beard neatly trimmed, had moved next to me. He rattled the ice cubes in his glass.

"There was a time when I regarded him as like a son. I don't have a son of my own, and César . . . My brother, Kate's father, felt the same way up to the day he died. You wonder if César turned sour over the years or whether we we're deceived. Both, maybe."

César and another man had separated from the crowd and were walking down toward the swimming pool. Both men wore Italian-cut black silk suits, and there was a similarity in the way they walked and held their heads, though César's companion was darker and shorter and broader through the chest and shoulders.

"Who is the man with César?" I asked.

"César's twin."

"They don't look much alike."

"Fraternal twins."

"When did you begin doubting César?"

"It was gradual," Warren said. "Incremental. Certain troubling occurrences, his gambling, whoring, scandals. He was still a son in my regard, but a wild, errant son, a prodigal son, if you please. But a couple of years ago it became clear that Katherine was unhappy. She didn't say anything, but we knew. It is not her nature to be unhappy. No, she was a joyous child and a joyous young woman. Any man who made Katherine unhappy just had to be a base son of a bitch."

César and his brother had reached the pool apron. They sat on a pair of deck chairs.

I said, "I don't understand exactly why Kate hasn't publicly told her story about what happened aboard the *Zodiaco.*"

"She's thinking of her son, of course. Sons, perhaps, in seven months' time. She doesn't want them growing up knowing that their father had cruelly attempted to murder their mother. You can understand that."

"Yes, but her reticence now could complicate her

custody case in court later."

"It will never reach court. There will be negotiations. César will eventually comply with our wishes."

"I hope so," I said.

"César will return to the Dominican Republic in a day or two, a much richer man. And Tony will immediately be back with his mother, us, his real family. It's just a matter of agreeing to terms, drawing up and executing a contract."

I noticed a disturbance on the fringe of the crowd. Three security men hired by the family had swiftly converged on a fourth man; two held the captive by his upper arms while the other seized a camera. They then force-walked him up toward the house. The man, middle-aged and dressed in a shabby tan suit, did not struggle or protest; this, obviously, was not the first time he had been bounced.

"A goddamned paparazzo got through," Warren said. "A bunch of them are out at the gates. Excuse me, Shaw." He turned and hurriedly walked up the lawn after the men.

The seizure of the paparazzo had been quietly and professionally accomplished; only a few in the crowd seemed to have noticed.

"Will they beat him up?"

A young woman, standing near the bar, was smiling at me.

"Will they thrash him within an inch of his life?"

"I think they'll just call the cops."

"Too bad." She approached, offering her hand (cold and damp from the drink she had been holding), and said, "You're Captain Shaw."

"Just Shaw."

"I'm Barbara."

"Barbara, yes, the other sister."

She laughed. "For my entire life I've been thought of as the other sister."

"Sorry. I mean the younger sister. The sister who lives in California."

"I just arrived this morning."

All four of the Adams women, mother and three daughters, were very attractive. Barbara was twenty-two or twenty-three, smaller and lighter complected than Kate and Eleanor, with dark blond hair and luminous blue eyes. You could see the family resemblance, but she had her own non-Adams variety of beauty.

"Have you seen Kate?" I asked.

"Not ten minutes ago."

"Is she coming to the party?"

"Not, she says, until César is gone."

"Why doesn't your uncle have César thrown out?"

"Ask Uncle."

I followed her glance down the sweep of lawn to the pool area; Warren had joined the Cardinal brothers. Perhaps the negotiations were under way.

"I remember," Barbara said, "when Kate brought César home to meet the family. I was fifteen, and I instantly fell in love with him. All he had to do was smile and tease me a little, and I was lost."

"And now?"

"I've grown up, but a lot of it is still there. A girl never loses all of the magic of her first true infatuation."

"That was what? Seven or eight years ago? César has frayed since then."

"Frayed?" She stared down toward César. "I still go weak in the knees when I see him."

"He tried to kill your sister."

"That's what she tells us."

"You don't believe it?"

"And you are the captain who rescued her. I read in the newspapers that there was a suicide note."

"You're running a little behind. That was just some of Kate's writing that César extracted and claimed was a suicide note."

"Whitman, wasn't it? 'O Captain! my Captain! our fearful trip is done.'"

"That's a different Whitman poem, I think."

She laughed. She was a beautiful young woman, poised and gently mocking, and sexy in an unaffected way.

"There's something between you and Kate, isn't there?"

"If so, it's between me and Kate."

"Sex, I know that. That you can intuit. But somethin! more, something"—she laughed briefly—"something greater?'"

"What do you do in California?"

"Didn't anyone tell you? They all disapprove. I'm an actress."

"Having any luck?"

"I'm a starlet whose time has nearly come."

Her uncle Warren was walking up the lawn now. Cain and his brother remained behind at the pool.

"What's the brother's name?" I asked.

"Alejandro."

"It's remarkable how little he and César resemble one another."

"Kate told me that there's particularly ugly gossip

about the two in the Dominican Republic. You know that it's not unheard of for fraternal twins to have different fathers."

"I didn't know that."

"True. A woman has sex with two men in the same day and nine months later, presto—same mother, different fathers. The gossip is that Alejandro is actually the son of a hunchbacked gardner. Not everyone in the Dominican Republic worships the Cardinal family."

"Do you believe that rumor? Does Kate?"

"No. It's such malicious nonsense. But it's very hard on Alejandro, their lack of resemblance. He loves César and imitates him in every way, but look at the man, that thick, clumsy body and rather brutish look. No fault of his. Kate says he's nice enough, intelligent and quite gentle, but he's stuck with a body he loathes. He wants to be exactly like César. But how can he be like César, when César is slim and graceful and athletic and brilliant, really. It's sad."

"You make it sound like the beginning of a tragic old fairy tale."

She laughed. "Did I overdo the pathos? Sorry. And now, good-bye, I promised to have a drink and a chat with your lawyer friend."

"Tom said that he was falling in love, but I thought it was the other sister, Eleanor."

"Now, at last, Eleanor is the other sister. Bye-bye." She walked away, turned after a few strides, smiled, and waved in a motion one might employ to wash a window.

She had seemed skeptical about Kate's version of

events aboard the *Zodiaco*. But then, Barbara had also admitted to a schoolgirl crush on César. He could still make her "go weak in the knees." It might be that she had long been jealous of Kate, was jealous now. Even so, I didn't like hearing a family member question Kate's veracity in so serious a matter, because late at night, I too wondered about the parts of her story that didn't quite dovetail.

The sun was low in the west now, illuminating the clouds in pink and rose and peach hues, and it ignited all of the flowers in the garden and on the trellises. For a moment, in the strange clear light, this party, these people, seemed from another time. The sun went down, the sky flamed briefly and then darkened. Fireflies rose from the grass and garden, and mosquitos came out of the woods.

I heard Petrie's voice. "Female mosquitos," he was saying, "are the ones that suck blood. The males are gentle creatures that dine only on nectar."

Petrie and a middle-aged man were standing at the bar, waiting for a bartender to make their drinks. The man with Tom was about his size but soft-looking, with sandy lank hair and blotchy skin and moist red lips.

"I'm a cartoonist in my spare time," the man said.

"Is that so?"

"Macabre cartoons, mostly, like the stuff done by Larson and Wilson. Once I sent to *The New Yorker* a rough that showed this dark, dank room in an old castle. You know, cobwebs, stone walls, and on the floor I had three coffins with mosquitos sleeping in them."

"Not bad," Petrie said. He knew I was standing

nearby, and now he flicked a glance at me with his eyebrows raised.

"*The New Yorker* rejected it. I also did one where a man is eating alphabet soup, and on the surface a word is spelled out in caps: HELP!"

"I know a cartoonist pretty well," Petrie said. "Martina Karras."

The bartender served them their drinks.

"Sure," the man said, "I know her stuff. She does that derivative, sentimental strip about swamp and woodland creatures. It's crap."

"Well," Petrie said, "her former fiancée is here tonight. Would you care to meet him?"

"No. Why would I care to meet him?"

"He's also my associate in this César-Kate saga."

"All right. Let's meet him."

Petrie, smiling, led the man to where I was standing. "Hugh Barlow," he said, "meet Daniel Shaw."

We shook hands. Barlow was a bit flustered by the trick Petrie had played, talking about me and Martina within my hearing, and he was further disconcerted in hearing my name.

"Shaw," he said. "You're the sailor who . . ."

"He's the Ancient Mariner," Petrie said.

"Kate has told me about her ordeal," Barlow said. "I'd like to discuss your part, if you don't mind. Would tomorrow be all right?"

"Fine."

"At my office?"

"I don't know about that."

"We'll videotape it."

"Why?"

"To put it all on the record, that's all."

"Wait. Are you talking about a deposition?"

"Oh, no, not really."

"Christ, Hughie," Petrie said, "Shaw's a bad lawyer, but he's still a lawyer. Did you really think you could run a filmed interview past him?"

"Well," he said to me, "would you object to having a stenographer present?"

"Yes."

"We'll talk tomorrow," Barlow said.

He shook my hand, shook Petrie's hand, nodded, and walked off across the grounds.

"That's Kate's lawyer?" I asked.

"Hugh Barlow, of Barlow, Hazelton, Schwartz, and Neale."

"I liked his cartoon ideas."

"Don't underestimate the man. He's a civil attorney, and they sometimes have difficulty expressing raw hostility. But he's more than hostile enough underneath, and plenty devious."

"Then why did you get the guy mad at you?"

"Because I think he's working against us. He doesn't like Kate bringing in criminal defense lawyers. Doesn't like us moving into his territory. He'll try to cut us out. I just wanted to let that Harvard Law shit know that though we may be yokels, we're mean yokels."

"He attended Harvard Law?"

"Yeah."

"But you attended Harvard Law, Tom."

"Right, but I was a *scholarship* student. He was to the manor born. We hated those bastards. But, I did learn a few things. Kate is worth about three point five million in stocks, bonds, property, trust funds, et cetera, and with more still to come through inheritance and the maturation of certain instruments."

"That much?"

"Down from about five point nine million a couple of years ago. César has eaten into the cake, plus there were some investments—bad investments—in the D.R."

"Kate told me that she wasn't rich."

"Yeah, well, that depends on your point of view, doesn't it? But she's certainly rich enough to excite the venality of our boy César."

"Warren was down at the pool with César and César's brother. They were negotiating the hostage exchange—little Tony for a lot of money."

"Nah. César wants Kate's big bucks." And then, impatiently, he said, "How long do you intend to maintain your *querencia* here?"

"I'm watching for Kate."

"She ain't going to show. She loathes her husband. She's locked up in the tower, awaiting her prince. Why don't you amble up to see her?"

"I may do that."

"Do it," he said, and he went off into the crowd.

I started up the lawn toward the house. César and his brother, twenty yards away, watched me. César nodded. He nodded, and then walked up the lawn at an angle that would cross my path. I halted.

"Mr. Shaw," he said in a pleasant baritone. "I am César Cardinal."

He was at ease, not smiling exactly, but with an expression that indicated a smile was impending. His handshake was firm and lingering; mine, reluctant.

"I have heard how you saved the life of my wife. I want you to know of my deep gratitude, my thanks."

His accent was barely perceptible. It would be hard to identify his native language from the accent alone; you just noticed that he spoke more precisely than most Americans. He hit every consonant, gave full value to each vowel.

I said, as I had said a dozen times in the past two days, "I really didn't save her. She saved herself."

"No. You saved her life. She herself says so, I'm told."

Cardinal had that facial symmetry that in women is called beautiful; in men, handsome. His hair, black at a distance, was a dark brown close up, and wavy. Straight nose, strong jaw, a wide mouth that had an almost feminine curve, and arched black eyebrows over gray-green eyes. He looked at me through a fringe of eyelashes. His eyes and lashes, like his mouth, might cause a woman envy. Ten years ago he might have been sneered at as "pretty." But he was in his late thirties now, darkly tanned, with crow's-feet at the corners of his eyes and deep lines, like scars, bracketing his mouth. He spent a lot of time in the sun. There really was no doubting the man's masculinity. It was on exhibit.

"Everyone is grateful to you, whether that embarrasses you or not; but no one is more grateful than I, and of course my son—when he is old enough to understand."

I shrugged.

"If there is anything I can do . . ."

"What do you mean?"

"I've heard that you quit your law practice and so

perhaps are temporarily . . . pressed. Perhaps I could help."

"Are you offering me a reward?"

"A gift. Gifts are given freely, generously, from the heart, not in payment for services rendered, and never with condescension."

"I see. I thought you were offering me money."

"I'm sorry if you've taken my gesture as an insult. It was unintended."

The insult had, of course, been intended, and we both knew it. He was placing me in a category. I wanted to call him on his attempted murder of Kate, but she had urged us all to remain silent about that. I wanted even more to smash my fist into his latent smile.

"So," he said, "I have thanked you, but I would have to thank you a thousand times more before you could appreciate the depth of my gratitude."

"Kate," I said, "thanked me once. That was plenty."

What was unmentioned, and I was sure would never be mentioned by César, were those long days and nights when Kate and I had been alone on the boat. The days of calm, the days of sailing, our time together at Woeful Cay, our intimacy.

"I haven't talked to Katherine yet," he said. "But she will tell me everything. And then, together, we will thank you."

The smile, so long held in reserve, finally was released, and he inclined his head, turned, and walked away.

I watched him weave through the crowd toward his waiting brother. We perhaps had underestimated César. Our contempt had reduced him to a sort of clown—gigolo, mambo dance instructor, cowardly killer of women. But the actual César was far more formidable than the one we had created out of our scorn. He was a hard man. And his vanity was the sort that impelled men to violence in the name of honor.

I went on toward the house and had just reached the steps when Kate emerged. She smiled, took my hand, and together we started down the lawn. Everyone below was looking up toward us. Kate had, without intending it, made a grand entrance.

"It suddenly occurred to me: why am *I* hiding? *He* should be hiding."

She stopped, kicked off her high-heeled shoes, and resumed walking barefoot. Kate had dressed and groomed herself for the party, she wore more makeup than usual, she had on a black dress, and wore a single strand of pearls around her neck.

"I've got to greet people," she said quietly. "We'll eat dinner together."

I freed her hand, releasing her into the twilight and the welcoming crowd.

The automatic lights came on: colored lights in the tree branches, unnoticed until now, other lights around the barbecue, bar, and patio area, and the pool lights down at the end of the lawn. It was not long before the lights were surrounded by fluttering coronas of insects, and shadowy nighthawks darted through the glow.

TWENTY-TWO

Kate did not eat dinner with me; she was shanghaied by her relatives and close friends, and seated at a banquet table that had been erected upwind of the smoky barbecue unit and away from the mosquito-humming woods. The food was presented buffet-style. Petrie filled his plate with a ribeye steak, a baked potato, asparagus, and a salad; I took only a salad and a few grilled jumbo shrimp. We sat at one of the umbrellaed tables near the bar. It was full night now, hot and humid, with the sky filled with faint stars and a pallid moon. César and his brother, two pariahs, sat at a table ten yards away.

"Good steak," Petrie said. "Prime beef." He filled his glass from a bottle of merlot.

I said, "Did you know that César and Alejandro are twins?"

"Warren must have a special meat supplier. Fraternal twins."

"They behave like honored guests."

"You can't buy a decent steak in the supermarkets anymore, haven't been able to for years."

"Barbara told me that there's a rumor in the D.R.

181

that their mother got pregnant by two men in the same day. One, a hunchbacked gardener."

"Not so loud, sport. The brothers will come over here and stomp the life out of you. It's bullshit, of course."

"The rumor?"

"What are we talking about?"

"Steak."

"Aren't you going to eat those shrimp?"

"No."

He reached over and, one by one, speared my shrimp with a fork and transferred them to his plate.

Somewhere in the trees concealed speakers began softly playing the sort of big-band instrumentals that did not require listening. Mosquitos whined in my ears. A glossy brown flying beetle landed on the table near Tom's plate; he picked it up, pretended to eat it, then tossed it into the grass.

"The party's going to die," I said. "Food always kills a party."

"It isn't much of a party anyway. Let it perish."

"Tom, I have moments, flashes, when I wonder what the hell I'm doing here."

"Amen, pal."

My tooth was beginning to throb. I had left both the pain pills and the antibiotic capsules at the guest house.

"I'll be back in a minute," I said.

"Take your flies and mosquitos with you."

I walked up the lawn, around the side of the house, and across the grassy courtyard. The stained glass windows of the little chapel were illuminated by an inside light. I angled that way, went up the stone walk, and through the door. The chapel was small and plain, with only a few old pews, a peaked ceiling, and an elevated platform at the rear. There was no altar, no religious objects or symbols on display, no burning candles or smell of incense. The space was dimly lighted by a pair of low-watt bulbs. Clearly, this chapel was nondenominational verging on the secular. The Adams family worshipped an austere god. Or maybe the god worshipped them.

I went to the guest house, sat on the living room sofa, took a pain pill and an antibiotic capsule with water, and closed my eyes. I was sweating, in part from the humid heat, but mostly because my fever had returned. It seemed that two sides of my mind were functioning simultaneously, the rational conscious side and a fevered lower level. Moths beat against the screened door. I could hear faint music floating up from the lawn behind the house—"Perdido." Had I misunderstood the relationship between me and Kate? She had never said that she loved me; I'd assumed it. Never said that we would be together, married, after her divorce from César. I had trusted my emotions and presumed that hers were identical. And maybe they were. Maybe it was the fever creating those doubts. On the one hand, on the other hand . . .

After a while I got up and went back outside. Some people were leaving the party, others were gathered in small groups on the lawn, talking, finishing their drinks, slapping at mosquitos. I saw César and Kate standing together in the shadows near the gazebo. César gestured; Kate shook her head. César reached out a hand; Kate stepped back. I watched them for a moment, then started forward, unsure of my intentions, prepared to simply lead Kate away from César or hit the man as hard as I could. But before I had gone a few yards, the two of them turned, went up the steps, and entered the gazebo. Some others in the crowd turned to watch them.

The gazebo, which earlier had reminded me of a huge birdcage, was backlighted by the bright lights down at the pool and tennis court, and César and Kate were darkly silhouetted, two sharply defined shadows standing a couple feet apart. César talked, gestured. Kate remained very still. The music prevented me from hearing César's words. It was pantomime, a pair of silhouettes enacting the old obvious drama of male-female conflict, with the taller silhouette pleading, the slender one resisting, both seeming confined in a giant cage.

Finally César abruptly turned, went through the screen door and down the steps, joined his waiting brother, and together they walked rapidly up the lawn.

Kate remained behind in the gazebo, head down, slumped a little, her silhouette a portrait of dejection. I hurried across the lawn, went up the steps, and through the screen door. She lifted her head to look at me. She had been crying. She tried to smile, failed, then took my hand, and together we left the gazebo and walked (aware that we were being watched) to a bench in a shadowy section of the gardens. Mosquitos came out from the woods. Fireflies flashed green in the air around us.

"Well," Kate said.

"Did he threaten you?"

"No. Threats aren't his way."

She wiped her wet cheeks with her fingertips. I gave her my handkerchief.

"He pleaded with me. He . . . courted me. It was like a seduction. He tried to persuade me that black was white and up was down."

"He denied throwing you into the sea?"

"Oh, yes. And he almost convinced me. He's a very convincing man, you know."

"You're susceptible, Kate. You once surrendered your mind to him. That can happen in a relationship. It's like hypnosis. You have to free yourself."

"He said that he had come for me, had just reached the deck, when he saw me climbing over the railing. He lunged, he said, almost grabbed me, touched my arm, but then I was gone."

"Let's pretend that's true. Why didn't he dive over the side to help you?"

"I asked him that. His answer was logical. Because then both of us would be in the sea as the *Zodiaco* cruised away. He had to remain on board to effect the rescue. He threw me life rings, he said, two of them, called to me, and then ran to the bridge."

"But you didn't see any life rings?"

"No."

"And the yacht never turned back."

"It did turn back, César said, but it took so long, and he was unable to return to the same location."

"Ships are well lighted at night."

"But a swimmer, so low in the water, has a low horizon. The lights quickly vanish."

"What about the false position he gave to the Coast Guard?"

"It was an error. An error he made during that frantic time. They searched, he said, for hours and hours."

"Do you believe him, Kate?"

"No. How could my mind falsify those events, that moment when he picked me up and threw me into the sea like a sack of garbage? Can memory be so false? I told him that he lied. He swore, he swore on our son's life, that he was being truthful. He would not harm me ever. He loved me. And he said that I had been in a precarious mental state for over a year, had drunk too much that day, and had impulsively . . . He told me that during my long, terrible hours in the sea, I had come to deny my action, I had hallucinated, and my mind had created a false . . . scenario. That happens, César said. And I suppose that sort of thing does occur under extreme duress, to children, maybe, and the mentally fragile. But, Dan, I don't believe that I tried to kill myself. It's all so clear and real to me; I'm standing on deck alone, and then César arrives, and he lifts me in his arms, and then I'm in the sea. I'm alone in the sea for a thousand years."

"Of course you remember it correctly. Kate, he hasn't made you doubt yourself, has he?"

"No. It sounded so plausible when he explained it to me. But as soon as he left . . .

"Did you tell him you're pregnant?"

"Yes. I owed him that. He was excited. It will be a girl this time, he said. And he told me that this new child was all the more reason why we should stay together, *must* stay together, for the sake of the children and our own happiness. And he took my hand, and he said, 'And we will be happy, Katherine, deliriously happy,

even happier than during our first years together.'
That's when I cried. Because it was impossible."

"Are you still in love with him?"

"I don't know. I don't know anything. A little,
maybe. I'm ambivalent. And I'm very tired. Walk me to
the house, please."

The lawn was still brightly lighted, but not many
people remained: just the catering crew, which had
put out the fire and were packing everything away,
and a few guests standing about, finishing a last drink,
exchanging a last fragment of gossip. They became
silent as we passed. I did not see César and his brother.

TWENTY-THREE

Damn my tooth," I said. "I'll have a drink." Petrie had appropriated a bottle of thirty-year-old single-malt Scotch whiskey, and we sat in the guest house's living room, sipping whiskey and waiting for Leroy Karpe to phone from the Dominican Republic. Tom checked with his staff lawyers several times a day, and this afternoon had received a message to stand by for an important call from Leroy at ten tonight. We figured that the importance was in getting him out of jail, but at present we much preferred him behind bars.

"Have you slept at all?" I asked Petrie.

"An hour here, an hour there."

"You look beat."

"Sleep is a vice. Anyway, I've got to stay awake to run this circus. Every time I close my eyes someone screws up. You, for example. You shouldn't have allowed Kate to meet with César."

"How could I stop it? She's free to do as she chooses."

"Not free as far as that guy is concerned. She actually used the word 'ambivalence'?"

"Yes."

"Meaning what? She loves and hates him, trusts and fears him, what?"

"That's about it."

"Christ. Look, pal, I won't say she's non compos mentis, but there's clearly a mental problem here with our Katie. I know, I know, she's gone through a shattering ordeal, something that might temporarily crack anyone's psyche. And that's why you should have prevented her from seeing César for even five minutes. She's just incapable of dealing with him at this time."

"Well, it happened, they met, it's past now."

"Nothing is past. The past is always sneaking up behind to bite you, like a savage cur."

"It's okay, Tom. She's still determined to get him permanently out of her life."

"Yeah? Step one in that admirable program: refuse to see the bastard ever again."

"Kate thought she owed it to him to tell him about her pregnancy."

"Jesus!"

"I know."

"'Good news, honey, the fetus and I survived your nasty murder attempt.'"

"I *know*. But she's confused, miserable, all torn up, though she conceals it pretty well."

"Not well at all."

"Look, every thought, every proposed action, presents her with a dilemma."

"Ah, we have dilemmas, do we? Dilemma, from the Greek: a choice between two equal alternatives. But are they equal? No, goddamn it, they are not *equal* alternatives! There is no dilemma present here, pal. She meets with her would-be murderer or she doesn't."

Petrie poured a splash of whiskey into his glass, then slid the bottle across the coffee table toward me.

"And now," he shouted, "that fucking Leroy is keeping me waiting, keeping me awake, getting me drunk, upsetting my stomach, testing my humanity!"

I didn't know if Tom's sudden temper tantrum was faked or genuine. I never could be sure. He was an actor inside the courtroom and out. He was more convincing at displays of anger and contempt, but, as Judge Samuelson once said, when Tom pleased, he could charm the vultures down out of the trees. I wondered if, tonight, his exhaustion and frustration had triggered an authentic rage.

He had shouted, but when he picked up his twittering cell phone, his voice became as smooth and soft as honey.

"Leroy," he said. "Where are you? We've been very concerned here."

He listened for a time, then said, "You did what? How? Not very smart, Leroy. Shaw and I have been working our asses off. We would have got you out of jail in a day or two."

Petrie glared at me as he listened to Leroy's voice. Leroy wasn't in the room to be intimidated, but I was.

"Look, pal," he said. "This is a very fluid situation, changing every hour. No. No. Not at this time. No!"

Petrie and Leroy Karpe formed a strange alliance: the criminal defense lawyer and the ex-criminal (sometimes not so ex), the insider and the outsider, the very smart, well-educated man and the swampbilly. Maybe

Tom saw something of himself in Leroy, what he might have become if not for a lucky toss of the genes. Years ago he had got Leroy freed from prison on serious drug smuggling charges, and later had become partners in Karpe's charter air service. Judge Samuelson—a treasury of Petrie observations—said that if Petrie was a warlock, as some suspected, then Leroy was his familiar.

"Stop and think, Leroy," he said. "Think of what a sane person would do in your position. Listen to me! Stop talking about bodyguards and nannies and little playmates—listen, for Christ's sake! No. No!"

Now Leroy was shouting: Petrie held the phone six inches from his ear and looked at it quizzically.

Then: "Where are you now?" A pause. "No, I mean *exactly* where are you. Mil Flores, but where in Mil Flores? You're *not* in Mil Flores, you're in . . . fine, and where is that, my old friend? Okay. Got it. But where, precisely, are you in San Marcos?" Another pause. "Are there streets in San Marcos? Streets, buildings, houses—is San Marcos a three-dimensional town where three-dimensional people can move about and find one another?"

I got up, went into the bathroom, and when I returned Petrie was quietly saying, "I'll kill you. I swear on the bowels of Christ, I'll kill you if you do." Tom, like Oliver Cromwell, sometimes swore an oath on Christ's bowels for special emphasis.

He removed the telephone to arm's length and stared at it incredulously. Leroy had hung up. He had hung up on Thomas Petrie, LL.D., his friend and mentor and benefactor.

"You're no better than he is," he said.

"Tom . . ."

He leaned back in his chair, prepared his facial muscles, and revealed a broad, tooth-capped, totally insincere smile. "Leroy escaped jail."

"How?"

"He crawled through a ventilator shaft to the jail roof, jumped to another roof, another, dropped into an alley, and was free."

"Leroy's lean," I said, "but that must have been some ventilator shaft."

"He's lean and supple, and like any good rat he can find his way through a maze."

"Where did this occur?"

"In a city called San Marcos, a few miles west of Mil Flores."

"He's stalking little Tony."

"Right. He's reconnoitering. He's observing, timing movements, learning the family's routines. He figures one more recon and he'll be ready. Leroy didn't say it that way, but that sure as hell is what he's doing."

"He was going to snatch the kid."

"Was, is—I don't know. I'm not sure I talked him out of it."

"What was that about nannies, playmates, bodyguards?"

"Each day Tony's nanny takes him for a walk along the beach in Mil Flores. Usually there are playmates, cousins, maybe, and naturally there's a bodyguard who trails the group."

"You think he'll go ahead?"

"I don't know. He hung up before I could get his promise to come home."

"He'll do it," I said. "He'll abduct the boy. For Kate, because it's right and noble, because he sees himself as some kind of freaky comic book hero."

"It could be that Leroy has slipped his leash."

"Leroy was never leashed, Tom. You dreamed he was."

"Maybe the police will find him before—"

"Why was he jailed?"

"I forgot to ask."

"Remember when he gratuitously torched the Ahriman house?"

"Keep your eye on the ball."

"Pass me your telephone."

"Maybe the bodyguard will kill him."

"Give me your phone, Tom. I'll get a reservation for a flight to Santo Domingo."

He passed me his cell phone. "Right. Go fetch the son of a bitch."

"Did he give you an address? A place where I can find him?"

"No. He refused."

I dialed an airline that flew between Washington and Santo Domingo, and got a reservation on a flight leaving Reagan International at noon tomorrow.

"Well, shit," Petrie said. "A nightcap?"

"Why not?"

He uncapped the bottle and poured three or four ounces of whiskey in each of our glasses.

He said, "I noticed that Kate hasn't been drinking. Because of her pregnancy?"

"Yes."

"You said she drank a lot before."

"Not a lot, but she liked a glass in her hand."

"As we do. But women can't handle booze. Their livers are smaller than men's. Bladders, too. Brains, natch. They're constitutional inferiors, you know."

Petrie was merely trying to provoke me into the absurd position of defending the organ sizes of the female gender. When I didn't respond, he said, "Leroy knows that César was flying up here to attend the memorial service."

"How does he know?"

"He says that there's something about Kate and César in the papers and on TV every day. It's a huge story down there. César is greatly admired—*mucho hambre.*"

"*Hombre,* " I said.

"What?"

"You pronounced the word *hambre* instead of *hombre. Hambre* means hunger in Spanish."

"No, it doesn't."

"So which do you mean, Tom? Is César regarded as much man or much hunger?"

"You are such a weaselly nitpicker," he said.

His glance warily flicked between my eyes and the glass in my hand. He was ready with his own glass. Moving deliberately, like an Old West movie gunfighter, I lifted my glass, drank the whiskey, stood up, and started for the stairs.

"*Buenos nachos, hambre,*" he said.

I went into my room and stood in the darkness for a while, looking out a window at the clapboard house next door. Lights glowed yellow behind the closed Venetian blinds. Katherine's mother had invited César and Alejandro to stay in that guest house. We were neighbors. A shadow, larger than life—a King Kong of shadows—moved from left to right behind the glowing blinds. César or Alejandro, I couldn't tell.

TWENTY-FOUR

Early the next morning, a little after six, I heard a commotion beneath my open window: voices, male and female; the snuffling and stamping of horses; metallic jingles and leathery creaks. I did not get up to look out the window, but, judging by the sounds, there were at least four riders.

I got up, pulled on khaki shorts and a faded blue tennis shirt, and walked barefoot down the stairs and through the living room and outside. There were no riders in sight, but I could hear the hoofbeat of several horses deep in the woods. The sun had risen above the treetops and it was a bright morning, still cool, still misty, with dew thick in the grass. I crossed the open central area and walked down past the house to the big lawn. César Cardinal was casually tapping a ball around the croquet court set up near the eastern fence line.

He wore unbelted white Levi's and a blue dress shirt with the top three buttons open. He appeared jaunty, unaffected by last night's conflict. César was the sort of man who disturbed others while himself remaining

195

undisturbed. He saw me walking down the lawn and stopped in mid-stroke.

"Shaw," he said. "Grab a mallet and ball."

"You didn't go riding with the others?"

"When one has ridden great horses, merely good horses are a bore."

"What's the difference?"

"The difference between driving a great car, a Ferrari or Porsche, and driving a Ford."

"I see."

"Shall we play a game or two?"

"Sure." I almost told him that I had not played the game for many years—that premature excuse for losing—but just walked to where the croquet equipment was stored beneath a canvas awning. I chose a green-striped mallet and green-striped ball. I expected, when I turned, that César would say, "A small wager? To make it interesting."

He said, "A small bet, Shaw? To make things interesting?"

"Sure. How much?"

"One hundred dollars per game?"

"Let's make it ten."

"All right. You first."

It seemed to me that in croquet it was better to follow; you could judge the irregularities of the course, the roll and "break," and you also had the opportunity to gain additional strokes by striking your opponent's ball.

"After you, Alphonse," I said.

"*Pues.*" He dropped his ball in front of the stake, tapped it into position with his mallet, and then drove it through the pair of wire hoops. His next shot was well short of the hoop off to the right; he had not judged how much the dew-wet grass slowed the roll. He corrected on his next shot and left his ball at a good angle to take him through and down toward the center hoop. Still, his ball was in the open, toothless and claw-less, sitting prey.

I went through the first two hoops, landed half a foot from his red-striped ball on my next shot, hit his ball, and then drove it across the lawn and into the weeds along the fence line.

"Villain," he said.

We proceeded around the course. We needed less than ten minutes to complete the circuit. I won the first game, César the next two. Sunlight dried the dew and evaporated the mist down by the swimming pool. There were snails in the grass, and earthworms, and grass-hoppers that flew off with a ratchety buzz. Hazards, too; pebbles, roots, and at one crucial position a pile of dogstools. Pausing to clean dogshit off a ball or foot would cause a serious loss of face.

After the first round it became evident that the two of us had tacitly agreed to ignore the events that had made us rivals. It was an undeclared truce. But that did not mean that we were more than superficially amiable. Each of us needled the other.

"You served in the army, Shaw?"

"Twelve years."

"Rank?"

"Captain when I got out."

"I hold an honorary rank of colonel in the Army of the Dominican Republic. I outrank you."

"An honorary commission is worth about as much as a honorary degree."

"It's an equivalent rank, matching my diplomatic status. In another few years I expect an equivalency of general."

"Well," I said, "then you'll have a command position in one of the Caribbean's great military powers."

César was relaxed and cheerful. I supposed that he was the kind of man who, in the Latino way, might remain relaxed and cheerful in front of a firing squad or prior to a duel more deadly than a croquet match.

"Is your country still ruled by a dictatorship?" I asked.

"Of course not. It never was."

"What about Trujillo?"

"*El Caudillo* was a lackey of the imperialist Americans."

I won the fourth game; he, the fifth. The sun was hot now and drew strong odors from the earth and banks of flowers. A rabbit emerged from a thicket, limped across the lawn below the croquet court, and began nibbling at clover. High above us a hawk carved ellipses into the enameled blue sky.

I tapped a long shot that, just before passing through a hoop, struck a stone and angled sharply away.

"Bad luck," César said.

"Everyone is surprised that you didn't bring Tony along to see his Adams relatives."

"Surprise, in that context, is a code word for disapproval. Anyway, his name is Antonio, not Tony."

"Kate calls him Tony."

"And her name is Katherine."

A few minutes later, he asked, "Have you ever killed a man?"

"I've been asked that question before."

"Have you killed?"

"Yes."

"While in the army?"

"No."

"How many?"

"Two. The second was the man who asked me if I had ever killed a man."

He grinned, addressed his ball, and drove it thirty feet and through a hoop.

"Aren't you going to ask me how many I've killed?"

"No."

"You aren't interested?"

"I'm interested, but I'm afraid I'd feint if you told me the number."

He again grinned at me.

I hit my ball too hard, and it rolled several yards past the wicket and stopped a few inches from the curled monument of dog turds.

"Bad luck," César said.

"I expect to visit the D.R. someday," I said. "May I call on you?"

"Of course. And when you visit me and Katherine, I'll introduce you to some great horses and great cars."

"Would you describe Kate as a great woman?"

"Certainly. Wouldn't you?"

"And Tony's a great boy. Do you own great paintings? Great objects d'art? How about—do you own many other great persons besides Kate and Tony?"

"Look out," he said.

But it was too late; I had stepped into the dogshit, which immediately released its awful stink. I moved away and, disgusted, rubbed my bare foot over and over through the clean grass. César did not laugh. I would have preferred laughter. He regarded me with an exaggerated—satiric—sympathy and concern.

"Perhaps you should thoroughly clean your foot at the garden hose. You don't want to contract hookworm."

"Hookworm?"

"This is still hookworm country, I'm afraid; the disease hasn't completely been eradicated. If a dog has the parasite—"

"Your shot," I said.

"The hookworm—is it the larvae?—penetrates the sole of the foot, matures in the body, and the adult worms hook on to the arteries and in the lungs and intestinal lining."

"I'll concede this game," I said. "Let's start another."

We had just returned to the starting point when we saw Barbara Adams, the Other Sister, walking down the lawn. He hair was snarled and she wore no makeup, and she was beautiful, as fresh and clean as the morning. She smiled at César as she walked toward us. She wore white shorts, sandals, and a sleeveless teal-blue blouse. She saw me, and yet she did not see me; I was a part of the staging, like the apple tree and the croquet court.

"César!" she cried. "Good morning!"

"Good morning. Shaw and I have been waiting for the arrival of a sleepy-faced nymph."

She stepped into his welcoming arms. César appeared disconcerted by the length and fierceness of her embrace. Finally she moved back and turned to me.

"Captain Shaw," she said. "Your poor jaw is still swollen. You should rest."

"I'm all right."

I was dissolved in her mind and eye as she turned again to César. "I didn't get a chance to talk, really talk, to you last night. We *must* talk, César. Please. Right now. It's been so long since I've seen you."

"After one more game," he said. "I should give Shaw a chance to win back his money."

"No. It's a stupid game, and this is such a beautiful morning, and I want to talk to you."

"How much are you down?" César asked me.

"Twenty dollars."

"One more game then, double or nothing?"

"Fine."

"Grab a ball and mallet, Barbara," he said. "Play along with us. You'll be the oddball."

"No! Don't be mean and stupid, César. Stop now."

Her annoyance was far out of proportion to the situation—one more game, ten minutes. She was not the same cool, poised young woman I had met last night. This was a different mood, a different Barbara. She pouted as César and I tapped our way around the course. He was well ahead of me, on the home stretch, when Barbara ran over, snatched up his ball, and threw it over the fence and into the woods. Then she grinned maliciously, well pleased with herself.

"End of game," César said to me. "We're even."

They walked down toward the swimming pool. After a few yards she reached out and took his hand. Barbara, like all of the Adams women, was long-waisted and had long legs and a narrow lower back that swelled into jutting compact buttocks. Great ass, I thought; dubious temperament. She laughed, moving close to César's side, and looked up at him in a manner half coquette and half whore. They went through the gate into the pool area.

I retrieved the ball she had thrown over the fence, collected the other balls and mallets, and replaced them in the rack. I found Petrie in the kitchen, frying eggs.

"Where have you been?" he asked.

"Playing croquet with César."

"Sure you were. Now pack your stuff, bud. I'll drive you to the airport."

"Tom, have you ever heard of hookworm?"

"Drop a couple slices of bread in the toaster, will you?"

I placed bread in the slots and lowered the toaster's lever.

"Hookworm, yeah," Tom said. "A really nasty parasite. Get the raspberry preserves out of the fridge."

PART III
Robachico

TWENTY-FIVE

César's brother, Alejandro, was a passenger on the flight to Santo Domingo. He was in first class, had boarded after me, and so I didn't know he was aboard until he came through the curtain and down the aisle into coach. He was unable to pull off his brother's graceful walk or casual ease as he slipped into the seat next to me.

"Small world," he said.

"Too small, sometimes."

"You have business in Santo Domingo?"

"Yes."

"What?"

"My business."

"You feel safe going to the Dominican Republic?"

"Yes. Shouldn't I?"

"It's Cardinal territory. All of it. You won't feel comfortable there. I'll pay your airfare for a return flight."

"No, thanks."

"It's known," he said, "that in five years César will be the president of the Dominican Republic. Maybe sooner. You don't believe that?"

"I do believe it. What will your job be then?"

He shrugged. "Minister of Internal Security, maybe."

"Is there such a post in the Dominican Republic?"

"Are you certain you want to visit my country? It isn't safe for you there."

"Why not?"

"Because you are spreading vicious lies about César and his wife."

"Kate herself is the original source of what you're calling lies. Call her a liar."

"It must stop at once."

"I can't stop it. The truth is out now."

"To have the man who is credited with rescuing Katherine spreading such poisonous gossip is intolerable. Haven't you a sense of honor, man, of decency?"

"Take the subject of honor and decency up with your brother. He's the one who tried to kill his wife."

"I see," he said calmly. "You are beyond reason, beyond persuasion. Very well." He got up, stared down at me for a moment, then walked slowly up the aisle to the first-class compartment.

Alejandro was not a credible version of his brother. It was not just their physical differences. César, like him or hate him, was complete, a strong character, while Alejandro appeared only half finished. He dressed like César, combed his hair the same way, used the same cologne, affected the same partial smile and dangerous air, practiced a careless manner that did not naturally suit him. César was a racehorse; Alejandro a plow horse. And his effort to turn himself into a duplicate César was a form of self-annihilation.

The flight was late in leaving Washington, was further delayed during a Miami stopover, and didn't arrive in Santo Domingo until dusk. It was very hot, ninety-five degrees with an equivalent humidity, and the pavement steamed from a recent rain. The Dominican Republic is very poor, but no capital city is so poor that it can't support in luxury an elite category of rich.

A taxi took me through wretched streets of the poor to a bright enclave of the privileged, native and tourist, and dropped me off at a good hotel on the seafront boulevard. It was dark when I reached my big fifth-floor room. I tipped the bellman ten dollars, gave him an extra five, and asked him to bring me several of the city's newspapers and a map of the island of Hispaniola.

Sliding glass doors led onto a balcony furnished with a table and chairs, a chaise longue, and potted plants still beaded with water from the rain. The moon had not yet risen, and the sea was black with a sprinkling of boat lights; other bright sodium-vapor lights glowed along the *malecón*, which itself was lined with swiftly moving car lights. The breeze carried an odor of vehicle exhausts along with the sour, rank smell of the sea. Sea water has a strong smell when it is warm and rich with plankton. And maybe rich in human wastes; many tropical cities in poor countries empty their untreated sewage into ocean waters.

I returned to the room with my shirt soaked with sweat. The air-conditioning vents issued a welcome chill. A television weatherman reported that a tropical depression far east in the Atlantic might or might not turn into a tropical storm, and that into a hurricane, which might or might not threaten the Caribbean in a couple of weeks.

I ordered a lobster dinner from room service, three bottles of beer, and then sat down to read Judge Samuelson's report.

*   *   *

I consulted a number of sources regarding César Cardinal et al., and those sources led me to others, but no one reading this report should assume that it's exhaustive or even particularly accurate. What we have here is a compilation of opinion and informed speculation and poorly recalled events (memory selects and condenses) and biases, both for and against César.

The Cardinals are one of the ruling families of the Dominican Republic and have been such for more than two hundred years. Their original fortune was established from the land (and, it is said, the importation of slaves), and they still have extensive land holdings: a cattle ranch in the highlands, large sections of agricultural land, a sugarcane plantation, and a refinery. They also distill a popular rum named Ron Cardinal. Wages and conditions for workers on their various possessions are, of course, abysmal, in conformance with standard practices in the Dominican Republic and other third-world countries. The Cardinals are oligarchs, and proud of it. So, then, they profit from the land and human sweat, but they are also diversified, with investments in other areas of the national economy—a tourist resort now under construction on the less developed north coast, a factory that manufactures baseballs, textile sweatshops, a gambling casino now under construction, et cetera.

César is generally regarded as the head of the family even though his father is still alive (suffering the effects of a stroke incurred two or three years ago). César controls the money and commands the widespread family tribe. (Nearly all of the properties are trusted to family members, brothers and uncles and cousins, Cardinal relatives by blood or marriage.)

It is no doubt true, as Kate says, that the family is now deeply in debt, perhaps precariously so. The D.R. economy, strong during a period in the nineties, has since crashed. They are not in danger of going broke, but could take a severe beating in some of their investments, with loans coming due, failed enterprises, César's gambling, etc.

César was and probably still is the golden boy of Dominican society. One of my sources grandly referred to him as the "Alcibiades of the Caribbean." An excellent student and schoolboy tennis and swimming champion, he was playing polo for the premier Santo Domingo club at sixteen, drove a race car at the same age in island competitions, and so on. He attended an elite private elementary school in Santo Domingo; a military academy-preparatory school in the same city, studied at Cornell University in the States (political science) for three years, then went to the London School of Economics for two more years. During his free time he skied at St. Moritz, climbed at Chamonix, gambled at Monte Carlo, and seduced women wherever he happened to find them.

Soon after leaving college, at twenty-three, he

entered his country's diplomatic service, and almost immediately was assigned to the embassy of the Dominican Republic in Washington—a rare posting for a rookie, and one that embittered veteran D.R. diplomats. But he was a Cardinal. You wouldn't dare send a Cardinal to Tonga or Tierra del Fuego. Opinion varies over his effectiveness: Some claim that he was a dilettante, a playboy who exploited his diplomatic status for personal ends. Others insist that he actually was quite effective in his job as Special Envoy; that he made many important contacts on his party and golf rounds; that, for César, everything should appear to be accomplished without effort, from hitting a tennis ball to concluding serious negotiations. Visible effort, hard work, *sweat*—these are plebeian virtues.

It is accepted, though, by both sides, that César was and is a wild young man. Not so young now, thirty-seven, but still reckless, a man who loves risk. His seductions and affairs in and around Washington were notorious, and often quite dangerous politically. Dangerous too in another way: he once was shot at by an enraged husband, and there were other attempted assaults, threats, scandals. We may imagine that César enjoyed all the fuss enormously. And he exploited his diplomatic immunity, not just in the usual ways—ignoring traffic and parking violations—but in more serious matters. There was the shooting incident mentioned above, nightclub fights, etc., but he was also peripherally involved in the murder of a young Baltimore woman of good family. She had been killed—slaughtered—in one of those frenzied attacks we read about, twenty-six stab wounds, mutilations, and so dismally on. César had been seeing this woman, as had a few other men, and César, with his arrogant contempt of police and his immediate claim of diplomatic immunity, became an early suspect. Things were eventually smoothed over. He had many friends in Washington. He did not lose his diplomatic accreditation, he was not expelled from this country, and ultimately another suspect was arrested, tried, and convicted of the murder. I mention this because he *did* invoke diplomatic privilege, and because it is possible for his critics to believe him capable of such a crime.

Now, as to his famous charm. One informant, a woman, said that César exerted a hypnotic effect on people, individually and collectively: he could, with equal success, charm a woman, a man, a child, a dog, or dominate a room filled with people of consequence. He has, she and others told me, "charisma." I personally have heard of certain charismatic personalities whom I later met with disappointment. They seemed ordinary to me.

Flashy, maybe, pretentious, but ordinary. I was not a victim of their charm. Of course, no one can live up to that sort of glorious advertisement—charismatic. (And surely the advertisements feed the legend, they are pre-persuaders.) But it does seem that one must be susceptible to the type (as some are particularly vulnerable to professional hypnotists while others make poor subjects); charisma, like beauty, is in the eye of the beholder. As we know, there have always been people who willingly abandon themselves (their souls) to politicians (Hitler) or religious hysterics (Savonarola) or military scourges (Napoleon), while the rest of us are left cold and wondering what the hell the others are seeing that we fail to see. Of course, not all "charismatic" figures are evil, and I don't mean to place César in the same category with the men mentioned above. Anyway, some of César's partisans insist that the man can charm you out of your skin. He is a hero to them, almost a minor god.

His life does seem to have calmed in recent years: the polo, race car driving, alpinism, etc., are infrequent events these days, though his image as a bold man of action remains—and haven't we been told that image is everything?

There are many conflicts in the varied views of this man César Cardinal. He is described as arrogant, corrupt, brutal, treacherous, criminal. And contrarily described by others as possessing the great virtues: honor, loyalty, courage, and generosity—he's a bloody Boy Scout, according to some. How can we reconcile these views? We can't.

My personal opinion, for what it's worth: César Cardinal is a case of retarded development. He remains, in his late thirties, the brightest and bravest and most popular and most talented and most daring boy in prep school. Maybe—pardon the cheap psychology—maybe he could never give up that delicious early taste of fame and admiration. His family's position of privilege and power didn't help.

He's still a boy inside, except, maybe, the pranks have turned into crimes and the selfishness has developed pathological overtones.

As you might expect, I learned some things about Kate during my inquiries: Kate before she met César,

Kate when they courted, and Kate and César when they married. Shall I follow up?

*   *   *

By the time the table was set and the food served, the bellman returned with three newspapers, two tabloids, and a broadsheet. I tipped everyone in sight: the waiter, the bellman again, a woman who brought in a bouquet of complimentary flowers, and finally, the busboy who cleared away the debris. There were two lobster tails cooked in a wine-garlic-butter sauce, a garden salad, potato, creamed corn, and a small wedge of cheesecake for dessert. The bill, excluding tips, came to one hundred and three dollars and sixty-eight cents. I felt, in the jargon of the times, violated. I drank two of the beers while eating, and carried the third to the sofa along with the newspapers.

My Spanish, never fluent and now rusty from disuse, was just adequate for piecing together the stories of interest. One tabloid, *Éste Semana,* a weekly published four days earlier, contained a dull rehash of Katherine's disappearance at sea and reported on the inconsolable grief of the Cardinal family, their sadness and pain that so gifted a wife and mother, a woman with so much to live for, should take her own life and dress all who loved her in mourning. There was a color photo montage of César and Kate and little Antonio on the cover, culled from snapshots and studio portraits. Inside, on page three, was a foggy picture of Kate, cool and serene, with the baby in her arms. She wore a gold cross on a chain around her neck, and there was a big ornate cross on the blue velvet background. Madonna and child? I was not unfamiliar with the sentimental excesses of the Spanish-speaking peoples, but this photo went too far. It evoked hilarity. Kate and little Jesus.

The other tabloid, *Ahora!,* reprised the by now familiar story, the idyllic cruise, the tipsy Katherine going up on deck for fresh air, the "incredible event"— the unimaginable, the unspeakable accident. The subsequent search, the despair, the days of waiting and praying. César, to the reporter, announced his intention of traveling to Virginia to attend the memorial services with his late wife's family. ("They are my family, too. Our two families are one, and mourn together.") He wished he might take his son, Antonio, north to the memorial service, so that the boy might share in the healing ceremonies, and meet again with his mother's family, whom he loved deeply and who loved him. Unfortunately, the boy was ill, not seriously, but not fit for the journey north and the strain of collective mourning. The Cardinals and Adamses were united forever in mutual affection and shared memories—memories that could not be soiled by the slanders of the envious.

The quotations did not much correspond to the César Cardinal I had met, but then, reporters are granted a certain latitude in regard to the truth. Still, maybe when speaking Spanish, César was tempted into flowery rhetoric. The language encourages it.

The broadsheet, *La Prensa,* published this morning, had a front-page article about César's pilgrimage to the United States to attend his wife's memorial service, his shock and happiness at learning that his beloved

Katherine was alive (he had never surrendered hope), rescued by a lone sailor becalmed in the desolate waters off the Puerto Rican coast. The couple's joy at again, at last, being reunited, could not be conveyed in mere words. Together, hand in hand, they had entered the small chapel on the Adams estate and silently prayed together. The couple had later emerged from the chapel to the weeping and cheers of the assembled families and friends, and then they had gone off to the secluded bliss of the marital chamber.

I tossed *La Prensa* on the floor with the two tabloids, and telephoned Petrie.

"Who?" he said in his usual abrupt way.

"Shaw."

"Oh, man," he said, "why did I allow you to lure me into the bramble thicket?"

"What's happening?"

"Stuff."

"Tom . . ."

"Barlow has pretty much succeeded in cutting me out. Kate won't talk to me privately, Barlow's always there. He and Kate are conspiring together."

"Conspiring how?"

"If I knew, it wouldn't be a conspiracy, would it?"

"Have you been able to get any sleep?"

"Not much."

"Go to bed."

"I'm all right."

"Where are you?"

"On the front porch of the guest house. There are holes in the screen. I'm being exsanguinated by mosquitos. It's quiet. I can hear mosquitos and owls.

There are still lights on in the big house."

"Is César there?"

"No. He left two hours ago."

"Has he been seeing Kate?"

"You mean, are the two of them going off alone together? No. But he's *seeing* her. At meals, at croquet. Tomorrow a group are going riding. We have a fine summer party going on here, pal."

"How does Kate behave toward César?"

"Cold. Very cold and haughty. But she isn't hiding in the attic."

"You can see her dilemma."

"Not dilemmas again. Okay, César is the father of her son, and the father of her child-to-be. But did he or did he not try to kill her?"

"Have you heard from Leroy?"

"No."

"Is that good?"

"No, it's bad."

"I'll start looking for him tomorrow."

"Do that."

"How are the media treating Kate and César?"

"How do you think? With a terrifying savagery. They're like a medieval army camped at the gates. I'm not kidding. Uncle Warren has hired a second security outfit to keep the brutes away. Even so, the party goes on."

"I suppose her refusal to talk to them has chummed the waters."

"Apt metaphor. The story is out now that Kate has accused her husband of throwing her into the Atlantic. She denies the rumors, but so what? The media sharks have been maddened by the scent of blood. And you, Bunky, you are about to become a key figure. You'll be infamous by noon tomorrow."

"That won't help me in my task down here."

"Indeed not."

"They'll be digging up a lot of old bones."

"Oh, yes, surely. That Kate. The time will come when you'll regret not beating her to death with a boat hook on the night she came calling."

"Try to talk to Kate, find out what she's feeling and thinking."

"You really believe that one can find out what a woman is feeling and thinking by *asking her?*"

"Get some sleep."

"Women love to tell you what they're thinking and feeling. And it's truthfully what they're thinking and feeling at that moment. But what will they be thinking and feeling after lunch, after a visit to the hairdresser, after coitus?"

"I'll call you tomorrow."

"Do that," he said, and he broke the connection.

TWENTY-SIX

There was a photograph of me and Katherine on the front page of *El Diario,* a morning newspaper. It was not a good photo; it had been taken from a distance, then enlarged and cropped, and made foggier still by being reproduced on newsprint paper. In it, Kate and I were sitting together by Petrie's swimming pool, she on a chaise longue, I at the patio table. I could tell by the angle that the picture had been taken by Natalie Coleman from behind the shrubbery that screened her place from Tom's. Nat's motive in taking and selling the photo was not worth puzzling over at the moment. It would be difficult for anyone to recognize either me or Kate from the picture. But there would be other photos of me, better ones, published in the papers and on TV. I was, after all, the solo mariner who had rescued Katherine Adams-Cardinal from the sea; and I was—according to the report—a man with a very shady background.

Daniel Shaw was a lawyer who had abandoned his failing practice to adopt the life of a sea vagrant. He was a former officer in the U.S. Army, and subsequently an investigator both for private attorneys and for the Bell Harbor, Florida, state attorneys office. More recently Shaw had been at least peripherally involved in as yet unsolved crimes that had triggered investigations by Florida police authorities. There then followed brief and inaccurate descriptions of the Peter Falconer-Raven Ahriman mystery: the murders in the Keys, the kidnapping and death of Falconer, and the curious vanishing of Ahriman; and an even more sketchy, speculative mention of last summer's Paradise Key swindle. The principal in that criminal enterprise, a man variously known as Victor Trebuchet, Anton Arbaleste, and Jean Halbert, had mysteriously vanished during a period when Shaw had been occupying an Italian villa next to Arbaleste's.

There was no mention of Petrie, the judge, or Leroy, but I figured that they would soon make their media debuts in what might come to be called *The Mystery at Sea* or *The Mermaid's Lament*. Cry havoc and let loose the dogs of reportage.

It was unlikely that anyone would identify me from the photo in *El Diario,* but Daniel Shaw had passed through customs and registered at a popular tourist hotel. And Alejandro might well arrange to have me tracked by the police or private agents. Finding Leroy without first being found by the media was going to be a problem. I couldn't rent a car, use my credit cards, stay in the better hotels, move about like an ordinary citizen. I had to behave like a criminal. I felt like one while reading and rereading my abbreviated biography in *El Diario,* though it did seem to me that, in Spanish, my suspected crimes and misdemeanors *(aventuras)* had a rather raffish slant, as if the writer admired more than condemned Daniel

Shaw. And maybe there was a certain sympathy because I had saved "La Señora," Kate.

For a while I considered leaving the Dominican Republic. Charter a light airplane. Seek anonymity and refuge with Finn at Woeful Cay. But there was Kate, and Kate's son, who might even now be stalked by Leroy. Petrie and I had lit Leroy's fuse; we were at least in part responsible for his actions.

I wore khaki shorts, sneakers, and a T-shirt on the sixty-mile bus ride along the south coast from Santo Domingo to San Marcos. The bus was crowded, cheerfully noisy, and at every stop itinerant musicians came aboard to play their instruments—bongo drums, flutes, a concertina—in return for a few coins. It was sauna-hot aboard the bus. All the windows were closed, and I was reprimanded when I tried to open one. There is a peculiar phobia about fresh air blowing in through windows in the third world; people think it will make them sick.

A sign outside San Marcos stated that the town had a population of fifteen thousand, but it was an old sign, and there were probably at least twice that number in the city proper and the shack slums that ringed it. The bus depot was located in the run-down old core of the city. I picked up my duffel, bought a local newspaper, and went out into the blistering sunlight.

Sweating, half blinded by sun glare reflected off shop windows, I wandered through chaotic back-streets packed with food carts and merchandise stalls and shoppers and celebrants and loiterers and drunks. I learned that there was a *feria* in progress in honor of the city's patron saint, San Marcos. Many of the buildings were painted in bright pastels—yellow, aqua, pink, green—according to whim. I passed some small hotels and boardinghouses, and finally selected a three-story hotel that overlooked a square thick with foliage and with an X of flagstone walks leading to a center bandstand. Hotel Montejo. The plaster facade had the mineral equivalent of psoriasis, peeling and crumbling in places, and a few of the top floor windows were boarded over.

I went up half a dozen concrete steps, through the door, and down a lobby sparsely furnished but lush with potted plants and flowers. The desk clerk, a black youth with a milky eye, assigned me to one of the better rooms, number 322, on the front corner, looking down over the plaza. It cost thirty-five dollars per night, high, I thought, but the clerk explained that prices were inflated each year during the famous Feria de San Marcos. He gave me some brochures, and advised me that the city provided numerous cultural and entertainment venues during the week: concerts, dances, exhibitions of folk art, poetry readings, sports events—boxing, baseball, and soccer matches with teams of a rival city—and a carnival that had been erected on the open ground east of town. I glanced over the register as I signed: no name had been entered in Leroy's scrawl. Of course, he would not use his real name. Nor did I.

The elevator didn't work. I walked up the stairs to the third floor, down a dim hall to room 322. It was much better than I expected, large and clean, and the tall windows admitted plenty of light. The furnishings were austere: no carpeting on the tile floor, no overstuffed chairs or couches, things that absorbed moisture in a humid climate. I turned a switch and two ceiling fans began to revolve. No air-conditioning. The room was relatively cool now, a little before noon, but I expected the heat would be ferocious later in the day. There was a triple-threat bathroom: bathtub, separate shower stall, and porcelain bidet. All of the faucets issued tepid, murky water.

I opened the windows, stood a moment in the blast of heat and cooking smells from the stalls below, then closed them. An eight-piece brass band wearing army uniforms was warming up in the bandstand.

The newspaper I had bought at the bus depot was mostly concerned with local politics and fiesta news. There was no mention of Leroy Karpe's arrest and subsequent jailbreak. That was not information that the police would be eager to release. There was not much news about César Cardinal, Kate, and the shadowy small-boat sailor who had rescued her from the *furioso* sea, and none of the information was recent. César and Kate had been gloriously reunited in Virginia. The news blackout held; neither César nor Kate, nor their factions, were talking to the media. The paper's columns were filled with speculation expressed in hyperventilating prose. One might infer that César and his wife had not yet exited the bedchamber.

I stretched out on my own temporary bed. *Where are you, Leroy?* He would be hard to find. I had often questioned his sanity, though I knew that he actually possessed a good, if untrained, native intelligence. He was shrewd and tough. He had spent years moving through the paranoid, clandestine, violent world of drug smuggling. He knew how to hide; when to run;

how and when to strike. Most of all, Leroy Karpe was stubborn. You'd probably need a saw, chisel, and hammer to change his mind.

* * *

Late in the afternoon I hired a taxi to take me down the coastal road to Mil Flores. It was only a few miles away in distance, but worlds away in other respects. We passed by the carnival on the eastern edge of San Marcos, passed bare fields that had been ruined for agriculture by incursions of the salt sea, drove by a small private airport, and then stopped at a gate manned by the police. Mil Flores did not welcome undesirable visitors. A policeman gazed in at me for a few seconds, straightened, ordered the gate raised, and waved my driver through. He recognized me as an American or perhaps European. Not, anyway, one of his country's desperate poor.

Mil Flores was an oasis of the rich in the desert of the poor. It was not really a town. There was a cluster of specialty shops, boutiques, a marine chandlery, and precious little garden restaurants clustered around the yacht harbor. There was probably a hundred million dollars' worth of yachts docked at the marina. We went on down a narrow road made of crushed seashells, glittering white and pink in the sunshine; passed between the broad sandy beach on the right and the walled villas to the left—high walls, made of brick, a few topped by razor wire or embedded with broken glass. Beyond the masonry walls there were green walls of trees and shrubbery, jungly growths that obscured view of the complexes within. But you could imagine fine houses, tennis courts and pools, shady courtyards where the Family and Guests gathered for cocktails. There were other villas perched on the green hills that rose up behind Mil Flores.

It was an insular little enclave where like associated with like. I had no way of identifying the Cardinal villa, and I chose not to arouse the driver's curiosity by inquiring. I'd told him that I sold real estate in Florida, and wished to see the famous community of Mil Flores before returning home. Mil Flores, he said, was a dream. And it was: a dream of quiet and shade and perfumed air and what real estate advertisements called "gracious living." It did not get more gracious than in Mil Flores. But I had no difficulty in believing that there was rot inside the dream, and that at least one would-be murderer graciously spent his summers there.

San Marcos, with its heat and noise and stinks and raucous poor-folk fun, was a shock. I paid the driver, and wandered the area near my hotel. Feral boys ran in packs, kicking soccer balls, hustling coins, mocking adults, chasing cats, racing through the streets. They were a nuisance, but few in the crowd seemed to care. Their mad energy was tolerated. I found a relatively quiet area of the square, sat on a bench in the shade of a tree that smelled like turpentine, and waited for the boys. Gringos in this kind of neighborhood were a magnet. Some kids would drift over eventually.

I had learned long ago that such boys made the best spies and informants in a strange city. They noticed without being noticed. Just wild kids. They watched, they listened, they moved freely and invisibly through enemy—adult—territory. They could become, with a smile and a few dollars, your underground army. The police couldn't locate Leroy. A gang of wild boys might.

After no more than five minutes, I noticed a group of six boys watching me from a corner of the plaza. All of them were black, with the oldest about fourteen and the youngest twelve. They approached with the kind of swagger you noticed with some stray dogs; bold, even aggressive, but ready to retreat.

"Qué pasa, muchachos?" I said.

Nada was happening. That was the formulaic response. They could be waging war in the middle of a class-five hurricane, but it could not be admitted that something was happening.

The leader was the biggest and oldest of the boys, a muscular kid with wiry hair and a macho attitude well beyond his years. I chatted with the kids in my poor Spanish. They teased me, I teased back. That was ritual. I then presented my proposition: one hundred American dollars—a fortune here—for whoever could locate Leroy Karpe. I didn't use the name, I described him: American, five feet ten, scars on his face, lank brown hair and staring blue eyes, speaks Spanish pretty well, will beat the crap out of you if he catches you spying.

The big kid, Juan Carlos, showed me his palm. I placed a twenty-dollar bill on it. Was it a deal?

Juan Carlos grinned. We shook hands. His hand was narrow but long, long palm and long fingers, and the grip was strong.

"Where are you from?" he asked me.

"Baltimore."

Did I know Sammy Sosa, a great player from the Dominican Republic, who played for the Orioles?

Of course I knew Sammy. We lived in the same suburb. We golfed together. His wife and my wife shopped together. Sammy owed me money.

The kids laughed.

I told them that I was staying at the Hotel Montejo, room 322, and when they found Leroy they should immediately let me know.

They soon dispersed, eager to fulfill their mission, to earn one hundred dollars, and I ate a late lunch in a restaurant that served a meal of fresh fish, rice, beans, rolls, and beer for nine dollars.

TWENTY-SEVEN

The police administration building and lockup were located in an old section of the city and appeared to date from the colonial period. It was four stories high, constructed of gray stone, with narrow iron-barred windows and, in front, a row of (fluted columns which supported a flat slab roof. Concrete steps led up to open eight-foot doors. Two soldiers in parade dress uniforms and armed with automatic weapons flanked the doorway.

I walked past the sentries and entered a cavernous hall that occupied the buildings bottom two stories. It was damp and chill inside, cold in temperature and aspect: stone walls, slit windows which admitted little light, tile floors, and a septic smell. Desks were scattered around a vast space that dully echoed with voices and ringing telephones and the clatter of old manual upright typewriters. A stairway made of thick timber scaffolding led up to the higher floors. I supposed that there were offices on the floor above, and above that the interrogation rooms and cells—with one cell, at least, that had a ventilation shaft leading up to the roof and to freedom for a snake like Leroy.

227

Thirty or forty chairs lined against the east wall were occupied by men, women, and children, most of them black or of mixed race, all of them shabby, all scared and miserable except for the children too young to understand the situation. Most of the men were separate, and handcuffed to an iron pipe secured to the wall. Two of the men had been badly beaten, perhaps by the cops, more likely by each other. The women—some with babies—were patient, woeful, as they waited to inquire about their husbands, fathers, brothers. And all around the great stone cave bureaucrats, police and civilian, lethargically attended to their tasks.

There was no place to sit. I leaned back against the cold wall and waited. Not far away, three uniformed men sat on stools behind a huge crescent-shaped oak desk. They looked bored. Each action was performed in slow motion. They did not appear harsh or contemptuous, just bored, enduring a tedium not much different from that experienced by the peti-tioners and waiting criminals.

I expected to be interviewed ahead of the waiting crowd. I was a foreigner, fairly well dressed and groomed, clearly not afflicted by the racial and economic and criminal troubles suffered by the others. But police pride was involved, and national resentments: let the gringo share the chill and stink for a while.

After twenty minutes of being ignored, the policeman in the center looked directly at me, stared, and then abruptly gestured. When I did not immedi-ately respond, he gestured again. Good God, man, can't you see I'm busy?

I walked to the desk. There was no place to sit. On

my left a woman was pleading to see her husband; and on my right an old man was reporting that his pushcart had been stolen during the night. The center cop, my cop, looked at me from under his brows, then opened a manila folder and pretended to read the contents. Perhaps he wanted me to think that he possessed my dossier. I waited out his bluff. He was a barrel-chested man in his forties, a hairy man, with a thick bush of black hair and thick eyebrows, and dark beard shadow and a tuft of curly hair visible at the V of his shirt. He slowly lowered the manila folder to the desktop. His voice was low and throaty.

"*Habla usted Español?*"

"*Un poco.*"

"*Pues.* Then we will speak English. Have you a cigarette?" I passed him a half-full package of Marlboros. He took one, lit it, and placed the pack on top of the manila file.

"So," he said. "What?"

"I want to report that my wallet was stolen last night."

"Thieves," he said mildly. "I hate them. Show me identification, if you please."

"All of my identification was in the wallet."

"*Merde,* "he said. "You know *merde?*"

"Its French for 'shit.'"

"*Caca, merde, caca.* You want to talk French?"

"Let's talk Spanish."

"I don't think so."

He fitted a sheet of paper into the ancient Remington upright typewriter on the desk, rolled it, and said, "What is you name, *hombre?*"

"Jack Frost."

He typed rapidly with his two index fingers. "You live where, Zach?"

"New York City."

"The street, the zip, the telephone?"

I invented all three.

"What is 'piss' in French?" he asked.

"I don't know. Piss?"

"Yes, piss."

"I mean, it's the same in French as English, isn't it?"

"Maybe not."

"There's the word *pissoir*. And in France a street toilet is called a *pissoir.*"

"You marry, Zach?"

"Single."

He typed with a fine carelessness. "*Pissoir.* I don't think so. Why are you here in my country?"

"Business."

"What business, Zach?"

"Look, Sergeant, I've changed my mind. My wallet is gone. There isn't much the police can do. You have more important jobs. And"—I looked at my watch—"I'm late for an appointment."

"Caca. What is the business, Zach?"

"I'm a reporter for *The New York Times*. I'm here looking for an American fugitive named Leroy Karpe. He was in custody here a few days ago, but he escaped."

"No. No one escape this place." He looked at me warily.

"He crawled out a ventilator shaft to the roof."

"No. There is no Leroy Karpe here, no escape. No ventilator. Where you stay, *hombre?*"

"The Hotel Bienvenidos."

THE BLOOD RED SEA

"Hotel Bienvenidos is at Santo Domingo."

"Yes."

"This Leroy is you friend?"

"No. He's a bad man."

"Leroy means the king in French, no?"

"Spelled L-e R-o-i, yes."

He asked half a dozen more questions and, smiling cynically, typed my half dozen lies. "I have never heard such *merde*." He tore the sheet of paper from the roller, picked up my package of cigarettes, said, "Wait," then walked diagonally across the room and started climbing the stairs.

The continuous murmur of voices, the ringing of telephones and metallic clatter of typewriters, the whir of desk fans, were all combined into a steady humming in the great cavern. The woman who had been on my left was now gone, replaced by another woman, this one balancing a baby on her hip. She too was inquiring about her missing husband, Jaime, who had been arrested three weeks before. Could she please see him? To my right, a dwarfish man whose head barely reached above the desktop was quacking something about the confiscation of his money and watch by a street policeman.

I regretted coming here. It had been futile. Stupid. Anyone who voluntarily entered the police machinery should not be surprised if it chewed him up. I was about to leave when the sergeant emerged from a door onto the landing, came down the steps, and crossed over to where I waited.

"Let's go, Zach," he said.

I followed him across the humming room and up

the stairs to a door that opened into a hallway that ran the width of the building. A long center hall, lined with doors on both sides, divided the building lengthwise. We walked roughly halfway down this hall and paused before a door. There was a number on the panel, but no name or declaration of function. The sergeant knocked lightly.

"*Venga,*" a voice called.

We entered a rectangular space that was furnished more like a living room than an office: there was carpeting, leather sofas and chairs, coffee and end tables, floor lamps, a tallboy cabinet in polished wood, and a mahogany desk behind which sat a man whom the sergeant addressed as "Jefe."

"*Este es el hombre, Jefe,*" he said, and then he retreated to the door and out into the hall.

The Jefe, a thin man wearing a suit and tie, glanced at me, then looked down at the sheet of paper left by the sergeant. He had a sallow complexion, black hair combed in a pompadour, wire-rimmed glasses, and a thin mustache of the type worn by suave movie actors in the thirties and forties.

"Sit," he said, without looking up.

I sat on a straight-backed chair near a corner of his desk. There was no nameplate on the desk. A CD player on a cabinet behind the desk, tuned very low, was playing what at first I thought was opera, but now realized were screams. Men screaming, women screaming. I heard, faintly, the agonized bellow of a man shouting, "No! No!" and screaming at a pitch that hardly sounded human. A pause, and then a woman screamed in a way that raised the hair on the back of my neck. It went on like that.

Finally the man pushed the sheet of paper toward me. "Is there anything here that isn't a lie?"

I was surprised to see that the sergeant, with his casual rapid-fire technique, had made no errors except for spelling "Jack" as "Zach." All of the typewritten letters were clotted with ink and dirt.

"I am single," I said. "That isn't a lie. And my name is Jack."

"Your name is Shaw."

Then a particularly chilling scream issued from the CD player, maybe a child's scream, pitched so high that it was barely audible, but expressive of an incomprehensible suffering.

The Jefe surprised me by smiling in a friendly, confidential way. "The recording causes anxiety in the people I interview," he said.

"Christ. I can see why. What do you want to know?"

"It's a deception," he said. "Actually a collection of screams recorded from television and movie dramas. You can sometimes hear music in the background. It's shocking how much human screaming goes on in those mediums."

I more than half believed him. His complicitous smile, genuine as far as I could tell, indicated that the screaming was a clever ruse that humorous men like us could enjoy together.

"Cigarette?" he asked, offering the package of Marlboros confiscated by the sergeant. I took one, lit it, and returned the pack.

"A drink?"

"No, thank you."

"What do you want, Mr. Shaw?"

"Shall I call you Jefe?"

"My name is Gavilán."

"Gavilán—that means hawk, doesn't it?"

"Can you think of a reason why I shouldn't have you expelled from my country?"

"One. I might be able to help you find Leroy Karpe."

"Go on."

"I came here today to talk about Karpe, but the sergeant told me that Leroy had never been arrested and certainly never escaped."

"We know about you, Mr. Shaw. We know that you saved the life of César Cardinal's wife. We are a sentimental people. There is much good feeling toward you in the Dominican Republic. Let's say that you have established emotional credit here. The television and newspapers have made you a hero; but they can just as easily make you despised."

"I've had my fifteen minutes."

"Do you know where this Karpe is?"

"No. But I want to stop him."

"Stop him from doing what?"

I thought for a time. I did not want to betray Leroy altogether. A half betrayal might suffice. The thing was to prevent him from snatching the Cardinal boy, contrive to activate an all-out police search, get him back behind bars—but for just a few months, not ten years.

"Leroy," I said, "is a former drug smuggler."

"We know that."

"He intends to smuggle arms into this country. He has made contact with revolutionaries."

"We have no revolutionaries in the Dominican Republic."

"Of course not. Even so, Karpe has made contact with the revolutionaries up in the mountains and plans to sell them weapons. Kalashnikovs, AR-15s, mortars, C-4 explosives, grenades . . . all of it."

"Tell me about these revolutionaries."

I was inventing wildly. "They call themselves *Los Hermanos Unidos.*"

He smiled. His face changed when he smiled, became gender and expressed a wry humor. "Can you see, I am trembling." He held up his hands and trembled for me. "Thank you for coming to see us, Mr. Shaw."

"Okay, look, forget the bullshit. Just find Leroy Karpe and lock him up."

"We are looking."

"Look harder."

"Do you intend to stay long at the Hotel Montejo?" He was showing off.

"I'm not sure. I'll let you know if I move."

"No need. We'll know." Still showing off.

"Am I under surveillance?"

"You registered at the Hotel Montejo as a Mr. Donald Duck. Donald Duck, Jack Frost—please, give more thought to choosing false names."

"I've been watched ever since I arrived in this country, haven't I? Alejandro Cardinal arranged the surveillance."

"You haven't made it difficult."

"I'll try to make it more difficult in the future."

"Why don't you trying wearing one of those rubber carnival masks? Donald Duck, perhaps. Bugs Bunny. You could hardly do worse than walking the streets with your own face, which has been on TV and in the papers for days."

"Those are bad photos."

He picked up the typewritten sheet, tore it into quarters, and dropped the scraps into a wastebasket.

I stood up. "Thanks for seeing me."

"Did it happen as the newspapers say? Katherine Cardinal swam up to your boat in the middle of the night?"

"It did happen that way, yes."

"Incredible. And these vicious rumors about . . . ?"

"César? All lies." I walked to the door and turned. "What is your job title, Señor Gavilán?"

"I am Chief of Internal Security in this district."

"Are those screams really culled from movies and TV?"

"Yes, really. From American movies and TV."

"Well, then, remember that I warned you about Karpe."

"You did. Thank you."

A policeman was waiting in the hallway; he escorted me down the hall and down the stairs and through the stone cavern to sunlight and fresh air.

TWENTY-EIGHT

The citizens of San Marcos burned all of their bad luck in a ceremony at the Plaza Major at eight o'clock the next night. An eighteen-foot-tall effigy named *Mala Suerte* was erected in the center of the square and ignited. The crowd cheered. A band played. The fire started up the legs, slowly at first, then blazing as it reached the waist. It was made of papier-mâché and crepe over an armature of wire, and the big scowling face indeed had the look of malevolent fate. Firecrackers and rockets had been placed in the torso and head, and when they ignited *Mala Suerte* exploded into flaming fragments that arced wildly through the night. Most of the rockets went awry, whistling off into the crowd and bursting into deadly blue, red, and white spears. Four or five persons were injured—one badly burned—and hustled into waiting ambulances. Finally all that was left of *Mala Suerte was* the red-glowing wire framework and pieces of smoldering papier-mâché scattered over the ground. The crowd seemed more puzzled than jubilant. They would have to burn an effigy of *Mala Suerte* every night to reduce this town's bad luck.

Juan Carlos and his gang of adolescent thugs saw me as I was leaving the plaza. The boy was angry. Where had I been? Was I not a serious man? They had been to the Hotel Montejo three times today looking for me. They had left messages with the desk clerk. They had found *el hombre perdido.*

"*Bueno,*" I said. "*Vamos a ver.*"

The kids led me through a labyrinth of dim crooked streets and filthy alleys to a section of the city known as La Cucaracha. It was a slum of corner bodegas and hole-in-the-wall bars and crumbling tenements that looked like giant beehives. The people here were celebrating the *feria,* too, but without much spirit; I had the notion that mournful, alcoholic fiestas took place every day in La Cucaracha. Few of the streets were paved. They would be dusty in the dry season, mud tributaries during the rainy months. They were dusty now, and on them I saw mostly drunks, feral children, barefoot prostitutes, day laborers without any labor to perform, and a few citizens who somehow managed to maintain dignity in this dusty hell. And there were pariah dogs—starving mutts so weak they stood with splayed legs and lowered heads—and here and there a fugitive pig or chicken. Music issued from some of the bars and three-table cafés. Beggars waited with the patience of stones on corners and in doorwells.

The boys led me to a final street, Calle de los Mártires, nearly identical to the other streets except maybe a bit more run-down, a shade more desperate. Juan Carlos pointed toward a yellow three-story building in the middle of the block. Another beehive. A fluttery orange neon identified it as the Hotel San

Francisco. Most of the windows were opaque with filth; a few had been broken and not replaced.

"*El está allí,*" Juan Carlos said. He—Leroy—was there.

"*Ahora?*" I asked. Now?

"*Creo que si.*" I believe so.

"*Crees?*" You *believe* so?

Juan Carlos conferred with the other boys, and after a rapid-fire slangy conversation that I couldn't follow, he told me that Leroy had been seen entering the building this afternoon at about three o'clock. That was six hours ago, and I had no way of knowing if Leroy was still there. He probably would not remain at one location for very long.

The boys watched me suspiciously. They expected to be cheated. It was the way of the world. I had given Juan Carlos twenty dollars; now I counted out an additional eighty in twenties and tens into his long palm; he could divide it among the others as he judged fair. Each boy solemnly shook my hand, said good-bye, and started quickly down the street.

"*A dónde vas?*" I called to Juan Carlos.

"*Al carnaval!*"

I diagonally crossed the street, pushing past hostile drunks and affectionate whores, and entered the *Hotel San Francisco. Número 1021 Calle de los Mártires. Se rentan cuartos.* The lobby was small, without carpeting or furniture except for the desk. I rang the bell, waited, rang it again every thirty seconds until a fat black woman in slippers and housecoat shuffled out of a side room. With her came a blast of cooking odors and the sound of a television.

"*Buenos noches,*" I said.

She did not reply. Her hands were placed flat on the countertop, and I saw that she wore cheap rings on every finger of both hands.

I placed a five-dollar bill on the counter and told her that I was looking for a friend. Leroy was easy to describe.

She shook her head.

I added another five dollar bill to the first.

"No está aquí, señor," she said loudly, picking up the two fives. Then she stepped back from the counter and pointed to one of the honeycomb of boxes on the back wall: 248. *"No conozco el."* She would not be accused of ratting on her tenants.

I went up a stairway littered with fallen plaster and insect corpses to a long, dimly lighted hallway that smelled of mildew. A fire exit was chained shut. Nail heads protruded from the floorboards. I went down the hall past room doors from which issued tinny music and angry voices and cooking smells, to the next to last door, number 248. I leaned close and heard inside the flutey voices of children.

I knocked, and a moment later a woman's voice said, *"Quién es?"*

"Un amigo," I said.

"Qué quiere?"

"Quiero ver a Leroy."

The chained door opened wide enough for me to discern half a face, a single inquiring eye.

"Leroy," I called. "Are you in there? It's Shaw."

"Admitir the son of a bitch," Leroy said.

The door was unchained; it swung open, and I stepped past the woman into a cubical room that was overcrowded with furniture and objects and people. There was hardly room for me to enter. Bed, dresser, table and chairs, cardboard boxes, battered suitcases, bedrolls on the bare floor, an ancient TV with a screen filled with snow. And children, three of them playing on the floor, and a crying baby on the bed. And Leroy and the woman.

"*Mi casa es su casa,*" he said.

He was standing on the far side of the room, a window on one side, a cardboard picture of a levitating Jesus on the other, an automatic pistol in his hand, and a toothy smile on his face. Leroy rarely smiled. He was never glad to see me. But the pistol was held in a relaxed way, at his side, and there was nothing dangerous in his smile.

"How did you find me?"

"I set loose a pack of kids."

"That usually works." He put the pistol down on a bedside table where some other objects lay: a cell telephone, a wallet, handcuffs.

The woman was of mixed race, what used to be called a mulatto (mule), and might have been pretty a few years ago, a few babies ago, when she was twenty.

The small children, two boys and a girl, had gone back to their game on the floor. It was a game that required much interpreting of the rules and scornful admonitions in lisping Spanish.

"That's Cristina," Leroy said.

"*Con mucho gusto,*" I said to the woman.

"*Igual.*" She nodded shyly, looked away, then drifted off through the debris that she probably regarded as her household possessions to the bed. She picked up

the baby, which had stopped crying on its own, but
now began again.

I said, "I'm glad I found you before . . ."

"Before what?" Leroy asked.

"Petrie and I have been going crazy."

"Poor fellas."

"Really, Leroy. Christ."

"So you and Tom were scared."

"You bet we were."

"You thought I was going to snatch Kate's kid."

"Exactly."

"But wasn't that the idea?"

"It was *an* idea, just one. But there wasn't a final
decision. Kate hadn't actually given us the go-ahead."

"It's her boy. She has the right. She has the right to
get her son away from that bastard César."

"Yes, but an abduction—that has to be carefully
thought out."

"You and Tom," he said. "Thinkers. Lawyers.
Maybe yes, maybe no, better wait to see which way the
wind is blowing."

"Thinking isn't a bad idea," I said. "You ought to
try it."

"But all's well that ends well. Right?" He was grinning.

"Leroy . . ."

"A stitch in time saves nine."

"No," I said.

I had merely glanced at the children when entering
the room. Now I looked more closely. Two of them,
a boy about five and a three-year-old girl, were, like
the baby, obviously Cristina's kids. They would be
regarded as black in the States, probably here as well,

and think of themselves as black. The other boy was fair-skinned, and his hair was a dusty brownish-blond. I could see Kate in his features, his mouth and eyes; and I saw César in the way he carried his head and in his imperious manner with the other two. He was a five-year-old dictator. He had been dressed like the other boy, in clothes that had been laundered so often that nearly all the color had been bleached away. The prince was dressed like a pauper.

"When?" I asked Leroy.

"An hour ago." He sat down on the edge of the bed.

"Where?"

"At the carnival."

"How?"

"That's a long story," he said.

"Tell me."

In Spanish, he said, "Cristina, give our honored guest a glass of rum."

She put the baby down on the bed, went to a cabinet, got out a half-full bottle (Ron Cardinal, according to the label), and poured two small jelly glasses to the brims. She gave one to Leroy and carried the other to me.

I looked at the bedside table: a 9mm pistol, a cell phone, an alligator skin wallet, and a pair of handcuffs.

"Did you kill the bodyguard, Leroy?"

"I don't know. I hit him pretty hard."

"With what?"

"A rock."

"How hard did you hit him?"

"He was down on the ground, twitching and jerking. Convulsions, I guess."

I carried my glass to a spindly cane chair. It was a

good dark rum. I drank half a glassful, and looked at Leroy. Now I recognized that he was scared. His grins were a manifestation of his fear. I had never seen Leroy scared until this moment.

I said, "We've got to figure a way to get the boy back to the Cardinal family. We can't just release him into the fiesta crowd."

"What are you talking about?"

"Maybe Cristina can take him to a police station, drop him off, run like hell."

"Give him back?"

"Christ, yes, give him back."

"I thought you came here to help."

"I will help. I am helping. We'll see that the boy is safe with his family, and then, Leroy, we'll get the fuck out of this country before they hang us from a lamppost."

"Go on," he said. "Run. I'll take care of it by myself. You've always been worse than useless, anyway."

I finished the rum, held up my glass to Cristina, and said, *"Otro ron, por favor."* She took my glass.

To Leroy, I said, "Why were you arrested?"

"Cops caught me walking around Mil Flores. They arrested me for trespass and stealing."

"What did you steal?"

"Nothing. That was just bullshit."

"They don't like vagrants in Mil Flores."

"I had plenty of money."

"And you escaped jail," I said. "Now they really want you. Did they photograph you when they took you to jail?"

"Photographed and fingerprinted."

"Great. You're probably a TV star at this very moment. You and Tony. Why is the kid having such a good time? He acts like his Uncle Leroy and Aunt Cristina have just taken him to play with his favorite cousins. Did he cry? Was he scared when you did whatever you did, and took him away?"

"That little boy over there," Leroy said with a fierce pride, as if Tony Cardinal was his own son, "has never in all his life known a bad thing. Never been hit, never been spoken to in anger, never was hungry or scared. He thinks whatever happens to him is good, what should be. He's never had a bad thing happen to him, and I aim to see that he never does."

The boy had been violently abducted (had he seen his bodyguard hurt?), taken to a miserable slum, and dressed in rags—and now Leroy was telling me that nothing bad would ever happen to Tony as long as *he* was responsible for his well-being.

Cristina brought me the glass of rum. I drank half of it immediately. You could not talk to Leroy once he had made up his mind. He was impenetrably stubborn. And he lived his disreputable, often criminal life, supported by a queer moral certainty. He was right and righteous in his noble effort to return Tony to his mom.

I finished the rum. I had drunk two glasses, maybe ten ounces, and I felt absolutely cold sober.

"I'll go out and scout around," I said.

"Do that."

"I'll be back in half an hour, an hour. I'll see what I can do to get us out of this."

"Like go to the cops?"

"No, no cops, Leroy. Try not to be more paranoid than nature made you. I'll be back. Alone."

"Don't slam the door," Leroy said. "Don't let the flies out."

I got up, thanked Cristina, and glanced at the angelic Tony, who was declaring another victory over the protests of the other boy. He was like his father; he had to win all the time.

I left the room, the hotel, the street, and the district.

TWENTY-NINE

The effects of ten ounces of rum on an empty stomach kicked in when I reached the street. Suddenly I was drunk. Not as drunk as some of those roaming the street, but drunk enough to suffer a slackness in my reflexes and, paradoxically, both a sharpening and dulling of my perceptions. Colors seemed brighter, noises louder, odors nastier, and the faces were like masks representing the baser human emotions. At the same time I felt remote from the colors, the noises, the stinks, the people; I occupied a different dimension. The *feria*, ordinary before, now seemed a hallucination. These were unhappy people desperately striving to be happy for one night, one week. Tonight was the fourth day of the *feria*, and nerves were raw, tempers short. It was a festive crowd that—on a rumor, a whim, some incident—could turn into a dangerous mob. Men offered me drinks from their bottles. Prostitutes beckoned, and one clutched at my groin as I passed. Adolescent boys jeered. A pariah dog snapped at my heels. I moved quickly, jogging at times, tacking up and down identical streets, through identical plazas, past crowds of identical people, heading south, toward the sea. I had forgotten my purpose. I only wanted to see and smell the ocean, walk the promenade, recover my wits. But my sense of direction was skewed. I jogged blindly through the maze of streets and alleys until finally I found myself back on the Calle de los Mártires. There was the Hotel San Francisco, and there, on the second floor, far right, a light burned in the windows of room 248. My watch informed me that I had been fleeing in a near panic for forty minutes. I was ashamed of my flight. It could not be blamed on the alcohol. I had been running away from the situation: mad Leroy, the bodyguard who had lain on the ground in convulsions, the kidnapped child—Kate's boy—and the trouble that was going to rain down on us as a consequence of Leroy's actions.

I went into a café not much bigger than a closet and ordered a Coca-Cola *grande*. Twists of sticky paper, dotted with dead flies, dangled from the ceiling, and their cousins walked on my table and the walls. Plaster madonnas and saints lined shelves behind the counter. I was breathing hard and soaked with sweat, but sober now, calmed, and prepared to deal with the mess. I'd probably have to kill Leroy. He never weakened, never deviated, never altered course. Traits that were admirable in the abstract were, with Leroy, grievous faults.

The café's proprietor delivered my warm Coke, accepted a coin, and returned to the counter. There were no other customers in the place, but a chunk of meat cooking on the grill was filling the place with smoke and a smell like burning trash. Cat, dog, roadkill?

I went outside and crossed the street to the hotel. A blanket-wrapped woman and two children were

sleeping on the lobby floor. There was no one at the
desk. I started up the stairs. Kill Leroy how? Or maybe
I could simply disable him somehow, knock him out,
tie him up.

I knocked on door 248, called, "Leroy," waited,
and knocked again. Silence. I knocked once more, and
inside Cristina said something that I couldn't understand. The door was not locked. I opened it, went
inside, and saw her lying supine on the bed, both
wrists handcuffed around an iron bedpost. The two
children and the baby were sleeping next to her. Leroy
and Kate's son were gone. I should have expected him
to run.

The key was attached to the handcuff chain by a
string. I unlocked the cuffs, and Cristina sat up, rubbing
her wrists and looking at me in a way that suggested
more fear than gratitude.

Leroy had taken the pistol, of course, and the money
while leaving the bodyguard's wallet and cell phone
behind. He knew that by now calls on that particular
telephone were being traced.

Cristina's three children, the boy, the girl, and the
baby, were sprawled out on the bed, sleeping with that
depth and trust that always astonish. Children played
themselves into a sort of coma.

Cristina fried half a dozen eggs, and we ate them
with a loaf of bread and coffee. The children did not stir.
There was enough food left over for their breakfasts.

After the meal, I took my coffee to the rickety cane
chair, and told Cristina that I was going to ask her
questions, and that she should answer truthfully. She
did not challenge my right to interrogate her. She was

simple, very poor, female, and alone. Passivity was her only defense.

Her Spanish was uncomplicated, and she spoke slowly and with many pauses. When she used slang that I didn't understand, I asked her to express herself in a different way.

"When and how did you meet Leroy, Cristina?"

He was a customer three—no, four days ago. Cristina's husband, who was in the United States working as a farm laborer, sent her money, but it was never enough, and so she sometimes resorted to prostitution to pay the rent and feed her children. Leroy was a customer, and then he simply stayed, which was all right, because he was good to the children and generous with money.

Did she know that he had been arrested by the police?

Yes. He had gone every day to Mil Flores. One day the police arrested him. But the night of his arrest he escaped from jail and came here. He thought it was very funny, how easily he had escaped, crawling through ventilator shafts to the roof.

Why did he go so often to Mil Flores?

To look for the boy, Antonio. He was trying to find a way to free the boy from captivity.

What did he say about the child and why he was being held captive?

He said that Antonio was the son of a beautiful and kind American woman whose husband had tried to kill her. The woman naturally wanted her son. Any woman could understand that. But the people who held him captive would not allow the boy to join his mother.

He told you that he intended to free the boy?

Yes.

Kidnap him?

Yes, it was the only way.

He asked you to help him?

Yes.

And you agreed?

Naturally.

And so earlier tonight you helped Leroy steal the boy?

Steal, no. You saw the boy tonight playing with my children. He was very happy. He came with us willingly. He never cried or tried to go back to those others.

Leroy hurt a man tonight.

A cruel bad man who carried a gun and handcuffs. He was there to see that the child would not be rescued.

Tonight Leroy handcuffed you to the bed.

Leroy said it was necessary.

All right. So you and Leroy rescued Tony this evening at Mil Flores.

Not at Mil Flores. At the carnival.

Who was with Tony at the carnival?

The bad man, a woman, and two children.

They were at the carnival, and you and your children and Leroy were there too, watching and following them.

Yes.

What was the plan?

There was no plan. We were waiting for the fortunate moment. That's what Leroy said.

And the fortunate moment came.

It did. The woman bought Antonio and the other children things to eat, and toys, and bought tickets to the rides. They went on the merry-go-round, and they were waiting in line to go on the Ferris wheel when Leroy made the lights go out.

Leroy made the lights go out?

Didn't he?

No. They went out in town, too, for a few minutes. It was his fortunate moment. And then . . . ?

Suddenly it was very dark, black. Leroy, I knew, would stop the bad man from interfering. I knew that. Antonio was not far from me. I went through the dark, took his hand, and led him away.

It was that easy?

Yes. Maybe the boy didn't know who I was in the darkness. Maybe he thought I was the woman with him. But he held my hand, and came with us. We walked through the night to the far end of the carnival grounds. It was easy. Antonio is a good little boy.

You had Tony, your children, and the baby. Did you wait for Leroy?

We waited at the gates.

And Leroy joined you there?

Very soon.

And Tony didn't cry or scream or try to run away?

No. It was dark, but my children were there with him. He talked with my Juan and my Maria. He wasn't frightened at all. Then Leroy came.

How did you get back here?

We rode a bus.

How long were you here in this room before I arrived?

Perhaps an hour.

And, Cristina, soon after I went out, Leroy took the boy and went away.

Yes.

Where was he going?

He didn't say. He left me money and told me to never, ever talk about this. But, since you are his friend . . .

And you're sure Leroy never said anything to you about where he might take Tony?

Well, to the United States. To return the child to his mother.

Cristina was too simple to understand exactly what she had done, what the consequences of her complicity in the kidnapping might be, how long she might spend in prison. She, taking her cue from Leroy's mad story, had merely done what was right and good, and people were not punished for doing good.

I asked her if she had ever heard of the Cardinal family.

Oh, yes, everyone knew of the Cardinales. They were like movie stars here in the Dominican Republic. Everyone knew and loved them.

Why did everyone love them?

Because they were rich and beautiful and important in the world outside this little island. They were respected, and so all the Dominican people were respected. Yes, they were all like Hollywood movie stars; their pictures were in the newspapers and magazines, and you frequently saw them on television.

"Cristina, I want to stay here tonight."

"All right. Do you want to . . . ?"

"No."

"If you want to, there's a room down the hall that we can use."

"No. Now, Cristina, the boy you helped abduct

tonight is named Antonio Cardinal. His mother is Katherine Cardinal, César Cardinal's wife. You have helped kidnap the son of famous movie stars."

She laughed. It was the first time I had heard her laugh. She didn't believe it. She couldn't believe it. It was too monstrous to be true.

She slept on the bed with the two children and the baby; I rested—I didn't sleep much—in the cane chair. The window glass glowed faintly with light, but it was dark in the room, very hot and stuffy, and the air was thick with the smells of poverty. Outside, the fourth day of the *feria* was dying; only a few drunken revelers remained, and eventually they too went away. Later, in the silence, I heard a whistle that sounded like harmonica tones; a neighborhood night watchman was letting those who paid him know that he wasn't sleeping in some alley, he was walking his rounds, alert for villains, blowing his whistle.

I dozed then, and at dawn was awakened by grumbling children and a crying baby. Cristina nursed her baby, then cooked eggs and fried bread slices for the boy and girl. They were not much interested in me. They'd awakened with other men in the room, the most recent being Leroy, and anyway, children do not find adults very interesting.

At eight I gave Cristina some money and sent her out to buy cigarettes and the early newspapers. She returned wide-eyed and trembling. The gravity of the situation was now clear to her. There were photos of Leroy and Tony on the front page of the local tabloid; and those two pictures, plus one of me, appeared in Santo Domingo's *El Tiempo*. The headlines were in

thick, four-inch black type: the local, *¡SECUESTRO!;*
El Tiempo, ¡RAPTO! Both words, along with *robachico,*
meant kidnapping. Leroy and I were the *secuestradores,*
the *raptores,* while little Tony, a cherub in his photo,
was of course the *victima.* I just skimmed the text:
nationwide manhunt, roads blocked, house-to-house
searches, millions pray, no ransom demand yet reported,
citizen patriots mistakenly kill man who resembled the
secuestrador, Leroy Karpe . . . this tragedy, following
upon the Señora Cardinal's terrible ordeal at sea . . .
in a bizarre twist, Caterina's rescuer named as one of
the conspirators . . .

Cristina watched me closely as I went through the
papers. The children, sensing her fear, were quiet.

"You said Leroy gave you money," I said.

"Yes."

"I'll give you some more. Are you from San Carlos?"

"No." She told me that she was from a village in
the highlands, about sixty miles from here.

"Go home," I said. "Today. Go to your home
village. You can't stay here. Do you understand?"

She understood.

"You and your children must get on a bus as soon
as possible."

She nodded.

"Just pack a few things and go."

I went to the bedside table and picked up the bodyguard's cell phone. I turned it on and brought up the
directory; there were about twenty numbers listed, two
beneath César's name; one, a house number; and a
number for Alejandro.

I lit a cigarette and dialed Petrie's cell phone. He

answered midway through the second ring.

"Leroy," he said. "At last, you son of a bitch."

"It's Shaw."

"Dan? Christ, give me some good news. Things are thoroughly bitched here."

"Where are you?"

"Still in Virginia."

"Can you talk now?"

"When I'm not sobbing."

"Listen, Tom, it's happened. We're in deep—"

"Kate and César announced their reconciliation last night. Except, they didn't call it that—their perfect union was never threatened, they're merely reuniting after a brief separation necessitated by certain well-known events."

"No," I said.

"That's right, bud. They're back together. They turned out a press release that's outrageously false even for press releases. They repudiate all the vicious rumors and gossip, say that . . . oh, Christ, you can guess. At this moment they are on a flight to the Dominican Republic, where they expect to live happily ever after with their two, yeah, two, children. Kate also announced her joyous pregnancy. Both hope it will be a girl."

"She was coerced."

"No, she was not. She's happy as a lark, pal, and so is her family, all of them. It was all a misunderstanding on Kate's part, you see, a natural consequence of her dreadful ordeal at sea. She has been suffering from post-traumatic stress syndrome fucking et cetera. Yes. Ain't it grand how the shrinks have given us a jargon with which to rationalize every crime, any betrayal?

Being thrown into the drink by her husband was merely a delusion, a product of her shock, anguish, and fatigue. She fell overboard when the *Zodiaco* skewed on a particularly high ocean swell."

"I can't believe this."

"Believe it. You've got to find Leroy."

"I found him."

"You did? Great. Now get out of there pronto."

"Found him and lost him. Tom—"

"Find him again."

"Tom, it happened last night. *It.*"

"Oh-oh."

"Leroy has the boy."

"Is that phone safe?"

"No. It's red hot, but never mind."

"You've seen the kid?"

"Yes."

"But now?"

"Gone. I don't know where. This town—the entire country has gone crazy. Cops everywhere, according to the newspapers, vigilante mobs, chaos."

"You've got to find Leroy and the kid."

"My picture is in the papers, probably on TV, too. They think I'm a part of it."

"I don't know you," Petrie said. "We said hello on the elevator a couple of times, that's all."

"I don't know how Leroy expects to move around out there with the kid. Their pictures are everywhere."

"But the kid was all right when you saw him?"

"Yes."

"But scared out of his teeny five-year-old mind."

"Actually, he seemed to be having a good time."

"Look, I'll phone the airport, see if César and Kate's flight has been delayed. Maybe, if I can talk to her . . ."

"About what? No, stay out of it. I'll see what I can do at this end."

"She knew we were going to do it for her, didn't she? Get her son back?"

"She never gave us the go-ahead. And now . . ."

"We have a defense," he said. "Kate claimed that she was nearly murdered by her husband, and she hired us to rescue her son from what amounted to captivity. Leroy acted alone, without authority. We'll throw Leroy to the dogs."

"Our defense will go over well in a D.R. court in front of a D.R. jury."

"Look, I'll fly back to Bell Harbor today. Call me at the office or at home. Keep in touch."

"If I'm able."

"Shaw? Take care."

"Send down a lawyer for me."

"I'll come."

"No, you stay clean."

"Clean? I'm chin-deep in the cesspool with you and the Pied Piper, and the level is rising. I'll come."

"They'd lock you up, too. No, hire a good criminal defense lawyer from Miami or Tampa, one who's fluent in Spanish. He can hook up with a law firm down here."

There was a long pause, and then Tom said. "Aw, Danny. You know that Jesus loves you."

Cristina and her children watched me closely during my conversation with Petrie. The children believed that I was responsible for their mother's fear, for the danger and disruption that had come to what they felt was their safe home.

I gave Cristina all of my D.R. money, plus four twenty-dollar bills, more than enough for their bus tickets. She also had the money that Leroy had given her.

"Go out," I said, "and buy tickets for a bus leaving soon. If anyone asks where you're going, tell them your mother is sick, your father is sick, the pigs and chickens are sick. But don't, for God's sake, mention Leroy or little Tony."

The girl started crying when her mother left the room, then the boy cried, and finally the baby commenced wailing. They calmed down when their mother returned. "When does your bus leave?" I asked her.

Nine thirty.

"Are you packed?"

Almost.

"Finish."

THIRTY

A gimpy old man and a boy showed up to carry Cristina's things—packed in cardboard boxes and plastic trash bags—to the bus station. She turned and gave me an accusing look from the hall, angry that I had forced her to leave and afraid, perhaps, that the possessions she had left behind might be stolen before her return. Then, carrying the baby, followed by the other two children, she walked stiff-backed toward the stairs at the end of the hall.

I closed the door, locked it, and went to a window. It was raining. Rain traced worm tracks down the dirty pane when the wind gusted. There was not much traffic: an old flatbed truck loaded with grain sacks, a motorcyclist, a cruising police car, a delivery van, a three-wheeled vehicle, probably a very old Isetta, another police car. A lone policeman in a rubberized rain cape stood on the corner. Cristina and the children appeared on the sidewalk below, looking left and right, and then cut diagonally across the street and down the opposite sidewalk.

In time, rain washed all the grime from the windows.

The panes blurred with water; it was like looking at the world through eyeglasses of the wrong prescription. The street had turned a muddy ochre, and there were rain-dimpled standing puddles and twisting rivulets linking puddle to puddle, and now and then a distant report of thunder. A white-haired old man, leading a burro overloaded with firewood, came down the center of the street, and his footprints and the hoofprints of the burro were quickly filled with mud ooze.

I smoked one of Leroy's cheap bitter cigars. It left a foul taste in my mouth that I failed to eliminate by eating a piece of bread. The policeman left his corner. Five minutes passed without another police car appearing. It was ten minutes to ten. A last, slow, sweeping look out of the window, and I slipped the bodyguard's cell phone into my pocket, went outside into the hallway and down the stairs and through the vacant lobby.

The street now was empty except for vendors setting up their stalls, men huddling in doorwells, and some boys kicking around a muddy soccer ball. It was raining steadily though not very hard, slanting silver in the dully luminous light, dimpling the mud puddles and ticking against store windows. I formed my suit jacket into a hood and started jogging east. There was nothing unusual in a hooded man running down a rainy street. A yellow dog, almost hairless with mange, his hunting instinct aroused, followed me for twenty yards and then collapsed into the mud. The air had a sulfurous odor. Other smells briefly intruded: cooking food, gasoline fumes, wet earth. Sounds, too: an unseen woman scolding an unseen child, a radio playing salsa, vendors calling to one another.

The street narrowed; farther on, it narrowed again into a trash-littered alley that eventually opened into a dreary plaza that looked medieval in the crepuscular light, the rain. A church occupied the entire north side of the square where the effigy of *Mala Suerte* had been burned. It was built of gray stone blocks and looked more like a fortress than a church. Stone steps led up to a pair of great carved doors. A dozen people, mostly women, some with babies, sought shelter from the rain—and refuge from the world—under the portico. It was raining harder now. My clothes were soaked through. I felt the weight of the cell phone in my jacket pocket. I knew I should get rid of it. My screams might be added to the Jefe's recorded collection if the police caught me with the bodyguard's phone in my possession. I was thinking this when a police car nosed out of a side street and began slowly cruising around the square. I stepped behind a column. Nearby the women waited for something or someone. None of the babies cried. The police car made two slow circuits of the plaza, then angled off down a side-street.

I went down the steps and jogged through the rain to a narrow street that doglegged off to the right. Secondhand shops, hole-in-the-wall cafés, a public scribe sitting at his typewriter beneath a canvas awning, food carts and curio stalls, a tobacconist's shop. Few people roamed the streets. It was early, and still raining hard.

A battered Dodge van with a cluster of loudspeakers on the roof was coming toward me, blaring out a political message (*"Votantes! Es el tiempo para elegir el hombre de justicia, hombre de honestidad y valor . . ."*). Behind the truck I glimpsed another police car, and immediately turned and went down a flight of concrete steps. The door below was open. I went through and into a subterranean bar that reeked of alcohol and urine and stale tobacco smoke. Four men, all thin and shabby, with the look of derelicts, stood at the bar.

I didn't know if the cops had seen me. When, after a few minutes, they did not appear on the steps, I ordered a beer from the bartender, a man who did not look much healthier than his smelly customers. He lifted a bottle out of a wash-tub of water, opened it, and placed it on the bar. He made change from a tin box on the back counter. Also on that shelf was a row of bottles: raw cane alcohol, cheap rum, cheap gin, and even cheaper spirits in bottles without labels.

The drinkers were morose. They would probably perk up after a few drinks; it was early. The ceiling was low, maybe six inches above my head, and the room was narrow, with the bar on one side and a twelve-foot-long trough against the other wall. A urinal. It was economical of motion and energy: you could drink at the bar and, when necessary, turn, take a step and a half, and relieve your swollen bladder. This was a get-drunk-fast establishment. No bar stools, no tables and chairs, no mirror behind the bar or pictures on the walls; just the bar, the urinal trough, and a minimal inventory of rotgut on a back shelf. My beer was warm and stale.

Running was futile. I had thought of making my way to the east coast, stealing a boat, and sailing across the Mona Strait to Puerto Rico, but I would never make it. The city was swarming with cops, all looking for Leroy Karpe, little Antonio Cardinal, and Daniel Shaw.

I went up the steps, looked around, and jogged

back to the church. The women and their babies were
still there, sheltering from the rain, waiting, and one
held out a cupped palm as I passed.

I switched on the bodyguard's cell phone, brought
up César's number, and punched the digits. A neutral
voice informed me that the number was not presently
in service. I tried the house in Mil Flores and a voice
answered on the second ring.

"*Quién es?*" I asked.

"Guillermo."

A servant, probably. I told him that I wished to
speak to Alejandro Cardinal at once, on a matter of
utmost urgency.

"*Y su nombre, señor?*"

"Daniel Shaw."

There was a thirty-second wait, and then a voice
said, "*Dígame?*"

"This is Shaw."

"I've been expecting your call. How much do
you want?"

"No, no, Jesus, you've got it wrong. I had nothing
to do with it. I tried to stop it. We've got to talk. I've
got to see Kate and César when they arrive."

"Where are you?"

"Do you know the old Church of San Benedicto?"

"Of course."

"Pick me up there as soon as possible."

"I'll be in a black BMW."

"And I'll watch for it."

"Do you pray, Shaw?"

"I'm thinking about starting."

"Try a quick prayer at the church."

THIRTY-ONE

The rain slowed to a drizzle; blue tears appeared in the clouds to the south. I had time to smoke two cigarettes before the black BMW arrived. There were three men inside: a driver, Alejandro next to him, and a third man in the backseat. The rear door opened as I descended the church steps. I got inside and closed the door, and the driver—a black man in gray livery—pulled away. He headed south, toward the seaside boulevard. Alejandro half turned and stared at me.

"You used Enrique's telephone to call me."

"Yes." I took the phone from my pocket and handed it forward. "How is the bodyguard—Enrique?"

"He is in a coma. Fractured skull."

"I'm sorry to hear that. Will he be all right?"

"God will decide."

I was mildly surprised to hear a Cardinal concede that God had any influence in a matter concerning the Cardinal family, but then I reminded myself that oligarchs were traditionally pious; after all, they were God's servants in maintaining the oligarchic social order and privileges. God himself might be an oligarch.

I said, "Maybe you could have someone pick up my things at the Hotel Montejo."

He ignored that. "Do you know where Antonio is?"

"I wish I could say yes."

"We can't waste time."

"I know that. Have César and Kate reached Mil Flores yet?"

"They are en route."

"Alejandro, I am truly sorry for this fucking mess."

"A fucking mess of your creation."

"I came here to stop Leroy."

"But you didn't stop him, did you?"

"No."

Alejandro turned away in disgust, and stared ahead through the windshield. His deadly calm worried me far more than a display of anger would have. The rage was deep and festering beneath his calm. I was sure that César would be even more dangerously calm. And Kate?

The man next to me lit a cigarette, inhaled, rolled the window down a couple of inches, and exhaled the smoke. He was young, maybe twenty, and had the mark of Cardinal on his lean, arrogant face.

We reached the *malecón* and the driver turned east, toward Mil Flores. The sky was clearing rapidly now. We passed the carnival grounds were Tony had been kidnapped and the bodyguard injured, passed the small airport, and hesitated only an instant at the gates before a policeman waved the car through. The sun was shining when we entered Mil Flores. Of course it was. Here the sea and sky glowed luminously. It was all bright and clean—the light, the colors, the sense of space, even the air one breathed. I thought of Cristina and her three children, the cluttered room and dismal streets, the lost souls of the Cucaracha district, and I was glad to be in Mil Flores despite the gravity of the situation.

We drove down the narrow seaside lane, the ocean and beach to our right, the high walls of the villas on our left; and then the driver turned into a paved driveway and halted before great iron gates. A boy inside the compound swung the gates open, and we proceeded down the drive to a parking area and garages.

"*Vámonos,*" Alejandro said.

The driver remained behind while Alejandro and the young man—one on each side—escorted me toward what looked like a small village. It was a much bigger compound than I had judged from beyond the gates. My first impression was of the jungly profusion of trees and plants, palms and hibiscus and jacaranda and mimosa and lemon and fig, big ferns, vines as thick as my wrist, plants that I had never seen before, plants enough to occupy half a dozen gardeners. Parts of buildings on my right could be seen through the wild growth, narrow two-and three-story houses with tall windows and terra-cotta tile roofs and iron-railed balconies. To my left was a high wall, and in the center a tiled courtyard the size of end-to-end tennis courts. White wood columns supported an overhead frame of lattice that was thick with leafy vines. Not much sunlight filtered through to the patio tiles. It was dim and cool there, with a strong smell of earth and vegetation.

"Wait here," Alejandro said, and he turned and walked toward the row of partly obscured houses.

"You're the one who saved Katherine," the young man said.

"I was there."

"That's maybe enough to keep you alive."

"And you're . . . ?"

"Roberto."

"César's and Alejandro's brother?"

"That's right. I'm the one who kills your friend Leroy if César and Alejandro fail. Which isn't likely."

"It won't be easy for any or all of you."

Roberto insolently stared at me for a time, then laughed, and said, "*Suerte*, cowboy. You'll need it." He laughed again, mockingly saluted, and went off toward the houses.

There were seven sets of tables and chairs spaced around the patio. The chairs were wrought iron, padded at the seats and backs; and the tables were large and square, with intricately decorated tile tops. You could feed forty people here and have plenty of space left for a band and dancing. At the back of the patio a flagstone walk led to another house, a tennis court and swimming pool, all barely visible through the trees and shrubs.

I sat down at one of the tables. The tile design, I saw now, detailed a coat of arms, a shield quartered in black, azure, white, and crimson, with a rampant horse, a Crusader cross, a falcon, and what appeared to be a sailing ship. The Latin motto I deciphered as "Serving God and King." The Cardinal armorial bearings? Maybe. But a lot of that stuff was humbug, commissioned by vain families from dubiously credentialed researchers.

A breeze rippled through the Cardinal jungle and dappled light and shadow trembled on the tiles. The breeze carried the sound of a woman's voice from somewhere near the pool area. A man wearing black pants, a white shirt and short white jacket, carrying a tray, materialized out of the heart of darkness. He murmured, *"Buenos días, señor,"* and then proceeded to efficiently set the table with plates, utensils, salt and pepper, butter, a glass and a pitcher of orange juice, napkin, cream and sugar, and an insulated pot of coffee. He went away, and returned a few minutes later with my breakfast: eggs, ham, fried potatoes, toast, and half a melon.

I realized, after my first taste of ham, that I was ravenous. I ate all the food, drank all the orange juice and coffee, and afterward lit a cigarette.

Two little girls were watching me from a patch of woods. I made a monster face, and the girls squealed in fear and delight, and ran away.

I lit another cigarette. The servant brought me an ashtray, cleared away all of the breakfast debris, and wiped the table.

A swallow swooped low over my table, skimmed the floor for an instant, then flew up through a gap in the overhead lattice. I smoked and watched. I saw more swallows, blackbirds, bright finches, and hummingbirds that darted about like fractured pieces of rainbow.

An old woman with white hair, wearing a robe and slippers, entered the courtyard, saw me and abruptly halted, then turned and retreated toward the row of houses. Somebody's granny. I heard her complaining to someone, heard a man's voice reply, and watched as César appeared on the path. He approached without haste. He wore khaki shorts, sandals, and a blue polo shirt.

There was no ceremony. César sat down across from me, crushed my cigarette out in the ashtray, and said, "You fucking imbecile."

"Right," I said.

"Where are they?"

"I don't know. I found them last night, not long after Leroy had abducted the boy. I left the room for a while, and when I returned they were gone."

"Who was the woman who helped this Leroy?"

"A prostitute."

"What is her name? Where does she live?"

"She's a very poor, simple-minded woman with two small children and a baby. She had no idea what she was doing."

"You think I can't find her?"

"Of course you can. But it will take a while, and maybe you won't be quite so vengeful when you do find her."

"This Leroy Karpe—tell me about him."

"Is Kate here?"

"Katherine is here."

"Leroy Karpe is . . . Christ, I'm not sure. Rough background, got into trouble when he was a kid, learned to fly in the army, smuggled drugs for a few years, runs a charter air service in Florida now. Look, the man thought he was doing Kate a favor. He's crazy. No, not crazy, but . . . unpredictable. No, not that, either. He's predictable enough if you know what direction he's headed. He won't hesitate, won't stop, won't deviate."

"Will he harm my son?"

"No."

"You have no doubt about that?"

"None. He would never harm a child. And, weird as this sounds, I think he loves the boy."

"Where will he go?"

"Notify every airport in the country to watch for him. He might try to steal an airplane and fly out of the country. He can handle a boat, too. He might steal a boat."

"This was your idea, wasn't it?"

"What?"

He stared at me until I said, "Yes. But it was only an *idea*. We had no intention of proceeding without Kate's approval."

"You, Thomas Petrie, Judge Samuelson, and this criminal Leroy were in this together."

"Try to understand the circumstances. Kate was certain that if she left you, she would never see her son again. And that's true, isn't it? Wouldn't you take your son from a foreign country if circumstances were reversed?"

"Katherine and I have talked."

"You tried to kill her."

"Katherine attempted suicide. How she remained alive in the sea so long none of us will comprehend."

"I want to talk to her."

"That is for her to decide. Are you in love with her?"

"Yes."

"And you believe that she's in love with you?"

"Yes."

"And your transcendent sexual interlude at sea has united you forever."

I did not reply.

"She told me. Katherine tells me everything. She was delirious. You took advantage of her mental state. She consented, but any honorable man would not have seduced a woman so anguished, so vulnerable."

"Bullshit."

"You say this Leroy was once involved in drug smuggling. In what countries did he obtain the drugs?"

"Mexico and Colombia, I heard."

"The Dominican Republic?"

"I don't know."

"Haiti?"

"I don't know."

"I am trying to determine if he might have old drug comrades who might hide him. Jamaica?"

"I really don't know."

"You know very little, it seems."

"Leroy didn't tell me his plan—if he had one."

"When did you last see him?"

"About ten thirty last night. Maybe a little later."

"So he's had fourteen hours to run."

"Yes, but I don't see how he can move around with his photo—and your son's—in every newspaper and on every TV station in the country."

"Where might he hide?"

"Leroy? In a slum hotel, in a culvert, in a tree . . ."

"Why didn't you kill him last night?"

"I thought about it."

"You thought about it," César said with quiet contempt.

"But it was too late then. He was gone."

"It was your duty to kill him."

"It was my duty to get the boy away from him."

"Could you do that without killing him?"

"Probably not."

"And so . . . ?"

"Leroy ran."

"You had the opportunity, and you failed."

"I suppose that's correct."

"And so now *I* must kill your friend."

"He's not exactly my friend."

"Have you no sense of honor, man?"

"Probably not as you define honor."

"So you leave your killing to others. To me."

"Is that how you see it?"

"Your cowardice has placed my son in jeopardy. I could kill you for that."

"You Cardinals certainly talk a lot about killing."

"I *would* kill you, except that you saved Katherine's life." He questioned me for another fifteen minutes, but there was little more that I could tell him. He was exhausted. That was not something that César Cardinal would reveal by word or gesture, but fatigue was evident around his eyes and in the pale grainy texture of his skin.

He stood up. "Come this way," he said.

"When will you allow me to see Kate?"

He turned away in contempt and walked slowly down the path toward the row of houses. I followed through the ferny wood, down a stone walk, and up an outside stairway to a third-floor apartment. There was a good-sized living room, nicely furnished, a bedroom and bath, and a room that might serve as a spare bedroom or study.

"Am I under house arrest?" I asked.

"You may go whenever you choose. But you're safer here."

"I still want to see Kate."

"Try to remember anything about this Leroy that will help us."

He left then, and I explored the apartment. My things had been picked up from the Hotel Montejo; the clothes were hung in a closet or packed in drawers, and my toiletry articles were arranged on a bathroom shelf.

I showered, shaved, and dressed in clean slacks and a sport shirt. My mirror image told me that I was at least as tired as César. We both, and Leroy, too, were running on adrenaline.

The compound had satellite television reception and so I was able to watch stations from the States as well as the Dominican Republic. I surfed through the D.R. stations for a while. One channel had suspended regular programming in order to follow the kidnapping; the others broke in now and then with news flashes that revealed nothing new. César had apparently issued a statement that cleared me of criminal complicity in the matter: it was repeated over and over that Daniel Shaw, the lone mariner who had rescued Señora Cardinal, was now an honored guest of the Cardinals and was assisting them in this difficult time. This fact alone, they said, should wholly discredit those vicious rumors about an absurd melodramtic murder plot on the high seas . . .

Leroy had become an international TV star. His jail mug shot frequently appeared. He did look like a child abductor or *robachico,* and worse. Pedophilia was suggested on one American cable channel. Information about Leroy's shady past was exposed. Cops and lawyers and psychologists discussed Leroy, often referring to him as "the gentleman." It had always amused me how, on American television, criminals—from mass murderers to political assassins to child molesters—were referred to as "the gentleman." Leroy, at last, was a gentleman.

THIRTY-TWO

At dusk I walked down to the beach. It wasn't necessary to traverse the courtyard; a walkway between the front of the houses and the screen of trees provided easy and relatively private egress. César and Kate must have entered that way this morning.

The tide was out, and fifty yards of beach stretched from the road down to the foamy wash of surf. No moon yet, just a few stars visible through a thin cloud haze, and the dark sea rolling on six hundred miles south to the Venezuelan coast. The beach was wide and steep, but I could visualize a hurricane's storm surge running up over the road and into the Cardinal compound. And a hundred-and-forty-mile-per-hour wind would pretty much defoliate their expensive designer forest.

I tried to sort out my thoughts, clarify things, but without success. Leroy and the boy; Kate and César; Kate and me—it was all a crazy muddle, Wonderland logic, and after a while I gave it up and lay back on the sand.

I remained on the beach for more than an hour, then crossed the road and returned up the walk. Patio lights glowed through the trees. I slowed, then halted, at the place from which the children had watched me this morning; there was a sort of tunnel through the vegetation and a part of the courtyard was visible.

They were quietly eating dinner. There were eight of them sitting at a long white-clothed table. A few colored paper lanterns hung from the overhead lattice, but most of the light came from the candles in three large silver candelabra. The tableau appeared slightly out of focus because of that misty halo of light in the surrounding darkness, and the people looked far off, diminished by perspective. Five men and three women, with three servants waiting like sentinels in the shadows. An old man sitting at the head of the table wore medals and colored ribbons on the breast of his dinner jacket. The Cardinal patriarch? The three brothers were present, César, Alejandro, and Roberto; the fifth man, in his late twenties, wore a priest's collar. A white-haired woman sat at the foot of the table. The matriarch. She wore a diamond necklace that flashed blue and white sparks into the night. Kate sat on the patriarch's right. A pretty young brunette sat between César and Alejandro. They talked rarely, and then in soft voices that did not clearly carry to me. The men wore tuxes; the women, evening dresses. It was a queer scene, formal and gloomy, and then there was a Gothic touch as a small black shape flitted through the candlelight— a bat. There were others. I realized that some odd structures that I had seen at the rear of the compound were bat houses. It was logical; bats, like the many birds I had seen today, were welcomed as a natural way to control insect populations.

A servant emerged from the shadows to refill wineglasses.

Kate placed her fingers over her glass. César sent him back to the shadows.

I wasn't sure whether I approved or condemned their rigid discipline in engaging in a family dinner while the boy was missing and in danger.

I moved farther down the walk and climbed the stairway to my quarters. A platter of chicken and rice, still warm under the silver lid, lay on the table. There was also a bottle of wine.

Forty minutes later there was a knock on my door. Kate, I thought, but it was César, still wearing his tux, pale and moving slowly in his tension and fatigue.

"An airplane was stolen tonight," he said.

"From where?"

"The Mil Flores airport."

"Wasn't it guarded, patrolled?"

"Of course it was. But nevertheless an airplane was stolen not long after it got dark. Is this Leroy qualified to fly at night?"

"He's instrument rated, yes. What kind of plane was it?"

"Do you mind if I sit down?"

"It's your place."

César sat on the sofa, closed his eyes for a moment, then looked at me.

I repeated, "What kind of airplane was it?"

"A Peregrine. It's a small aircraft of Italian manufacture. Two seats, one behind the other. Underpowered. We contacted the owner. He said that there was plenty of fuel aboard, and the craft is airworthy."

"When, exactly, was it stolen?"

"It was reported stolen twenty minutes ago. When, actually, it was flown away . . ."

"Have other airports been notified?"

"Authorities here, in Haiti, Puerto Rico, and Jamaica have been alerted."

"What about Cuba?"

"I hadn't thought of Cuba. We shall notify the Cuban air traffic people."

He rose from the sofa, moved to the door and opened it, hesitated, then turned. "Enrique died."

"The bodyguard?"

"Dead. His skull was shattered."

"I'm sorry to hear it."

"It was not necessary to hit him so hard."

"No," I said, though I didn't know how you calculated exactly how hard you hit a man with a rock.

"He has three children."

I didn't know how to reply.

"Perhaps," César said, "you'd like to consider contributing to his family's pension fund."

Kate arrived fifteen minutes later. I hadn't expected her to come. I assumed that César had forbidden her to see me, or that she herself would refuse. Clearly, everything had changed between us. We had each, in different ways, betrayed the other.

"Hello, Dan," she said.

She had changed into slacks and a sleeveless blouse, and her spikey hair was concealed beneath a paisley scarf. She had lost much of her suntan over the last week and looked pale, pale and thin and beautiful.

"Did the master let you out?" I asked.

"Don't," she said. "Don't use that tone."

"Sorry. Care for some wine?"

She shook her head.

"Kate, I'm sorry about Tony. I tried to stop it."

"But you set it all in motion, didn't you?"

"Please, no selective memory. We, you and I, set it in motion."

"You and your friends. God!"

"Can you explain to me why in hell you went back to the man who tried to kill you?"

"Do I owe you an explanation?"

"You damned well do."

"Maybe."

"Let's walk on the beach."

She hesitated. "A short walk."

The tide was still receding, leaving behind billions of glowing green specks on the wet sand. The beach, extending east and west as far as the eye could see in the moonlight, was like a miniature duplicate Milky Way. Surf, fighting the outgoing tide, broke fifty yards offshore and died foaming below us. We removed our shoes and walked east, away from the lights of Mil Flores and San Carlos, toward a zone of darkness. Two men, silhouetted by town lights, followed us.

"We're being watched," I said.

"They're protecting us."

"They aren't chaperons? *Dueñas—dueños?* Is there such a word in Spanish as *dueños?*"

"Yes, but it doesn't mean chaperon, it means owner or master."

"So César has designated them as your owners

temporarily? What would they do if we stopped here and embraced, kissed?"

"They would watch, and report back to César."

"And if we lay on the beach and made love?"

"They would watch, and report to César."

"What would they do if I began strangling you?"

"They would shoot you, and then report to César. Is that what you want to do, Dan? Strangle me?"

"Didn't our time aboard *Roamer* mean anything to you?"

"It meant everything. You saved my life. You always say you didn't, but you did. And you saved my mind. I'm not exaggerating. I was very near to madness, and you coaxed and teased me back."

"That's it?"

"What do you want me to say?"

"Figure it out."

"You want me to say I love you."

"Do you?"

"Well, I do. Okay?"

"I find your declaration somehow unsatisfactory."

"We've gone far enough," she said. "Let's sit down."

We walked up the sloping beach to a stretch of dry sand. The two silhouetted men halted. I saw the flare of a match, then the pulsing red glow of a cigarette coal.

"Kate, you can't stay with César."

"Oh, it's so easy for you men, isn't it? Pack your bags, honey, grab the kid, follow me."

"You can't stay with him."

"Dan, for God's sake, don't you have any idea of how selfish you're being? My son was kidnapped last

night by that . . . that idiot Leroy. Tony's in danger.
And you want to talk about love, us, a future!"

"Kate—"

"I was wrong about César. I lied to you."

"You didn't. But you're lying now."

"I mean, I lied without really knowing I was lying.
My mind . . . I hallucinated while all alone on the sea,
vivid, real images. My mind put together a story, a
narrative, to explain it all. No one will ever know what
I went through."

"Did you hallucinate all you told me about César?
His gambling, his cheating, his absences, his taking
your money, your determination to leave him?"

"Every marriage has difficulties."

I laughed.

"You have no right to conduct this inquisition."

"You told César that we slept together on the boat
and at Woeful Cay?"

"Yes."

"Do you remember telling me that men of César's
milieu might kill a mistress, but not a wife . . . unless
she was unfaithful."

"You take everything so literally."

"Do you love César?"

"He's my husband, the father of my son, the
father—in seven months—of another child."

"You didn't answer my question."

"Yes. I love him."

"Kate, did he or didn't he throw you overboard?"

"I honestly don't remember it like that now. It
couldn't have happened like that."

"Your brain has been thoroughly scrubbed."

"I want to go home now."

One of the bodyguards preceded us and the other followed as we walked down the beach and up into the Cardinal compound. It was a hostile parting. I believed that Kate was lost. Lost to me surely, but, more important, lost to herself.

"Goodnight," I said.

"Goodbye," she replied.

THIRTY-THREE

A servant knocked on my door at seven o'clock the next morning. He said that the Señor—César—wished to see me at once. I dressed, went down the stairs, and stepped out onto the patio. César sat at one of the tile-topped tables with Alejandro and an army officer who was introduced to me as Colonel Felipe Guzman. He was a tall man who looked in his late twenties, with unmilitary long hair and a glossy black handlebar mustache.

Everything—the banquet table, the chairs, the china and silver and crystal, the serving stations—from last night's dinner had been removed, though the lanterns strung from the overhead lattice still burned red and blue and yellow. It was cool at this hour in the courtyard, and a lingering fog that smelled of the sea was visible here and there, ghosting through the shrubbery.

I sat opposite César. He looked even more tired today. A telephone, a pad of paper, and a fountain pen lay on the table. The pad was covered with notes in a neat, small hand.

"An airplane crashed on the upper slopes of the Pico Duarte last night," he said quietly.

"A Peregrine?"

"We don't know. But what else? No other aircraft has been reported stolen or missing."

"You think," I said, "that Leroy was heading for Haiti and something—"

Alejandro impatiently said, "We want to know what you think."

I mentally pictured the island of Hispaniola: the Dominican Republic occupied the eastern two thirds; Haiti, smaller and much poorer, the west. The Pico Duarte was the highest mountain on the island, in the entire Caribbean, at 10,414 feet, and the Haitian border was a little more than fifty miles west of the Cordillera Central.

I said, "I can't believe that that Leroy is stupid enough to attempt to fly over a ten-thousand-foot mountain at night in an unfamiliar small plane."

"I thought we agreed that he's very stupid," César said.

"Not in an airplane," I said. "Not when flying." But I immediately realized that that really wasn't true; Leroy could be defined as a man who took chances.

The colonel offered cigarettes around the table. I accepted one; the Cardinal brothers refused with the contempt of men who do not share your particular vice.

"Does Kate know?" I asked

"No. We just learned of it. Last night a commercial aircraft flying from Cap Haitien to Santo Domingo reported receiving an emergency distress signal from the mountain. Such radio signals, I'm told, are triggered in the device—a small metal box—upon severe impact. The air crew managed to get a rough navigational fix on the signal. It is in a remote location, high in the Cordillera."

"Are there search aircraft out now?"

"They went out at dawn. So far they report no sighting of the downed airplane, and no signal. The device might have failed."

He spoke precisely, in normal tones, while explaining to me the details regarding the near certain death of his son. His voice and demeanor hadn't changed, but it was as though he were stoically suffering extreme physical pain. Grief is a kind of torture.

I had not, in our few brief encounters, seen that side of César that people emphasized: the charmer, the suave ladies' man and bold man's man. I could not reconcile that half-mythical César with the pale, distracted, rather fussy man who sat across from me. Of course, the circumstances were grim; this wasn't a time for swashbuckling; but I wondered if his attempt to murder Kate and the subsequent events—as much as the kidnapping of his son—had destroyed a sort of reckless innocence in the man.

"You're going to the mountains?" I asked.

"Of course."

"I'd like to come along."

"Be ready in thirty minutes."

"Thanks."

He gathered up his telephone, pad, and pen, got up, and walked slowly toward the house at the north end of the complex. Now he had to inform Kate that their son was most likely dead.

Alejandro remained at the table for a moment, staring hard at me, then he got up and followed his brother.

"This is very difficult," Colonel Guzman said.

"Yes."

"Tragic."

"Well, maybe the Peregrine didn't crash. And even if it did crash, it could be that the boy will be found alive."

"True," he said. "We must turn to our faith."

It seemed to me that he spoke about faith with a certain irony.

"Faith, in moments like these, is our strength and our salvation."

Guzman was young for a full colonel, even in the D.R. army, and his English was almost without accent. I supposed that he, like many members of his class, had attended college in the States, and he probably played polo and an excellent game of tennis, and he might spend his winters skiing in St. Moritz or the Dolomites. His tailored lightweight summer uniform fit perfectly, and his shoes—not army issue—gleamed like polished obsidian. They were thousand-dollar shoes, hand-lasted; no doubt he could order an identical pair simply by faxing his London boot-maker.

"Awkward for you, I imagine," he said.

"Yes."

"And for me, in a different way."

"Why you?"

"I'm engaged to Maria Cardinal."

"César's sister?"

"César's, Alejandro's, Roberto's."

"And they don't approve?"

"They're a possessive clan, especially where the females are concerned. And they think she's too young. She's eighteen."

"Well, César and Alejandro . . . Why haven't they killed you?"

He laughed. "Her father gave me permission to marry Maria. He's still head of the family, though not the man he once was. There's no open conflict between me and César, just a sort of cold and permanent disapproval. And also, I am not sufficiently in awe of—"

He abruptly got to his feet. "Speak of the vixen."

"Who are you calling a vixen?"

I stood up and was introduced to Maria Cardinal, the girl I had seen at the dinner table last night. She was dark-haired, very pretty, with a V-shaped smile and a slightly tilted look to her eyes. She offered her hand.

"So you're the notorious Captain Shaw."

"Just notorious Shaw."

"You don't look like the devil."

"What does the devil look like?"

"Like Felipe here, with yellow eyes and a thick black mustache."

She turned to Guzman. "Are you going with them?"

"Yes."

"Don't. Stay here with me. They don't need you."

"I can help with the military aspects of the search."

She assumed a pouting expression. "Well, then, I'll go too."

"You can't, Maria, there probably won't be room on the airplane."

I excused myself, went up to the apartment, quickly packed my things in the duffel, and then spent a few minutes studying my map of the island. The Pico Duarte was about midway between the Dominican Republic's north and south coasts, fifty miles east of the Haitian border, and maybe one hundred miles north-east of Santo Domingo. There were a couple of nature preserves in the area. You could assume that much of the Cordillera would be thickly forested. Assume, too, that the heights would frequently be obscured by clouds and subjected to considerable turbulence, downdrafts and updrafts, wind shear, and furious local storms. Mountain weather. Leroy, I believed, would not attempt to fly over the Pico Duarte, not when it would be fairly simple to circle the range to the north or south where the elevations were lower. So then, for some reason he had been unable to accurately navigate his course to Haiti. Night, clouds, perhaps rain, and an unfamiliar airplane with dubious instrumentation (compass off a few degrees, altimeter affected by the change in air pressure), no radar, no direction-finder . . . And so Leroy—Leroy and Tony—had flown into the mountain. That seemed to explain it. A series of factors, events, none of which alone would kill you; but put them all together and you were lying on a mountain slope with ravens picking at your eyes.

It occurred to me as I was going down the steps that maybe César was permitting me to go along on the search so that he could swiftly execute me when Tony's death was confirmed. He would view it as a just execution.

*   *   *

An airplane was waiting for us on the runway of the little airport west of Mil Flores—the same airport that had reported the theft of the Peregrine. It was a small, twin-engine turboprop painted a military brown, with military insignia on the wings, tail, and fuselage. The pilot, Perez, was a young man with captain's bars on the epaulets of his uniform. There was seating for eight aboard the plane, but there were only six of us besides the pilot: César, Alejandro, their younger brother, Roberto, Colonel Guzman, Kate, and me. There was not much talk. The pilot warmed the engines for a while while doing his instrument check, spoke to the controller, released the brakes, and began taxiing south into the ocean breeze. It was a short runway, but he easily cleared a red fence at the end, and we were rising above the foaming surf and metallic blue sea; then, still climbing, the pilot banked to the west. We flew over the carnival where Leroy had killed the bodyguard and kidnapped the boy. San Marcos, from the air, looked clean and orderly, clusters of stacked cubes in a maze of streets and alleys, dotted here and there with green parks. A soccer game was in progress at the stadium.

Kate became sick. She had never suffered motion sickness aboard *Roamer*, but her pregnancy was further along now, and her son was missing and presumed dead. She had not looked at me at the house, on the ride to the airport, or when we boarded the airplane. She refused to meet my gaze.

Then Santo Domingo was below and to my right, and after that, the fair-sized city of San Cristóbal. We were flying over land now, though the coastline and sea were still visible. There were other coastal towns, Nizao and Baní, and then the pilot banked the airplane and angled, still climbing, northwest toward the interior. Much of the land below was under cultivation, mud browns and bright greens, and corrugated steel roofs flashed with sunlight.

César and Alejandro sat together behind the pilot. Colonel Guzman and Kate were together on the other side of the plane, Roberto behind them; I sat alone on a jumpseat at the rear. No one talked. We were soon flying at five or six thousand feet, and the air in the cabin was relatively cool and dry.

Then we were flying into the highlands. The land rose beneath us, fanning out into long ridges and broad shadowy valleys that converged toward the Cordillera. I saw muddy rivers and thin bright threads of creeks winding down from the mountains. Most of the land in the valleys was cultivated, and there were towns and villages here and there, linked by mostly unpaved roads bulldozed through the terrain. Ahead I could see green mountains.

The pilot banked, and followed the larger of the valleys, which gradually widened and leveled into a plateau with a town at its center. The pilot did not have to lose much altitude; the land had steadily risen during our flight, and now it was just a matter of lining up with one of the two runways that formed a concrete X. Then we were down and the pilot taxied the plane near a cluster of steel Quonset huts.

A military helicopter and a black Cadillac with blue-tinted windows were waiting. Kate, Roberto, and the pilot walked across the concrete and got into the car. César, Alejandro, the colonel, and I climbed aboard the helicopter. It had gun mounts but no guns, and the interior had been fitted with high-backed airline-style seats. This pilot was older than the first, a black man, and he wore a fleece-lined leather jacket despite the heat.

"Has the airplane been sighted?" César asked him.

"No, sir."

"The signal?"

"No one has received an emergency signal."

"Let's go," César said.

The colonel, ahead of me, turned in his seat and offered me his silver flask. I drank, nodded my thanks, and returned the flask to him. It was a good, smooth dark rum—maybe Ron Cardinal Supremo.

THIRTY-FOUR

We flew along the east face of the cordillera at ninety-eight hundred feet. Twisting columns of smoke, a glowing red eye at the center of each, rose up here and there far down on the lower slopes. People were practicing slash-and-burn agriculture. They cleared a patch of land, managed to harvest a crop or two before the soil gave out, and then moved on to the next piece of wilderness. But the steep, high slopes were still wild, with rain forest a dozen shades of green, palms arching above the canopy, and waterfalls arcing over rocky buttresses. The summit of the Pico Duarte, six hundred feet above, was wreathed by a swirl of gauzy mist. Its ridges descended out of the mist, and there were high bowl-like depressions, striated rock walls, and talus and scree slopes like deep scars in the landscape. It seemed to me impossible that we could find the rubble of a small airplane on this great mountain.

The helicopter began describing large circles. Each loop, at the far west end of the arc, brought us so close to the mountain that particular details emerged out of the mass—a dead white tree that looked carved out of bone, a dry ravine, a fractured stone wall, a thin silver waterfall. The pilot shouted something that I couldn't understand, but I guessed he was telling César that we were near the area where the emergency signal had been recorded late last night.

Two civilian airplanes were also searching the mountains. They appeared out of nowhere, out of the empty blue sky, bright flecks which rapidly became a red Cessna and a yellow Piper, and then they were well to the north.

We tacked back and forth across the face of the Duarte for nearly five hours, flying at different altitudes and angles and distances, but we saw nothing, none of us, and finally the pilot returned to the airport. César wanted him to refuel and go out again, but the pilot said that the light was poor now, with all but the highest slopes in shadow. You needed penetrating sunlight to pick up the flash of aluminum or broken glass. And too, the peak often started clouding up at this time of day.

The Montaña was not much of a hotel, but it was the best in town, situated in a parklike grove near a small lake. It was built in a pastiche of modern and colonial styles, utilizing the worst features of both schools, and the windows wouldn't open and the air-conditioning didn't work and the courtyard restaurant was flooded from recent rains. My room was a sweatbox on the fifth floor with a view of the smoky cloud mass that had settled over Pico Duarte.

I showered, shaved, dressed in my wrinkled suit, and went down to the ground-floor lounge. A male trio, up on the corner stage, was singing of unrequited love and vengeful murder and eternal remorse. There were some couples in the booths that lined the wall, and Colonel Guzman was sitting at the bar.

"Can I buy you a drink, Colonel?" I asked, sitting on an adjacent stool.

"Yes, why not?" he said.

He was drinking rum; I ordered a Scotch.

"It's going to be tough," I said.

"It will be found if it's there."

"What happened to the emergency signal?"

He shrugged. "The device failed."

"But a signal *was* picked up by a passing commercial airliner?"

"So they reported."

"Is it likely that they could get an accurate fix on the signal?"

"Certainly. Although it's also possible to make an error."

"And it's possible that they really didn't receive an emergency signal after all, that they were confused by another radio transmission."

"My turn," the colonel said, and he ordered two more drinks from the bartender, though I hadn't yet touched mine.

I had seen the country now, and to locate the wreckage even in a relatively compact search zone would be enormously difficult. You'd need luck. The rugged terrain, much of it almost vertical, the thick forest and canopy, made a sighting of the wreckage a long shot. As the helicopter pilot had said, you needed a certain angle of sunlight, a certain position overhead, a flash of metal or glass or color.

"Why do you say that the plane will be found?" I asked him.

"It will be found because César will never quit. It may take ten years, but we'll find it. César will. He will bury his son." After each sip of rum, the colonel dried and shaped his mustache with a forefinger.

I said, "I feel responsible, in part."

"From what I've been told you are responsible—in part."

"Then why are you drinking with me?"

"It isn't my duty to punish you."

"It's César's duty."

"Yes, but he can't."

"Why not?"

"How can he kill you? You saved Katherine's life. Her life and the life of the child she's carrying. You see his predicament."

"Kate said he tried to murder her."

"That's nonsense. I know César. He loves the woman. She's lovely, of course, but a nervous type."

"A liar?"

"Nervous, high-strung, imaginative. A creative type."

"So then, you don't think César will kill me."

"No." He grinned and brushed his mustache. "But I'd watch out for Alejandro and Roberto."

"At least you don't intend to kill me, Colonel."

"Not unless I'm ordered to," he said, grinning. "Is it my turn to buy?"

"Mine." I held up two fingers for the bartender.

Guzman had been half drunk when I'd joined him; I was several drinks behind. My infected molar began to throb.

We had two more drinks, and then I said, "I've got to get something to eat."

"Eat? And ruin a good drunk?"

"Good night, Colonel."

"Wait, Shaw. I know some girls in this town. Young, clean, passionate girls. Expensive, but worth it."

"Some other time," I said, and I made my way to the lobby and elevators, and went up to my room. It was very hot, I was drunk, my tooth hurt, and the air-conditioning didn't work. I unplugged a heavy floor lamp, carried it across the room, and smashed out all the glass in both windows. No one phoned my room to inquire. No security men knocked on the door. My last thought before falling asleep was *This isn't such a bad hotel after all.*

Next morning Colonel Guzman was reading a newspaper in the lobby. He grinned at me. "How was she?"

"Who?"

"Mina. The girl I sent to your room."

"Did you pay her?"

"Certainly. My treat. Don't tell me she asked you to pay."

"No."

"I didn't think so. Mina's honest, for a whore. I'm told there was a ruckus in your room last night. You didn't . . ."

"Throw Mina out of the window? No."

"So you got along, then?"

"We had a great time," I said.

The colonel was pleased. He brushed his mustache left and right, and said, "Let's go to the bar for a Bloody Mary."

THIRTY-FIVE

Civilian airplanes were in the search area early that morning, and so too were a pair of military helicopters brought in from a base in La Vega. A babble of voices and static erupted on the radio's search frequency. The airspace along the mountains was much too crowded for safety, and Colonel Guzman, in the copilot's seat, did nothing but scan the skies for other aircraft while César, Alejandro, and I studied the mountain flanks for a glimpse of the wreckage.

It was a fine day, clear, with a deep blue high-altitude sky and ranks of puffy trade wind clouds scudding across the sky from northeast to southwest. There were thermal updrafts as the land heated, but nothing that caused the pilot difficulty.

I had studied the terrain for almost five hours the previous day, by eye and through powerful binoculars, but it all looked unfamiliar today, not as I remembered. I recognized some of the distinctive features (a bare ridge extending southward from the summit of Pico Duarte, a vast scarred area where a landslide had taken place years ago, a burned area), but nothing was positioned as I recalled. And new features were exposed in the early morning light, seen and then lost as the helicopter changed altitude or angle.

The forest was luminous in the light following sunrise, dozens of greens, from pale yellow-green to green-black, all glossy bright, and here and there the leaves (flashed with reflected sunlight. Some of those flashes looked as though they might be reflections off aluminum or shattered glass, but when we moved closer, and our angle changed, they vanished, and other blurs of light appeared elsewhere.

We returned to the airport for fuel. A mobile kitchen had been set up on the runway apron, and two women served us eggs and bacon and coffee. Our pilot went off to talk to the pilot of another helicopter, one that also had come in for refueling. César, Alejandro, and the colonel took their plates off to the shade of a Quonset. I ate alone. Colonel Guzman, friendly last night, was hungover, and constrained in the company of the Cardinal brothers. Neither César nor Alejandro had spoken to me, and their glances my way were blank, empty of hostility or curiosity or even recognition.

We searched the shadowed western side of the range on our return. César thought that maybe Leroy had made it over the mountain before crashing. There were often dangerous downdrafts in mountain country, and nighttime temperature inversions when the cool mountain air rushed down into the warmer valleys.

Trees close to the summit were dwarfed, bent and gnarled by the prevailing winds, and the highest areas were bare except for yellow grass.

The west side of the cordillera appeared less steep,

and the forest thinner. We could see the low mountains of Haiti some fifty miles away, brownish and furrowed in the distance, and glimpses of the sea to both the north and the south. There would not be many days as clear as this one. We saw no sign of wreckage.

Again, we returned to the airport for fuel. The kitchen had prepared hot sandwiches for the search crews, roast beef, ham, and chicken, and there were soft drinks and cans of cold beer. I got a chicken sandwich and a beer, and carried them to a wedge of shade.

César, Alejandro, and the colonel stood twenty yards away. My Spanish was good enough to understand most of their conversation. Colonel Guzman told them that a company of soldiers had been dispatched from the east coast; they would arrive this afternoon or tonight. Arrangements had been made to hire mules and guides from villages on the lower slopes of the mountain. There were trails that led up into the high country. You couldn't see them from the air, but they tacked up through the forest to within a few hundred feet of the Duarte's summit. The mules would carry tents and enough supplies to last for a week or ten days. The ground search would commence tomorrow morning.

César, hands on his hips, eyes concealed by dark glasses, asked if the soldiers were city boys, or country boys who could be expected to function well in that terrain. *"Hay peones,"* the colonel said. Alejandro, who himself looked like a peasant with his thick body and blunt features, remained silent. He too wore dark sunglasses, and it seemed to me that he stared at me all through the discussion.

I thought that sending a ground search team into the high country was futile unless first the wreckage had been sighted. They would find nothing wandering around blindly. I believed that it was equally futile to take the helicopter out a third time today; the sun had moved beyond the summit and the entire east flank of the Duarte was in shadow now. No penetrating sunlight, no reflections, no combination of light and shadow to create a three-dimensional landscape.

But I was wrong. We sighted something on the first sweep. The helicopter was flying at eight thousand feet, maybe a hundred yards from the slope, and César and I simultaneously shouted at the pilot. A silvery object had been visible on a talus slope partly overgrown by scrubby growths. We saw it, and almost immediately lost it. The pilot turned, flew slowly north, and then hovered when César and I again shouted. It was an irregularly shaped steel or aluminum panel with a black numeral 2 visible near the jagged edge. Through the binoculars, I could see other bits of wreckage, additional glints of metal, a powdery sweep of broken glass, a shredded tire.

It was on a slope of shattered rock about three hundred yards long and one hundred yards wide. The wreckage was strewn almost the entire width of the slope, from forest fringe to forest fringe, and on top were giant pillars of rock whose crumbling, over time, had formed the talus field. Forest could not grow there, but spikey shrubs and long grasses had taken root.

I couldn't recall passing this particular place on our searches. There were other talus and scree slopes on the mountain. But this one was lower than where we—everyone—expected to find the Peregrine, almost two thousand five hundred feet beneath the Pico Duarte summit, and not at all close to where the emergency device had emitted its signal.

The helicopter hovered as we looked for a spot to land. The talus slope was too steep and surrounded by thick forest. César, leaning forward, shouting to the pilot, hooked his thumb up—climb!—and we swooped up a couple hundred feet and again hovered. Now we could see that there was an uneven rock platform on top of the rock pillars. There appeared to be enough room to land; room for the skids and machine, clearance enough for the big rotor blade. The pilot and César argued. The pilot shook his head. César insisted. The pilot refused. Then Alejandro withdrew a small pistol from his pocket, moved forward, and held the muzzle against the pilot's head. It was absurd; the pilot could not be shot while flying the machine. But maybe he envisioned being shot later. The matter was settled.

The pilot had no confidence that he could perform the difficult maneuver. Within a few seconds I was drenched with sweat. The colonel rolled his eyes at me. Only the mad Cardinals were calm. Three times the pilot started to land, once touching a skid down, and three times he panicked and flew out into open space. On the fourth pass he brought it down. We felt first one skid, then the other, impact the rock ledge. We waited: the machine did not fall over the rim, the rotor blade didn't shatter against a boulder or tree. We were down. The pilot did not want to switch off the engine. César leaned forward, removed the key from the ignition, and put it in his pocket.

"Entonces," César said.

César, Alejandro, and I got out of the helicopter. Colonel Guzman remained behind with the pilot. There was a few yards of open space near the lip of the rock shelf. I felt a touch of vertigo, and thought how easy it would be for César or Alejandro to push me over the edge. An accident. Who would question it?

There was a vertical drop of about one hundred and fifty feet to the top of the talus slope, but the land to the left and right of the pillars was not nearly as steep, and there were forest growths that would help in our descent. I could see no sign of wreckage from atop the pillars.

César led the way, he traversed left along the shelf, paused a moment at the far end, then vanished over the side. Alejandro followed. There was a four-or five-foot drop from rock to soil. We descended in single file. There was a gulley adjacent to the rock pillars (and probably another on the far side), carved out by the flow of water. It was dry now, but I could imagine a torrent there during a rainstorm. We grabbed roots and rocks and shrubs to control our descent. The slope was steep all the way to the top of the talus. There, the fractured slabs and blocks of rock made the going easier. César, quick and agile, increased the distance between himself and Alejandro and me. He was an alpinist; this was not difficult terrain for him.

The wreckage was hardly recognizable as an airplane. The pieces—few larger than my hand—were strewn across the entire rock field. Bits of aluminum, rivets, wiring, glass powder, shreds of fabric, the mangled tire I had seen through the binoculars, machine parts, a scrap of leather, nuts and bolts, half a wing strut, a chunk of the engine block, a splintery piece of the wooden propeller. Most of the objects were half concealed among the grass and shrubs.

He had come straight on toward the mountain, saw it too late, banked steeply to his right, and hit hard, very hard, and the airplane virtually exploded. There were no signs of a fire. He had almost made it. An earlier view of the mountain, quicker reflexes, and he might have succeeded in sweeping low over the talus, and then out again and back to safety.

César, forty feet below, found the body parts. Alejandro and I descended. There was an arm and a hand, almost intact, and a part of the shoulder. The skin was brownish black and had a papery look, and the flesh was desiccated, very nearly mummified.

We stood together in silence, looking down at the partial corpse. This crash had taken place—what?— three years ago, five, ten?

César, his teeth clenched in a rictal grin, nodded his head over and over again. Yes, yes, yes. The wrong airplane, the wrong body. Tony could still be presumed alive.

"Maybe we can find some identification," Alejandro said.

"You look," César replied, and he turned and began ascending the slope.

Alejandro and I followed.

"Did you see?" Alejandro said. "His flesh looked like beef jerky."

THIRTY-SIX

My room window had been replaced by the time I returned from the mountain. From it I could look out over
the hotel grounds. There was the pond they called a
lake, encircled by a flagstone walk with wooden benches
placed on the grassy banks. A fountain in the center of
the pond spewed a rainbowed geyser of water thirty feet
into the air. Ducks floated in the rain of spray, and there
were scattered trees in the parklike grounds. An arched
wooden bridge spanned the little creek; a white marble
sculpture looked like a giant drillbit. A fringe of trees
blocked my view of the golf course, though hazy green-
blue mountains were visible in the distance.

I went to the window in the late afternoon, after I'd
packed some clothes, and saw a solitary figure walking
around the pond. Kate. She wore a short-sleeved
sweater and a pleated skirt, her hair was covered by a
paisley scarf, and she walked with her arms folded over
her breast, as if chilled. She completed her round and
without hesitation began another.

By the time I reached the pond she had completed
her circle. I fell into step alongside her. I didn't have

the feeling that I was intruding; rather, I sensed that she welcomed my company. We walked together at a good pace, a little better than three miles per hour. I now recognized that the ducks I had often seen from my window were decoys, tethered to the bottom, placed there probably in the hope that they would attract wild ducks.

It was a quarter mile walk around the pond. We strolled counterclockwise, and after a couple of circuits I became familiar with the objects that marked our progress: the little wooden bridge; a sun-and-shade-dappled patch beneath a eucalyptus tree; a loop in the path that brought us close to the tall marble sculpture; a shrub with partly closed bell-shaped yellow blossoms. The sun was low, its shafts of light steeply angled, throwing long shadows and tinting the pond water pink. An irregular breeze now and then sinuously curved the fountain geyser and filled the air with a fine mist. Once we heard voices on the golf course beyond the fringe of trees, but we saw no one. Kate looked straight ahead or down at the path. I glanced at her from time to time, at her cleanly incised profile, her dark eyelashes, the curve at the corner of her mouth.

Small lizards sunned on the warm flagstones. Most scuttled away into the grass as we approached, but a few were sluggish, and we were careful not to step on any. There were dozens of them, but they all vanished when the sun went down. And soon after sunset a flock of insolent blackbirds gathered in the eucalyptus. They shrieked at our periodic invasion of their territory.

Kate showed no sign of fatigue. She walked with a mechanical precision. I was not wearing good walking shoes; my feet hurt, began to blister, and the tendon supporting a bad knee became sore. Both of us were perspiring. We went on as the sun incandesced crimson and appeared to turn oblong before vanishing behind the mountains, though the sky remained blue and the clouds still glowed with sunset pastels.

The sky deepened to indigo. Stars appeared, singly at first, then they coalesced into clusters. Kate often looked up at the sky as we walked. I wondered if she were remembering our time aboard the boat, when I had taught her the names of some constellations and told her the myths behind the names.

It was still warm, though I knew that at this altitude it might turn chilly within a couple hours. We crossed the little wooden bridge, passed the eucalyptus, the marble sculpture, the shrub whose yellow blossoms had fully opened and whose perfume identified it as jasmine. We went on.

The moon had not risen, lights from the hotel complex did not reach us, and so we walked through the faint starlight. If Kate was tired, she didn't show it. Her pace had not slowed. Bridge, eucalyptus, sculpture (dimly luminous in the dark), the jasmine bush. I calculated that we had walked seven or eight miles around the pond.

At last Kate halted. Maybe she had tired herself enough so that she might sleep tonight. We embraced. Warm, sweaty, we embraced, and then she kissed my cheek and stepped back, and in the starlight I recognized her special wry smile. She turned and walked up the lawn toward the hotel. I could now see the fatigue in her posture, her walk.

I sat on a bench for twenty minutes, smoking, waiting for the warm breeze to evaporate my sweat, and watching the duck decoys—just shadows—bob and turn and curtsy at the ends of their tethers.

*　　*　　*

Eight taxis were lined up outside the hotel entrance the next morning. I knew the mountain roads were dangerous. None of the eight cars looked well maintained, and so I picked the one that displayed the fewest religious medals, decals of Jesus, miniature portraits of Mary, and glow-in-the-dark statuettes.

I was negotiating the fare when an airport limo pulled beneath the portico. The driver jumped out, opened a rear door, and waited, cap in hand, as Barbara Adams exited. She wore a royal blue suit, matching heels, wraparound sunglasses, and a wide-brimmed straw hat. She paid the driver with a lovely disdain, and preceded the bellman toward the hotel entrance. A different persona was evident each time I saw her. Today she looked like a film star, or a royal from some Mediterranean principality, or the Other Woman in a rich and ugly divorce proceeding. Barbara's hauteur did nothing to dispel an aura of sex and scandal.

PART IV
Consequences

THIRTY-SEVEN

It was not good to be home. Bell Harbor hadn't changed during my absence, but I had. Failure changes one. I had not prevented Leroy from abducting the boy, and then, when I had the opportunity to take him away from Leroy, I had failed again. And those failures had triggered a chain of misfortune that left Karpe and Tony dead on the Pico Duarte.

Judge Samuelson told me that he'd expected me to return to work. I wasn't a good lawyer, not yet, maybe never, but hell, if you had to be good to practice the profession the telephone pages under Attorneys would be blank.

"You're so tan," Candace said. "Have you been using that spray tanning lotion? I mean to try it."

Augustine Piñero, the punch-drunk ex-bantamweight who shined shoes in the Dunwoody Building lobby, hadn't known I was gone. "How'd you get them shoes so dirty since yesterday?"

I had given up my apartment in June, and so I slept on my worn Naugahyde office couch, now and then peering through the Venetian blinds at the world outside. I only went out when necessary. I had a TV, a hot plate, a microwave, a coffee brewer, a little refrigerator, a computer, and a telephone. I had it all.

I tried to avoid the assimilation of relevant information, but information seeped in nevertheless, all discouraging. The IRS had audited my account and discovered serious discrepancies in the last three returns. Finn Cooley phoned from Woeful Cay: my boat, *Roamer,* had sustained serious damage during a recent storm—send a check. Martina Karras, my ex-fiancée, was pregnant and deliriously happy. Martina was pregnant, Kate was pregnant. It seemed that all the women I saw were pregnant, young ones who followed their big bellies down aisles in the supermarket, older fertile women who carried a babe in one arm and pushed another down the street in a buggy. And then there was Thomas Petrie. Every day he dropped in from his top floor suite of offices to needle me.

"She's cuckoo," he said. "You're the only one who didn't know it."

"She suffered," I said. "She's still suffering. Her son is missing and presumed dead. Lay off."

"I like your suit," he said. "Salvation Army?"

"We screwed up big time, Tom."

"Leroy did."

"I did, you did, Leroy did."

"Okay. *Mea culpa.* But Kate set it all in motion, pal. She's ultimately responsible because of her big lies."

"You think they were lies?"

"Yeah. Don't you?"

"No. We don't know that they were lies."

"She's admitted they were."

"No, she hasn't."

"All right, false memories. Hallucinations, spelled l-i-e-s."

On another day, Petrie said, "Leroy Karpe—dead or alive?"

"You tell me."

"Dead, probably. We're partners in the charter company. I have his power of attorney. He hasn't taken a dime from any of the accounts. No checks, no ATM withdrawals, no credit card charges, no contact with his family down in Ochopee—if they can be believed. What has he been doing for money?"

"It hasn't been long."

"I think he crashed that Peregrine into the volcano."

"If so, César will find it. He's still looking."

"Have you tried getting in touch with Kate?"

"No."

"You lie."

"She refuses to talk to me."

"Shit, kid, I'm sorry. You're really in love with the neurotic bitch, aren't you?"

"Tom . . ."

"Anyway," he said, "Leroy Karpe—with the boy— remains missing. There hasn't been any activity on his passport. I had the judge check with his State Department pals."

"Leroy is resourceful. He can live underground."

"Nah," Petrie said. "Mistah Karpe, he daid."

* * *

Judge Samuelson had taken on more cases than he wanted or could properly handle. He was too old, he said, to work twelve-hour days. He was taking on no

new clients, and eliminating—when cases were disposed off—some of the old ones. I spent a few hours
each day helping him with the paperwork, and at five
thirty or six each day I went next door to have a drink
with Levi in his office.

"Tom Petrie," he said one day, "hates to be deceived."

"Who likes it?"

"Because he recognizes that, in most instances, one
actually deceives oneself. I mean, one collaborates in
the deception."

"I believed Kate. I still do, most of the time, though
late at night I have doubts. Like remembering that Kate
lied the first time we talked, faking amnesia."

"I believed her, too," the judge said. "So did Petrie,
so did—to everyone's misfortune—Leroy."

"And now, Levi?"

"I'm not sure. Like you, I believe her story most
of the time. But we'll never know for sure, will we?
There are hardly any indisputable facts. And now the
water has been so thoroughly muddied that we must
live with our doubts. Can you imagine trying this case
in court? Attempted murder. No witnesses. She said, he
said—wait, she said something else, and he changed his
story as well. No reputable prosecutor would even try
for an indictment."

"Petrie thinks that Leroy is dead."

"If so, the boy is dead, too."

"Yes, and I'm ultimately responsible. I had a chance
to stop Leroy and I failed."

"Responsibility is spread so thin among so many,
Daniel, that to claim ultimate responsibility is self-indul-
gence. You, me, Tom, Kate herself, César, Leroy, blind

fate—it can never be sorted out. Kate arrived at your boat in the middle of the night with a chilling story. It went on from there."

"That goddamned Leroy!"

"Yes, let's pin it all on Leroy. Especially if he's dead."

"Got any work for me?"

He pushed a folder forward on his desk. "Will you draft a motion of dismissal on this? Grounds of prosecutorial misconduct. The judge in this case won't buy it, but we go through the motions. Pun intended."

"I'll do it tonight."

"You probably ought to spend more time outside these walls. Get out, see people, take a lady to dinner."

I took several ladies to dinner, and they were as bored with me as I was with them.

*   *   *

"Your Kate is dead," Candace told me. She had come into my office immediately after arriving for work. "I heard it on the car radio. There was an airplane crash. Mr. Shaw?"

"Thanks, Candace."

"I'm sorry."

"Thank you."

Candace, tiptoeing, closed the door softly, as you might exit a hospital room that contained a dying patient.

I turned on the TV and flicked the remote among the cable news channels. It was all politics, disasters, war, celebrity profiles, business reports, a claimed extraterrestrial sighting in New Mexico, exotic diseases, and finally a tentative report about Kate: Katherine Adams-Cardinal, Virginia socialite, who had not long ago survived twenty-six hours at sea before being rescued by a yachtsman, had been killed in a helicopter crash in the mountains of the Dominican Republic, where, tragically, she and other members of the Cardinal family had been searching for the wreckage of an airplane assumed to contain the remains of her son, Antonio, and her son's kidnapper, Leroy Karpe. Also killed was the pilot of the helicopter, and Colonel Guzman, a Dominican Army officer in charge of the search operation. César Cardinal, husband of Katherine and father of the kidnapped child, was severely injured in the helicopter crash and reported to be in critical condition at a Santo Domingo hospital.

Later reports offered little that was new, but there was a lot of background material about Kate's ordeal at sea, her rescue, the abduction of her five-year-old Antonio, and the murder of a bodyguard. Leroy Karpe, an aviator from Bell Harbor, Florida, suspected of the murder and the abduction, was presumed dead in the crash of a stolen aircraft, along with the Adams-Cardinal child. Karpe was convicted of drug-related charges in 1994. The wreckage of the downed airplane and the remains of Karpe and Antonio Cardinal had not been found. The search continued.

My phone commenced ringing. Reporters from the States, the Dominican Republic, and even Europe, called and asked my response to the news. You rescued her less than a month ago, and now . . . I responded profanely half a dozen times, and then pulled the phone cord from the jack.

Petrie came through the door carrying a bottle of Scotch and two glasses. He sat down across from my desk, poured the whiskey, lifted his glass, and said, "To Kate, then."

It was early, I didn't want the whiskey, but I could hardly refuse a drink to Kate.

"What can I say?" Tom said.

"It won't stop," I said. "It just keeps going on."

"I could quote Shakespeare. 'Life . . . is a tale told by an idiot, full of sound and fury, signifying nothing.'"

"That's a comfort. Thanks, Tom."

"Turn on the TV."

"I've heard enough."

"César, according to CNN, was seriously concussed, badly burned, suffered a spinal injury, and lost an arm in the helicopter crash. He's not expected to make it, but he is still one tough son of a bitch."

"Then maybe we also should drink to César," I said. "Let's wait until he's verifiably dead."

Judge Samuelson came through the door that connected our offices. He sat down on the couch, crossed his legs, and sighed.

"Drink, Levi?" Petrie asked.

He shook his head. "Daniel, I'm sorry."

"We're all sorry," Tom said. "The gods are sorry."

"I liked her. I didn't know how much I liked her until this."

"We had nine days aboard *Roamer.* Perfect days."

"Is that a consolation?" Petrie said.

"Not much."

"Are you going to her funeral?"

"If it's held in Virginia."

"It won't be. They'll bury her in the D.R."

"No doubt."

"Christ, it might be a multiple interment. Kate, César, Tony, the fetus."

"I think, Tom," the judge said, "that you are the most insensitive man I know."

"Not an original comment," Petrie said.

"What are you going to do, Daniel?" Levi asked.

"I don't know. My boat is being repaired down at Woeful Cay. I can't go sailing anyway, it's hurricane season. I'll hang around here for the winter, I guess."

"I have plenty of work for you."

"Fine."

"You can stay at my house," Petrie said.

"Thanks, Tom. I will, until I find a place in town."

"Another drink?"

"Why not?"

"Levi?"

"No. I've got to be in court in an hour."

"What's the case?"

"Domestic abuse."

"You accept a lot of shitty cases, Judge."

"I inherited this one from Daniel. But I turn down a lot of shitty cases, too. A few days ago a woman came into the office who claimed that the government had planted a microchip in her womb."

"Another microchippie?"

"The same one," I said. "I saw her in the outer office on Wednesday."

"Why didn't you warn me?" the judge asked.

"She has a right to counsel."

"This is what I like," Petrie said. "One exceptional lawyer—me—and two hacks, sitting around discussing our ignoble profession."

I got up from my desk. "See you two later."

"Where are you going?"

"I'm going to take a long walk."

"Sure," Petrie said, "why don't you go for a long, stoic, manly walk."

*　　*　　*

Four hurricanes slammed into Florida that season; there was a great deal of wind damage and flooding, and predictably the insurance companies contested a lot of claims. It was a good time for lawyers, small-print time, and the judge and I accepted many new clients. Usually, stern letters from legal counsel were enough to obtain a settlement, but a few cases we had to litigate. We were busy all winter and well into the spring. We earned some money, the judge and I, and we received satisfaction from beating the insurance company racketeers in court.

I rented a Bell Harbor apartment on a month-to-month basis. I worked hard, played some tennis, tried out for a part in the town's amateur theater group (and was denied the role), dated a couple of women who declined a second date. I was burned out and they knew it.

I encountered Nestor Naranjo, the chief prosecutor in the SA's office, and asked him how he was proceeding in his investigation of me for the murder of

Anton Arbaleste et al. He couldn't recall our conversation on the matter and concluded that he must have been tormenting me for fun.

Phil Karras, Martina's uncle, the man who killed his wife with a shotgun, was sent by the court to a mental institution for further evaluation.

In June I received a postcard that pictured a smoking volcano isolated against an azure sky.

Danny boy,

Having a wonderful time.
Wish you were here.

Love, Gertrude

I didn't know a Gertrude, but I was familiar with Leroy Karpe's handwriting.

THIRTY-EIGHT

Leroy and Tony lived in a town some forty miles from the Costa Rican capital, San José, in a rich agricultural valley. You could see the volcano pictured on Leroy's postcard from anywhere in town. Sometimes it appeared very close, just beyond the rooftops; other times it looked very far off in a bluish haze; and once it completely vanished behind thick swirling clouds. It was an active volcano, quiescent now, but villagers suggested that it could blow—or at least smoke—at any moment.

The house was built on a flowery courtyard; room led to room around the perimeter, and there was an iron gate in front, doors behind the gate, and all the windows visible from the street were barred. It was a nice house in a nice neighborhood in a clean and prosperous small town.

Five lived in the house: Leroy, Antonio, and three servant women: a cook, a housemaid, and a girl of seventeen or eighteen who took care of the boy. I determined, from my several days of spying, that it was a happy household. The women were well treated and apparently decently paid. Tony, now six years old, attended a small school six blocks from the house, and seemed to like it there and at home. The girl delivered him to the school at nine thirty Monday through Thursday, and picked him up at two o'clock, and together they walked down the cobbled streets to the house. Tony, clutching his lunch pail, stumbling now and then, chattered all the way home.

Leroy Karpe, known locally as Larry Park, worked for a big agricultural corporation called Mundo Verde Sud, S.A. One day I followed him out to a dirt airstrip in the middle of vast fields planted with corn and soybeans and wheat. He flew a red Stearman biplane. It looked like a World War I fighter, with its double wings, open cockpit, and old design. The Red Baron would not have been surprised to see that plane, but he certainly would have been startled by the power of the engine and the craft's maneuverability. Leroy had hired on as a crop duster. It was dangerous work and no doubt paid well.

That day I watched him dust a particularly constricted field that was bordered at one end by electrical power lines and at the other by a row of big trees. Warehouses and farm equipment sheds reduced air space along the field's width. Leroy had to dust a long strip, then abruptly, steeply, climb to avoid the trees, bank at an acute angle—wings almost vertical—swoop down to within a few yards of the ground, and resume dusting. It was the same at the other end, only the hazard was power lines and towers instead of trees. There was not a moment without risk. But after a while I began to have confidence in Leroy's skill. He made it look routine. It probably was, for him. I drove back to town when he landed to take on another load of chemicals.

Leroy was a wary man, a fugitive killer and kidnapper, and I was not sure that he hadn't seen me as I followed him or the girl and Tony or watched the house from a street corner. If so, he said nothing, made no move, but went on with his strange—for him—domestic existence. He played catch with Tony on the street in front of the house. All five of them went to a movie theater two or three nights a week, and afterward ate flavored ices from a streetcorner vendor. One Saturday some of Tony's schoolmates, accompanied by mothers or nannies, came over to the house for a courtyard party and games. Leroy was affectionate toward the girl. I assumed that they slept together.

He had sent me the postcard, invited my visit for reasons I didn't understand. I held back. I watched and waited and considered for three days. Finally, late one afternoon, I walked up to the gate and rang the bell. After a moment, the door opened and the housemaid peered out at me.

"*Quiero ver a Larry,* " I said.

"*Su nombre, señor?*"

"Shaw."

"*Chaw?*"

"Shaw."

"*Momentito, Señor Chaw,*" she said, and she returned to the interior of the patio.

Déjà vu: I was reminded of that other door, that other woman, in San Marcos.

I heard her voice, Leroy's voice, and then he shouted, "Come on in, Senor Chaw."

I went through the gate, through the open door, and into the blue-and-white-tiled courtyard. There were potted plants scattered around, bamboo lawn furniture, a marble birdbath, and several twig cages that held small, brightly colored parrots. Vines of white and pink bougainvillea crept up the walls, in some cases obscuring windows, and there were eight doors, three on the left, three on the right, and two more in the rear section.

Leroy, grinning at me, was sprawled out on a lounge chair. "Christ, Chaw, what have you been waiting for?"

"For the right moment. Did you spot me?"

"Only three or four times."

He was wearing wrinkled khaki shorts, sandals, and a T-shirt with ¿No legusta? (Don't you like it?) printed on the front. Leroy had lost a little hair and acquired a potbelly in the eleven months since I'd seen him.

"Sit," he said. "A beer?"

"Sure."

"Something to eat?"

"No, thanks."

He called to the servant and told her to bring two cold beers, then regarded me with something like fondness. "Chaw, you son of a bitch!"

"You prick, Leroy."

The skin around his eyes crinkled when he laughed. This was not the man I had known for years, the sullen, resentful, often violent Leroy Karpe. No, this man had a pleasant expression and relaxed ways. He was the genial host, the contented family man. Leroy, nearing forty, had apparently metamorphosed into his opposite. I did not wholly believe in the transformation.

The servant came out of a room bearing a tray

upon which were two bottles of beer and two frosted pilsner glasses. She placed them on the table, poured the glasses full without their foaming over, performed a little curtsy, and drifted away.

I said, "I saw you dust a field yesterday."

"Yeah?"

"You can fly, Leroy."

"You just found that out yesterday?"

"Risky work. I suppose it pays well."

"It does."

"How did you get the job? No papers, illegally in the country, a fugitive?"

"I'll tell you how I got the job. In the last year two pilots were killed, two planes lost. They needed me more than I needed them."

"Where's the kid?"

"Tony's napping. He usually sleeps for ninety minutes after school."

"You have quite a manage. Joined the smug middle class at last, have you, Leroy?"

"I was pretty sure you wouldn't rat me out," he said.

"I thought about it."

"Nah."

"Why did you send me that postcard?"

"It was an invitation you accepted. Because I think maybe things have cooled down. It's been almost a year. The kidnapping, the bodyguard I hurt—"

"The bodyguard you killed."

"He's dead? Shit. I knew I hit him too hard. Christ. Would you believe I'm sorry for that?"

"I'll believe anything these days. How did you and Tony get out of the D.R.?"

"Stole a plane, flew to Haiti."

"The Peregrine?"

"Yeah."

"You flew over the Pico Duarte at night?"

"Not in that crate. You'd have to be crazy to try it. No, I flew over a low section of the cordillera, at about eight thousand feet. And it wasn't night, it was after dawn."

"You flew where?"

"To a little town called Croix des Bouquets, not far from Port-au-Prince."

"What about papers?"

"The little airport in Croix des Bouquets doesn't have any customs people. Anyway, this is Haiti we're talking about—a hundred-dollar bill is your passport to anywhere and anything. I sold the airplane to a guy at the airport for fifteen hundred dollars. A bargain. It was worth maybe five thousand."

"But the Peregrine was reported stolen by the kidnapper of the Cardinal boy."

"Sure, reported stolen all over the Dominican Republic. Word didn't reach Haiti, at least not very quick."

"Everyone thought the Peregrine had flown into the mountain."

"Yeah?"

"You didn't know that?"

"No. Why should I?"

"You don't read newspapers, watch television? You weren't interested in what was being reported about you and the boy?"

"We were out of Haiti before dark. Got a ride on a tramp freighter, stops in Jamaica, the Caymans, and Panama."

"There's still the problem of papers, Leroy."

"You make it sound like it might be hard to move around Latin America without papers. We, Tony and me, we jumped ship after dark. Got on a bus. Crossed into Costa Rica. And here we are, here you are, and our glasses are empty. Ramona! *Dos mas!*"

"Everyone," I said, "thought you dived that Peregrine into the mountain."

"Why the hell they think that?"

"During the night a commercial flight picked up an emergency signal. It was natural to assume you had gone down."

"Did they find *that* plane?"

"No."

"Not even with a signal and a navigational fix?"

"The signal stopped transmission and never started again."

"Strange stuff. I guess it helped me, though."

"Sure. They stopped looking for you except on the Pico Duarte."

Ramona came out with two bottles of beer and two more frosted glasses. She daintily went through her pouring ritual, placed the empty bottles and used glasses on the tray, performed her little curtsy, and drifted away.

It was five now, and the sunlight angled in low over the western wall, slicing the courtyard into equal triangles of light and shadow. I could not see the volcano from here, but it seemed to me that you could feel its weight, its mass, its dominance of the plain. One of the parrots, a blue, yellow, and orange bird, squawked harshly, said, *"Cómo no?"* and ruffled its feathers.

Leroy turned and smiled. I followed his glance: the pretty young girl and Tony had emerged from a room. The boy blinked sleepily as he crossed from shade into sunlight.

"Hey, cowboy," Leroy said.

The boy grinned shyly. He was wearing a cowboy suit: boots, chaps, denim trousers beneath the chaps, a western shirt, and a big hat.

"Where's your horse?" Leroy asked.

"I don't got a horse," Tony replied.

"I make sure he doesn't forget his English," Leroy said to me. And then, to the boy, "Lots of horses in Virginia. Remember Virginia?"

"I think so."

"Remember this guy? Señor Chaw?"

Tony studied my face in a serious way. "He's not a cowboy."

"He's a sheriff."

"I don't think so."

"Well, maybe you're right."

Tony had grown since I'd last seen him. He was taller, not so chubby, not quite so awkward, and there was something in his eyes—awareness of self, maybe— that had not been there before.

"Give me a hug, Bronco Tony," Leroy said, spreading his arms.

Without hesitation the boy smiled and stepped forward, hugged and kissed Leroy, then stepped back.

"Now Luz is going to give you a bath. Because you smell of the trail, Bronco Tony, you smell of cowhide and cowpies and rattlesnake sweat. Run along."

The boy, giggling, turned and trotted across the courtyard and into his room.

"Luz," Leroy said to the girl, "have Ramona bring out more beer."

When she was gone, I said, "Doesn't the kid miss his family?"

"Well, I guess so, but he doesn't talk about them much. It's like private, his memories. But right now I'm his family, in loco—what is it?"

"Loco parentis."

"And so are the women, especially Luz, his family."

"I never saw you as a man who enjoyed the company of women."

He shrugged, looked away. "People change, I guess."

"It can't last, Leroy. It has to end now."

"I know. That's why I sent you that card."

"What do you have in mind?"

"Like I said, some of the heat's got to be off me now. The bodyguard, snatching Tony. I want to go back to Bell Harbor, but I won't go back unless I know I won't be extradited to the D.R."

"I can't help you there, unless you want to hire me as your lawyer."

"Tom Petrie's my lawyer. Look, here's what I mean: you take the boy to the States. Virginia. Catch a flight tomorrow."

"Stop right there. There are a lot of people who still think that I was involved in the abduction. Leroy, I am not going to get on an airplane to the States with Tony at my side."

"All right. Have Kate fly down here and pick up her son. Maybe she can fix it so that I don't get prosecuted."

"Leroy, what is this bullshit?"

"She can fix it."

"You really don't know?"

"No jail time for me. That's the deal."

"Christ, man, Kate's dead."

"What?" he said. "No."

"She's been dead for almost a year."

He turned pale. He turned a ghastly white and stared intently as Ramona brought out more beer and a platter of food, and he continued staring at me after she'd gone. He looked more like the old Leroy now, mean and angry, stubborn as sin.

"She was killed in a helicopter crash. Kate, the pilot, a Colonel Guzman. César was badly injured."

He shook his head in wonder and bitter denial.

"They were searching for the Peregrine. They were searching for Tony."

"This isn't right," he said. "It's not right."

"How could you not know that she had been killed in a helicopter crash? Everybody knows."

"I didn't know."

"And César and Kate got back together. The night you snatched Tony, they were on a flight to the Dominican Republic."

The news that César and Kate had reconciled disturbed him almost as much as hearing that Kate was dead. He got up from the table, hurried across the courtyard, and entered one of the back rooms. Would he return with a gun? Kill the messenger? He came back clutching a sheaf of newspaper clippings. He gave them to me, sat down, put a palm over his eyes. There were at least twenty pictures of Kate that he had cut out of various D.R. newspapers: Kate smiling, Kate regal, Kate holding little Tony, Kate in a tennis outfit. Most of the pictures, on newsprint, were blurred, but two, clipped from slick-paper tabloids—one a full page— showed her in all her sculptured beauty.

I dropped the sheaf on the table.

"That's that," Leroy said.

"I can probably help you," I said. "Or at least I'll try. I'll call Kate's uncle in Virginia, and have him come down to pick up the boy. Petrie might be able to negotiate a deal for you."

"What kind of deal?"

"I don't know. Talk to Tom. But you'll probably have to stay here for another year or two, let things cool down some more."

"I'll think about it."

"Do that."

"Come back tomorrow. We'll have lunch."

"All right."

I got up and walked across the courtyard. I turned at the gate and for a moment watched Leroy intently study the photographs of Katherine Adams-Cardinal.

THIRTY-NINE

I returned to the house a little after noon the next day. The gate was unlocked, the door ajar, and Leroy was sleeping. One of the parrots screeched *"Chinga tu madre!"* when I entered the courtyard, then cocked his head and watched me with a cold yellow eye. I sat in one of the wicker chairs. Women were talking in a back room. Small lizards that looked like beaded ornaments were splayed against sunlit patches on the viney walls. Leroy shifted his weight, rocking the hammock. I was surprised that he had not been awakened by my entry. Leroy Karpe had always been a wary man, taut-nerved and defensive even in sleep, ready for the worst.

Tony, no doubt, was at school; women were cleaning the house and gossiping; and Leroy, rocking a little, slept the peaceful sleep of the just. His face was creased and jowly, his hair whorled, lips moist and slack.

I went outside, walked to a corner bodega, bought six bottles of beer and a packet of cigarillos, and returned to the courtyard. Leroy's sleep was not so tranquil now, he grimaced, and I could see eye movements behind the lids.

His eyes opened. He stared at me. "Christ. Señor Chaw."

"Sorry I woke you."

He ran his fingers through his tangled hair. "Nah. I was dreaming."

"About what, Leroy?"

He got out of the hammock, walked to the table, and sat in the chair across from me. "I was flying. Dusting. The plane stalled and pancaked. My seat belt was jammed. That's when I woke up—before the fire I knew was coming."

"Got an opener?" I asked.

He took a coin the size of a half-dollar from his pocket and deftly pried the caps off two bottles.

"The thing was, there was someone with me in the plane, but I didn't know who it was, who was going to die with me in the fire."

"Tony, maybe?"

"Kate, I think. Yeah, it must have been Kate. You told me the helicopter burned when it crashed."

"You didn't tell Tony that his mother's dead, did you?"

"Not my job."

"Right."

"I was up all night. Couldn't sleep."

I took a cigarillo from the pack, offered one to Leroy, struck a match, and lit them both.

"It's pleasant here," I said. "Cool, flower smells, bead-work lizards—I counted seven lizards."

"There's dozens. They keep the flies down. We had a cat but all he did was hunt lizards, never mice."

"*Cómo se dice?*" the bigger and more colorful of the two parrots squawked, and then, almost sadly, "*Madre de Dios.*"

Ramona appeared and asked Leroy if her services were required; he asked her to boil a pot of shrimp.

"Have you decided, Leroy?"

"Yeah. I guess I can't keep Kate's boy."

"No."

"What kind of deal do I get?"

"I can't say. But I'll tell Warren—that's the uncle—that there's to be no prosecution. Whether he'll promise and then stick to his promise, I don't know. But you ought to get in touch with Petrie soon. And stay away from the Dominican Republic forevermore."

"Fuck it," he said. "I don't care. Get it over."

"I'll phone Warren this afternoon. He can be in Costa Rica sometime tomorrow. I'll meet him at the airport or at his hotel, and drive him down here to pick up Tony."

Leroy opened two more bottles of beer with his coin. I could not read his expression. He loved the boy, that was evident; it was not hard for me to imagine the two of them in the open cockpit of the Stearman, ascending through the clouds, flying off to a new life in a new country.

"That César's alive, though, you said."

"He lost an arm, was badly burned, and has a lot of pain from a spinal injury. That's what I heard."

"Well, he did it. He finally killed her."

That, of course, was absurd. César might or might not have thrown Kate into the sea, but he certainly was not responsible for her death on the Pico Duarte.

Together they had obsessively searched for their son's remains. Ultimately, we were responsible, me, Tom Petrie, and Leroy—Leroy most of all.

Ramona came out of the kitchen annex with a tray containing a bowl of small shrimp, bread and butter, plates, napkins, sliced lemons, and a bottle of hot sauce. The shrimp had been deheaded and deveined, but we had to peel the shells. We ate in silence for a time.

"Who'll raise the boy?" Leroy asked.

"Kate's family. Maybe her married sister. I don't know."

"He's got no mother."

"No father, either, this way."

"As long as César doesn't get him."

"That won't happen. The Adamses will have custody, and they've got plenty of money. Tony will have a good life."

"You're full of shit, you know that?"

"Sure I know it."

"How can you say he'll have a good life? How can you say that about a little kid?"

"The odds are in his favor."

"They'll ruin him with a fancy education."

I glanced up to see if Leroy was being ironic. He wasn't, of course; Leroy and irony were hostile strangers.

"They'll give him everything he asks for, ponies and cars and prep school, and send him off to some la-di-da whorehouse like Yale. Turn him soft and whiny and snobby."

"But he'll always be Bronco Tony in your heart."

"Still the smart-ass wise guy, huh, Shaw."

"I guess."

"You know I never liked you."

"I never liked you, either. This is business."

He grinned. "I'm getting old. I'll turn forty in three months. Me, forty. If I wasn't getting old I'd probably decide to kick out all your teeth."

"Pass the hot sauce, Leroy."

"It wasn't all crap, the past, was it? We had some good times together."

Was Leroy Karpe going to become nostalgic? His good times had been hellish, largely composed of fear and danger and violence. He might eventually view his rampage in the D.R. as one of the good times we shared.

I scooped a few shrimp from the bowl, peeled the shells, dipped them one by one in the hot sauce, and ate them.

"Do you have a phone, Leroy?"

"No."

"Well, you can call me at my hotel from a pay phone if you want to know how things are going."

"Just get it over."

I finished my beer. "Ah, those good times," I said. "Those halcyon days of yore." I got up and started walking toward the gate. I had gone only a couple of steps when I felt something strike my back. My shirt was wet. Blood? I turned: Leroy had thrown a handful of shrimp at me. A dozen of them, moist and pink, lay on the tiles.

I went on across the courtyard and through the gate. Even when I was halfway down the street I could hear Leroy laughing and the parrot squawking, *"Madre de Dios!"*

FORTY

I drove the rental car directly back to my hotel in San José, and went up to my room on the fifth floor. Too much of my life was spent in hotel rooms, eating hotel food, waiting for someone or something. It was nine thirty in Virginia when I made my call. A servant told me that Mr. Warren Adams was not available at the moment; would I care to leave a message? I gave my name, the hotel's name, and my room number.

The Cardinals were playing the Cubs in a night game at St. Louis. I observed the neurotic rituals of both pitchers and hitters. Baseball was a slow game in fast times.

The telephone rang. I listened to a conversation between an international operator and the hotel switchboard, and then Warren Adams came on the line.

"Who is this?"

"Shaw," I said. "How are you doing, Warren?"

"What is this about?" He clearly was not pleased to hear from me.

"It's about Tony."

"I hope this isn't some kind of cruel drunken joke."

I pictured him: tall, erect, with his shaved head and neatly trimmed Vandyke beard; the man who had sacrificed his own life and career to watch over his brother's family. "Tony is alive," I said.

He did not speak. I waited for the line to go dead.

"How much?" he asked.

"I knew you'd think that. I didn't expect you to say it."

"How much is the ransom? I have to know, if I'm going to transfer money down there. Or do you expect me to carry cash in a brown paper bag?"

"I expect you to listen, and reason, if that's not asking too much."

"This is cruel, Shaw. Extremely cruel."

"Goddamn it, the boy is alive."

"Put him on the phone."

"I don't have him. The kidnapper, Leroy Karpe, has him."

"Your friend. Your partner."

"Look, I'm just acting here as the go-between."

"Yes. Trying to extort ransom for the return of a boy who is dead. Profiteering from a corpse. Is Katherine down there too? How much do you want for Katherine?"

"I didn't think you'd be this stupid," I said. "Leroy Karpe and Tony safely got out of the Dominican Republic. The Peregrine did not crash. They made it to Haiti, and from there made their way to Costa Rica. Tony is here. Karpe wants to make a deal: you come down and get the boy, and in exchange you don't press too hard for legal revenge. It won't cost you a dime beyond airfare and expenses."

"This is despicable."

"Oh, well, fuck you then, Warren." I hung up the telephone.

The Cubs were getting thumped by the Cards. I phoned room service and ordered a steak, salad, baked potato, and a bottle of Bordeaux. I figured I might as well enjoy a last good meal before cops started pounding on the door.

Warren called me back in thirty-five minutes, long enough for him to consult whomever he elected to consult—police, Kate's mother, other family members, the lawyer Mr. Barlow.

"How do I know you're telling the truth?" he asked.

"Pujols is up with a man on first. That guy can hit."

"Can you give me any proof?"

"He doesn't seem to have a weakness. High, low, inside, outside, straight or crooked pitch, he hits everything."

"Shaw . . ."

"Take a chance, Warren. Spend a few bucks. Fly down here. I'll take you to the boy. You do *want* the boy, don't you? You and Kate's mother and Kate's sisters, and all the cousins and friends? Isn't that right? You all want to raise the kid, make him happy, provide him with an excellent education, watch him become a stockbroker or CEO. Or do I have it wrong?"

"I'll get back to you."

"Can't you, for Christ's sake, stop weaseling and make a decision? You'd better act soon, Warren, because Leroy's a nervous guy, an impulsive guy, and in a couple of days he and little Tony might be selling trinkets on the beach at Cartagena or Rio."

"I'll make flight reservations."

"A reasonable first step. There are plenty of flights to Costa Rica—it's a tourist paradise."

"Is there a Sheraton in San José?"

"Yeah, the Regencia. Do you want me to reserve a room for you?"

"I'll do it at this end."

"Fine."

"Shaw, I apologize if I've offended you. It's just . . . after so much, after everything . . ."

"See you tomorrow, Warren."

"Tomorrow," he said softly, and he hung up.

I had been nasty to Warren Adams. My nerves were shot. I sometimes saw flashes of light at the corners of my eyes. My dreams were ugly, my heart skipped beats, I saw enemies everywhere. I tasted acid at the sight of a policeman or a hard guy. It had gone on too long.

FORTY-ONE

I started calling the Hotel Regencia at noon the next day, and called again every forty-five minutes after that. No, Mr. Warren Adams had not checked in; no, there was not a reservation in his name. I tried the other good hotels in San José with the same result. I telephoned the house in Virginia; no answer. Was the son of a bitch backing out, abandoning the boy? I could not believe that. I ate, watched television, waited for the phone to ring. In the early evening I called the Regencia and other hotels to ask if they had a César or Alejandro Cardinal registered. On my fifth call, the Hotel Suisse, a small but elegant place near the national palace, a desk clerk said, yes, the Cardinal group of three had arrived that morning. Would I like to be connected to their suite? No. I told her that I was a travel agent who wished to confirm that everything had proceeded smoothly for my clients. There was no need to disturb them or mention my inquiry.

There it was. Warren had notified the Cardinal brothers that Leroy and the boy were alive and in Costa Rica. I hadn't mentioned the little town, San Martin, nor the house, nor Leroy's job, but a man like César would have no difficulty in finding them.

It was nine thirty and dark when I reached San Martin. I parked my rental car a block away from the house and stood in a doorway for ten minutes, watching. A dome of light glowed in the air above the courtyard. A window on the east side of the building was lighted. It was very quiet; no music, no voices, nothing.

I walked down the center of the cobblestone street, hesitated, looked around, and then went on past the house to the corner. The gate did not appear to be locked, and the door behind it was slightly ajar. I waited on the corner for a few minutes, smoked half a cigarette, and returned down the street, opened the gate, pushed open the door, and entered the courtyard.

Leroy, blood all over his T-shirt and shorts, was lying on the tiles beneath a hammock. He looked dead, but his eyes opened when I lifted his shirt. There were two small holes in his lower abdomen, bowel shots. You wouldn't gut-shoot a man unless you wanted him to suffer greatly.

"I'll call an ambulance," I said.

He licked his lips. "César."

"Was he alone?"

"Alejandro."

"Who pulled the trigger?"

"César."

"He just walked in and shot you?"

"Sleep. Woke me. Bang-bang."

"Where is Tony? The women?"

"Movies."

"Is the pain bad, Leroy?"

"Not. Now." And he died.

Leroy Karpe, swampbilly, soldier, drug smuggler, aviator, arsonist, kidnapper, crop duster, dead man. R.I.P.

His eyes, half closed, reflected crescents of light from an overhead bulb.

There was some blood on the hammock, but no holes; the slugs were in his body. A small pistol lay on the tiles among shards of broken glass. I picked it up. It was a .22 Taurus with rosewood grips. The Taurus firearms were manufactured in Florida and sold both domestically and abroad. I slid out the magazine; four .22-long rifle hollow-point bullets remained in the clip, and there was another in the chamber. Hollow-points mushroomed upon impact. I found two brass shell casings on the floor.

Leroy belched softly as air escaped his lungs. Already his eyes had a gluey look, and I thought I saw a blueness, the color of a new bruise, around his mouth.

I kneeled and examined the amulet Leroy wore around his neck. I had never noticed it before, though Petrie had mentioned an amulet months earlier. Maybe Leroy wore it only when he was feeling unlucky. It was in a little leather pouch tied to a rawhide loop. Inside the pouch I found a gold frog no bigger than a grape. It might have been a pre-Columbian object that Leroy had picked up during his drug smuggling days. A lucky frog.

I stood up and looked around. Nothing alive in the place except me, the parrots, and the courtyard lizards. Leroy was a man and, in the time it takes to exhale, he had become trash to be taken out and buried.

I slipped the pistol into my pocket. It would cost me my freedom if I were caught with the murder weapon—a quarrel between the kidnappers. It was stupid of me to keep the gun, but I figured that César and Alejandro might now be looking for me.

I shut the door behind me, closed the gate, and walked down the dark street toward the town plaza. A thin dog, ribs showing, followed me for a while, looking for a handout, a friend, some company on a dark night.

The plaza was brightly lighted, and there were clusters of people standing on the corners or sitting on park benches and lined up at the theater's box office for the second showing of *Los Matónes de Durango*. I did not see César or Alejandro among the crowd, and I had neglected to ask Leroy if he had told the Cardinal brothers where Tony was. If asked, he would no doubt have simply said, "Fuck you." Or maybe not: this was the new Leroy Karpe, potbellied, cheery, head-of-household Leroy.

People, blinking their eyes in the light, began emerging from the theater. There was the housekeeper, the maid, Luz, the pretty girl who served as Tony's nanny. But no Tony. The three women walked to the corner, bought three flavored ices from a vendor, and began slowly strolling toward home. I intercepted them halfway down a dimly lighted street.

"*Las tres señoritas guapas,*" I said.

They halted, giggling at my flattery. Ramona, who had served Leroy and me beer yesterday, recognized me.

"*Dónde está Tony?*" I asked.

Ramona spoke for the three of them. It was a wonderful thing. Señor Park had always said that one day Antonio's beautiful mother would come for the boy, and that had miraculously happened this evening. They were both so happy, mother and child, as they kissed and hugged and wept.

What did Antonio's mother look like?

Oh, slim, very beautiful, and young—she must have had Antonio when she was almost a child herself.

This was a family enterprise: César, Alejandro, and their sister, Maria, posing as Tony's mother.

Was the father present?

Yes, yes, the father, a crooked ugly man—why would she marry him? And a big man, Antonio's uncle.

And you allowed those people to take away Antonio without first consulting with Señor Park?

They looked baffled. Señor Park had said every day for months that Antonio's mother would one day appear. Was there something wrong?

You should have talked to Señor Park.

But *they* said that they had already seen Señor Park, and were taking Antonio to the house so that Señor Park could say goodbye to the child.

Yes, yes, it's all right, I told them. Señor Park was very happy that little Antonio had been united with his mother and father at last. So happy, in fact, that he had given me money to give to the women, so that they too could celebrate this wonderful occasion. I gave Ramona about thirty dollars in Costa Rican currency. Eat something, I said, talk with your friends, buy something for yourselves, enjoy this fine Saturday night. Señor Park will be very disappointed if you return to the house before midnight.

They were pleased and embarrassed. They thanked me and their patron, Señor Park—a kind and generous

man—and they praised the Holy Mother for this
miracle that at last had reunited mother and son. They
would go to the church and give thanks.

One more thing. Did Antonio seem happy?

Oh, yes. Tony is always happy. He's a happy little boy.

I exceeded the speed limit all the way to the San José
airport, left the car in a parking lot, and trotted into
the major terminal. Not many people waited for flights
late on a Saturday night. Two men were mopping the
floor, a woman passed out leaflets, a security guard was
sneaking a smoke behind a pillar. I studied the flight
schedules: an AM plane was due to depart for Miami
in ninety minutes; an AeroCarib flight was scheduled to
soon leave for Kingston, Havana, Santo Domingo, and
San Juan. Concourse B.

I walked to the west side of the terminal and up
an inclined hall. Ahead was the security checkpoint.
César and Alejandro were waiting in line. It was a
shock to see César. Ramona had called him a crooked,
ugly man, and he was: he had been devastated by the
helicopter crash. He limped; an empty pinned-up sleeve
indicated the missing left arm; and the left side of his
face and neck (and presumably his torso and left leg)
were patched by puffy-looking skin grafts.

It was an equal shock to see Barbara Adams there.
The Other Sister was at the front of the line, holding
Tony's hand. So the woman posing as the boy's mother
had not been Maria Cardinal, but Barbara, sexy now
in a red dress and high heels, leaning over to attend to
sleepy Antonio, kissing his tiny hand, glancing up at
César with a loving smile. She wore a big diamond ring
that sprayed white sparks when the light struck it from

a certain angle. I would have bet *Roamer* that it was Kate's engagement ring. ("He didn't want me wearing that ring when I drowned.") Barbara and César. It was crazy, but there was a certain interior logic to the craziness: her girlhood crush—her obsession—had been realized. She had at last taken her sister's place. Now she would lie at night beside her beloved César. His infirmities, I thought, would not put her off, they would more likely reinforce her adolescent infatuation, her misty dream of romance.

The line moved forward. César, unaware that he was being watched, winced at a sudden increase in pain. The warped man, the burned man, the mutilated man.

I was aware of the pistol in my pocket. It occurred to me that I could kill him now and possibly get away with it. Empty the pistol, five shots, drop it, run out of the terminal and into the parking lot . . .

Often you can sense another's stare. César did, and he half turned, found me, and returned my stare. We gazed at each other over thirty feet of open space. All we had in common was Kate. We stared, the line moved forward, and César smiled faintly. His face was half a mask, the burned side impassive, the other side smiling. He nodded. I returned his nod. Then he limped forward, and I went outside and disposed of the pistol in a trash can.

I bought a ticket on the AM Miami flight. There were no problems. I was not stopped by the police, nor taken aside by security, and I was home in Bell Harbor early the next morning.

FORTY-TWO

I telephoned the San José hotel the next day from my office in Bell Harbor, told the manager that I had left suddenly, and authorized him to deduct my room bill and other expenses from my credit card. And I asked that he send on my luggage. He said that of course they would do that, immediately, but my bags never arrived.

I phoned the Adams place in Virginia half a dozen times, but only the servants would talk to me. Barbara and César had been married. Barbara—Mrs. César Adams-Cardinal—was now resident in the Dominican Republic. The Other Sister had at last got her man, what remained of him.

Soon after my return, Tom Petrie, the judge, and I gathered together at a Bell Harbor restaurant, they to mourn the passing of Leroy Karpe, me to keep them company. We drank too much before, during, and after dinner.

"Well, you fucked up again," Petrie said to me.

"That isn't fair," Judge Samuelson said. "You know nothing about it."

"He didn't fuck up? Tell that to Leroy's ghost."

"Leroy fucked up," I said. "He spent his entire life fucking up, and finally got the payoff."

"Please," Levi said. "The waitress doesn't want to listen to your profanity."

"She doesn't mind," Tom said. "Do you, honey?"

"Yes, I mind," she said. She performed a neat pirouette and went off to the kitchen.

"Poor Leroy," the judge said. "He was such an unhappy man."

I said, "I believe that Leroy was fairly happy during the last few months. He had Tony, the three women, his daily aerial circus in the Stearman. It mellowed him."

"See where happiness gets you?" Petrie said. "He'd have lived to ninety if he'd stayed mean and unhappy."

There was some truth in that. César and Alejandro would not have found it easy to walk into the house and shoot the old, the hard, the paranoid Leroy Karpe.

"Christ," Tom said. "Now I've got to track down his heirs. Leroy really should have died destitute. It was his nature. But he left a fairly substantial estate."

"How did it happen?" I asked. "Kate dead, Leroy dead, others dead, César warped and crazed. And little Tony an unqualified and unchallenged Cardinal. No—an Adams-Cardinal again."

"It happened," Levi said, "because of our hubris." The judge was too polite to say *your* hubris; he, after all, had been the only one of us to oppose the mad idea of kidnapping the boy.

"Get out of here with the Greek words," Petrie said.

"Arrogance, then."

"It was a good idea badly executed. Everybody—even me—is subject to the immutable Petrie Laws of Incompetence. We just fucked up. Sorry, honey, mine's the duck."

PART V
Somewhere Safe at Sea

FORTY-THREE

It was hot at Woeful Cay in early July, hot everywhere in the Caribbean, hot in Florida, where I had once again given up the practice of law and said goodbye to my friends.

There had not been as much storm damage to *Roamer* as Finn Cooley's phone call had led me to expect. His boatyard crew had done a good job in repairing her. Some flying object had put a hole in her bow above the waterline, but the workers applied a fiberglass patch and painted the entire hull; you could see the patch only when the light struck from a certain angle. The rudder had sustained damage and the engine compartment had been flooded, and they too had been put in proper order. We launched her on my second day at Woeful Cay.

The resort had been beaten up by last year's storms: trees down, one pier turned into splinters, some roof and flooding damage at the hotel; and several of the fake thatched cottage roofs had been peeled off by the wind and sent westward. But, except for a certain bare look, the island had been restored to its former sleepy and shabby ambience.

I stayed in the same cottage that Kate and I had shared a little more than a year earlier. I found the copy of *Le Rouge et le Noir* that she had been reading. Many of the pages contained notations in Kate's small, neat hand. The notations, like the text, were in French, and I was unable to translate many of them, but they seemed ordinary enough. I'd always thought that readers who wrote comments and queries in the margins of books were a little strange. Were they talking to themselves, the author, a subsequent reader? I was the subsequent reader and I couldn't make much of them. Maybe she had been talking to Julien, the novel's antihero.

Finn presented me with a large manila envelope on the evening of my arrival, while we were waiting for dinner in the restaurant. It was from the judge. Inside was a note from Levi and another sealed manila envelope.

Dan,

Candace abruptly quit her job. She moved to Miami with her Cuban. I have been trying for days to reduce the astonishing chaos of her desk and our files. There were enough cosmetic supplies in her desk to open a beauty salon. Why would she file the enclosed envelope—received almost a year ago—in a portfolio marked *Pending*? Anyway, here it is.

Levi

The return address on the interior envelope was Hotel Montaña, the Dominican Republic.

"Aren't you going to open it?" Finn asked.

"Later. It's just a bill from a hotel in the D.R. I broke a couple windows, and they forgot to include the charges when I checked out."

"You broke windows? Tell me about that."

"I was drunk."

"Maybe I should start counting your drinks."

"I'll be sailing Wednesday," I said, "if the weather's good."

"It should be okay. Where are you going?"

"I want to finish the cruise I started last year. To the Virgin Islands, maybe on to Martinique."

"Son of a gun. I wish I was coming."

"Come along."

"Don't tempt me."

The dining room was empty except for two young couples down from Ohio for a week at the cheap off-season rates. They seemed disappointed and bored: no people their own age, no parties, no limbo dancing and steel drum bands, none of the advertised Caribbean color except for the dark blue sea and the clear blue sky.

"It's hard to figure," Finn said. "This Barbara Adams marrying her dead sister's husband, the guy who threw her sister into the sea. Plus he's fifteen years older and crippled bad."

"The heart is strange," I said.

"The head is even stranger."

The waiter arrived with our food: I was having a strip steak, Finn a red snapper that had been caught just a few hours before.

An elderly couple who had been drinking in the lounge noisily entered the dining room and immediately protested the location of a table assigned to them by the hostess. She offered another, which they rudely rejected; they finally accepted a table near the two young couples.

"Well, what's the truth?" Finn asked. "Did César actually try to kill Kate, throw her overboard like a sack of garbage?"

"Finn, I just don't know."

"If not, if she made it up, then that makes her a little crazy, doesn't it?"

"She was unhappy; her marriage was breaking up at the time. Then twenty-six hours alone in the sea, terror and hallucinations . . ."

"Kate wasn't crazy, she was a fine lady. César chucked her over the side."

"Maybe. But I'm learning to do without opinions."

"Why did Kate go back to him?"

"Opinions are almost as dangerous as convictions."

The old couple began complaining about the service; they wanted menus, more drinks, and no back-chat from the waitress. And they tried to enlist the two young couples in their little insurrection.

"Christ," Finn said, "there were a lot of casual-ties for such a simple operation. Kate, the bodyguard, Leroy, the helicopter pilot."

"And Colonel Guzman. And César's sister, Maria, who was engaged to the colonel."

"Right. I forgot about them."

"And César."

"Him, too, I suppose."

"And Tony."

"Yeah, I guess you can call the kid a casualty."

The male senior citizen fumbled his cocktail glass, spilling its contents on his lap. He blamed the waitress.

"I'd throw them out," Finn said, "but there's no place for them to go."

"I'd throw them out anyway."

"That's an opinion."

After dinner we went into the lounge and were served coffee and brandy at a corner booth.

"It was a kind of miracle," Finn said. "Beautiful Kate swimming up to your boat in the middle of the night. A gift from the sea. Only good should come from a good thing like that. It's like God saw her safely to the boat, then went away, and the devil took over."

"He left, and humans took over. But I'm through picking at scabs tonight, Finn."

"Right. Sorry. Well, we can drink to Katie."

"We could drink to all of them."

"Nope, just Kate."

Later that night, back in my cottage, I opened the envelope sent from the Hotel Montaña. It did not contain a bill, as I'd assumed, but an ordinary white envelope, sealed, with Kate's handwriting on the face. Probably a member of the hotel staff had found it in her room after the helicopter crash, placed it inside a larger envelope, and posted it. Last words from the dead, misfiled under *Pending*.

Dear Daniel,

Didn't we say a lovely goodbye during our walk around and around the pond? You under-stood the importance of a silent farewell. We

had said all there was to say to each other, words
of love first, and then later hard words, bitter
words. And so we both understood that silence
might cleanse and heal the wounds caused by
our words.

My mind has partly cleared and continues
to clear.

I must now tell you this, the truth, as I have
finally and painfully discovered it. Remember,
you accused me of faking amnesia after my rescue. But I was not wholly false—there *were* blank
areas in my memory, hours and hours of nothing. You, more than anyone, know how much I
suffered, and yet your knowledge comprises just
a fraction of the actual. My doubts caused you
to doubt. My confusion confused you.

I never lied to you, Dan, I lied to myself. I
simply could not believe that what I knew to be
true *was* true, and so I embraced the lies presented to me by César and others. Poor woman,
she made it all up out of God knows what crazy
imaginings. Can you understand that there are
times when one is not strong enough to bear a
horrible truth?

I mean to say that what I told you at the beginning is what I tell you now: César did coldly
and cruelly—he was smiling!—throw me into
the sea that night. I know it surely in my heart
and memory and dreams.

The fog has lifted and I know it. I know it.

I have not accused César, though he knows
that I know. Now I must stay here and search

for my poor lost boy until he is found alive or dead. Then I will come to you, if you still want me. Do you? I believe you do. Let's anyway agree that our silent farewell at the pond was not a farewell after all, but was instead a kind of profound greeting.

Love, Kate

Three days later, not long after sunrise, Finn came down to the harbor to see me off. He presented me with an expensive bottle of French champagne.

"Take care," he said. "The sea is always looking for a mistake, a weakness."

"I know."

We shook hands. Finn thumped his fist against my shoulder. "Bon voyage," he said.

"Thanks, Finn."

"Wait, Christ, I almost forgot." He gave me Kate's platinum wedding band. "One of my workers found it tucked under a mattress."

"An honest workman."

"I added fifty bucks to your bill, and gave it to him as a reward."

"That's fine. Thanks."

"Well, hell," he said. "Send me messages in bottles."

❊   ❊   ❊

It was dismal sailing for ten days: I fought headwinds, nasty squalls, contrary seas, minor equipment failures, and bouts of seasickness. It was calmer when I reached the Puerto Rican trench. Not as calm as last summer; I would never again see anything like that. Stars and a horned moon were visible through a thin haze but there was no meteor shower this year, and the sea did not flash with an equal phosphorescence. I consulted my log for *Roamer*'s position on the night of Kate's mysterious appearance, checked my GPS, and then motored to 19.5 degrees, twenty-nine minutes north; 66 degrees, twelve minutes east.

I thought about the day when I'd caught the dorado, cut it open, and found Kate's wedding band. She had tossed it out of a porthole. But it had glittered as it fell through the galleries of deepening blue, and the fish had seen it as a tasty morsel.

I dropped the ring over the side. It sparkled with bioluminescence, spinning, and vanished into black water on its five-mile journey down to the abyssal plain. My little ceremony was a disappointment. What was the point? I was glad that at least I'd had the sense to leave Finn's champagne in the icebox.

I raised sail, made some adjustments to the self-steering apparatus, and sailed east at a sluggish three knots. Later that night a pod of dolphins appeared and provided escort for several miles. There was enough light so that I could see their goofy dolphin smiles. They were sheathed in phosphorescence. They rhythmically leaped and dived, leaped and dived, silent except for their soft exhalations, and then—*Roamer* was too slow—they went off to seek more exciting diversions.